MONSTER GIRL GALAXY

BOOK ONE

AUSTIN BECK

COPYRIGHT

DEDICATION

Dedicated to my sole harem member...Kelly.

I opened my eyes and felt my head explode in pain from a vicious headache. A whirlpool of nausea followed the discomfort in my gut.

The night before had been a doozy, it would seem. I turned my throbbing head to my right and saw a naked girl lying beside me on the king bed. She had one leg under the sheets and one leg out. The sunlight pierced through the crack of the closed curtain and lit up her curves nicely. I had no fucking clue what her name was, but I knew she was a sexy beast.

We had met in the hotel bar on the first floor the night before. I was exhausted from my match, but when a hot lady wants to get in your pants you let her do it. We drank...a lot, and then ended up here in my above-average room where we drank some more from the little fridge filled with overpriced spirits. Then we went at it for two hours before we passed out. She was insanely good at pleasing a man and a worthy ring rat. Ring rats is a wrestling term for girls that hang out around wrestling shows and want to fuck all the wrestlers. Rock stars have their own groupies and so do pro wrestlers. It was a nice perk to have I must say.

I am Dalton Wade, and I am a KAW superstar. KAW being the legendary Kick Ass Wrestling promotion based out of Las Vegas, Nevada. I go by the ring name "The Cooler," and I am a babyface. What does that mean? Babyface is wrestling jargon for the good guy.

I am the guy that the fans cheer for, and the other guy, the heel, is the villain that the fans dislike. I have been a professional wrestler for ten years and have worked hard to get where I am. I have spent 50 weeks out of each year on the road living out of a suitcase in ratty motels, mostly. Sometimes, like last night, I would get lucky and stay at a decent spot. I spent every other night in the ring in controlled chaos. I have gotten damn good at the profession. I paid my dues night in and night out during my early career. Three years ago, I rose from being a mediocre mid-carder to a main event draw. Not only were my skills in the ring pristine, but my mic skills rivaled my actual wrestling ability. The ability to do a promo that got the crowd going was just as valuable as putting on a good technical show in the ring. Over my career, there were guys that were great at one or the other. It was rare for a wrestler to excel at both.

Those who did so were the guys that headlined the weekly prime time cable shows and monthly pay-per-view spectacles. The Cooler led merchandising sales as well. All over the packed venues, you will see fans wearing "The Cooler" shirts with my famous tag line "It's My Way or the Highway!" Life was good for me. I was one of the most popular wrestlers in the world, and I loved every second. The rush of hearing my theme music explode as I walk through a curtain to be blanketed by thousands of cheering fans was amazing. It was exciting and bizarre to see fans of all ages and types going nuts as I walked by. I would see a cheerful kid with a Cooler sign only to be met by a blonde bombshell flashing her tits for me just a few rows down. This life was a strange one, but it was the one I had chosen. Hell, maybe the life chose me.

I hadn't even developed a healthy addiction to pain killers yet or become a raging alcoholic. Pro wrestlers were usually both. It was unavoidable in most cases. We put our bodies through extreme stress night after night. We had to wrestle with pain and injuries. You always had another guy ready to take your spot if you slipped at all.

Wrestling is scripted, but the moves hurt, and the falls to the mat rattled your bones. However, I admit to one naughty thing. I am a steroid user. Big shock, I know. In this business, you need to look like a beast and be able to perform like a beast. Steroids will get you there and is an unofficial requirement if you want to make it to the top. I had a prominent doctor that helped me do them right. I wanted the right balance. I didn't want to grow tits or shrink my balls to the size of skittles.

I am six foot four inches and weigh in at 280 pounds of pure muscle. With my looks and mic skills, being a babyface was par for the course. My blonde hair was still long but not as long as it was in the early days when it draped halfway down my back. The more successful I got, the shorter my hair got. The blonde locks are shoulder length now. It is doubtful that it will get any shorter soon. The women seem to love it the most at this length. My smooth-shaven face and baby blue eyes to the appeal.

I figured I would have the eventual surprise heel turn that most wrestlers have at some point, but the brass with KAW hasn't wanted that yet. Why rock the boat? The money was pouring in just fine as is. In two days, I would have a huge payday. The biggest pay-per-view event of the year was coming up, and I was in the main event. The PPV was called Factory of Pain, and I would defend my belt in the World Heavyweight Championship match. This wasn't your run-of-the-mill match. It would be a no holds barred match in the gargantuan Mega Cage monstrosity.

These types of matches were the bane of my existence, but this would be one hell of a payday, and the world would be watching. This would be one of the most purchased pay per views in the history of professional wrestling and would help seal my legacy as one of the greatest wrestlers of all time, so I figure I can put my reservations to the side and suck it up and give the fans the best match they have ever seen. The bout was against the mega-heel Death Row. The funny thing is, Death Row wasn't even acting the role — he was a mega asshole in real life. Our dislike for one another wasn't a "work" at all. I despised the guy, but he was good at his job, so he got the push from the brass even though he was a dick. He brought in almost the same amount of merchandising revenue that I did, and he received almost the same amount of pop when he walked through the curtains. This title match made perfect sense for the fans and the business. The marketing had been nuts for the event.

Our faces were everywhere I looked, and we delivered heated promos at one another at each live event. They were easy to do, because we despised one another, so there was no acting involved. There were to be no physical altercations in the ring or outside of the ring between us until the night of the match. However, a few days earlier on Monday Night Ass Kickin' in Madison Square Garden, Death Row went rogue and followed me down the ramp without my knowledge and slammed a steel chair on the back of my head. He didn't make impact with the middle part of the seat which was the proper way to hit a man in the head with a steel chair to avoid injury. He hit me with the steel bar at the top of the chair. This wasn't a work; this was a shoot 100%. The term "shoot" means not scripted in the wrestling world. A shoot is when shit goes off the rails.

The brass was livid with the motherfucker. Had I received a concussion, there would be no main event, because my ass wouldn't be wrestling in it. Any other wrestler would have been fired immediately. If I would have pushed for it, Death Row probably would have been. However, no big match meant no big payday. Not to mention the flack I would receive from getting the man fired, even though it was completely justified.

Even though Death Row's stunt was reckless and pissed

off everyone, the fans loved it. The buzz for the match proceeded to get bigger and bigger.

I walked into the Staples Center with my duffle bags early on the morning of the match. I had a meeting with the president of the KAW, John Johnson, Death Row, and the referee about the match plan. Usually, something of this nature would have been discussed earlier, but things haven't gone normally for a while now. We weren't even sure of the outcome yet. Was I going to keep the belt or give it to Death Row? I had no fucking clue.

Chuck, the errand boy of the big man John, met me near the entrance.

"Cooler, how's it going? Are you feeling well?"

"I can't complain. I got a good night's sleep, and I am ready to put on an excellent match. Hopefully, Death Row feels the same way."

Chuck nodded and motioned for me to follow him. "Can I get you anything, champ?"

I shook my head. "Nah, I'm good right now. I am just ready to get everything squared away with the match. I enjoy being able to chill a few hours before the bell rings...especially before one of these types of matches."

"It will be amazing! I can see it now!"

Chuck was in his late 40s. He was short and chubby with

a quickly dissipating hairline. Nonetheless, Chuck was a good guy. He was a yes man through and through, but his excitement was sincere. I have yet to have any issues with Chuck, which is a rarity in this business. You always had beef to some extent with most everyone. We engaged in a few minutes of bullshit, small talk on our way to John's office, our meeting area. I was eager to get this whole thing drawn out. We reached a door with the word Chief stamped temporarily on it.

Chuck placed his hand on the nob. "You are the last one here."

I scoffed as I looked at my watch. "I am ten minutes early. What the hell?"

Chuck opened the door, and there was a big rectangular table in the center of the room where everyone sat.

They all stopped talking and turned their attention toward me.

"Ah, Dalton, thanks for coming in so early this morning. We are ready to get started," John said as he waved me over.

There was an empty seat between the referee, Casper, and the boss. I chose that one. I had no interest in sitting beside Row.

Row sat with his enormous arms crossed. He was wearing blue jeans with a black Metallica "Ride the Lightning" shirt and sunglasses. Row's jet-black hair was tied into a ponytail that went to the middle of his back. His goatee was longer than usual, and he appeared to have a new tattoo on his left forearm. It looked to be some sort of bladed weapon with a snake wrapped around it.

"Fuck man, we have been waiting long enough for your diva ass to show up," Death Row scoffed.

I rolled my eyes and kept my attention on John. I just wanted to get everything squared away, so I could spend the rest of the day getting my mind right and prepared for what would take place. I took my job very seriously, and I cared about my fans. I wanted to give them a great match that they would remember for a long time.

"All right guys, I want tonight to be exceptional. You are the two best pro wrestlers in the business right now. There will be ALOT of eyes on you guys tonight. It's important that we give those eyes a good fucking show. Understand?" John glared at us both.

Row laughed. "You don't have to worry about me, boss. Twinkle toes here is in over his head, I think."

I turned and looked Row directly in the eyes and pointed. "I have had enough of your bitch mouth. I bring my A-game night in and night out. I'm ready for this shit. Now shut the hell up, so John can talk."

John and Casper laughed uncomfortably, and Row's face showed fiery anger. He kept his mouth shut, though.

John and Casper took us through all the basics and technical stuff we needed to know.

John sighed as he looked at Death Row. Dalton will retain the belt tonight."

"What the fuck are you talking about, John?" Death Row leaned forward and growled.

"It's simple, the fans aren't ready to see Dalton lose the belt right now, and PPV buys are higher with him as the champ. I understand it upsets you. You'll wear that belt one day, but it just won't be today. I hope you understand," John replied calmly and directly.

"I have worked my ass off these past few months. I deserve the win tonight. Is this about the unsanctioned chair shot I gave him? Am I being punished? That shit was epic and added to our feud. Which will add more buys to the PPV," Row asked with his hands raised.

"Nope, this decision has nothing to do with that, believe it or not. It is best for our fans and bottom line if Dalton stays champion for a bit longer. Like I said, you will get your run soon enough. I can assure you. Enough about that, let's get a plan in place for tonight."

Death Row slammed his fist on the table with an enormous amount of force. The impact caused a shock wave that knocked over John's coffee onto his paperwork. John's face turned blood red as he cleaned the area up as best, he could without saying a word.

John finally turned to Row and pointed at him. "I will give you that one, but just that one. Believe me, I will happily replace your ass in a heartbeat if I have to."

Death Row held up his hands. "I'm sorry boss, please continue."

"Well, you two are professionals and know what you are doing in the ring. I am fine with you guys controlling things if the action stays exciting, and it ends like we want it to. I think the ending should be Dalton performing one of his finishers, the double deuce off the top of the Mega Cage. We have fiddled with the ring a bit to handle the impact from that fall a bit better and reduce injury potential. It shouldn't be a problem for professionals like yourselves."

———

As I sauntered toward the curtain, I wore my usual attire: a white t-shirt, blue jeans, and black boots. My attire had always been very plain and unremarkable, however when you put my body and charisma in the clothes, it works.

My custom heavy metal anthem began blasting out of the speakers scattered all over the arena. Gooseflesh appeared on my massive arms as I made my way onto the stage under the enormous high definition display. Camera flashes bombarded my vision, and the roar from the fans was deafening. Before I walked down the ramp toward the ring, pyrotechnic blasts fired over and over behind me. When the smoke dissipated, I began strutting down the ramp toward the Mega Cage. I locked eyes on Death Row, who stood calmly in the middle with his arms crossed and a devilish grin on his hardened face. The Mega Cage was a monstrosity of height and steel. The top of the cage was twenty feet above the mat.

My stomach dropped a bit as I pictured myself doing a backward double deuce moonsault onto Death Row below. I had two finishers, and the double deuce was my high-flying aerial maneuver. My other move was "Prepare to Die" where I kick my opponent in the stomach and perform a lightning quick DDT driving their head into the mat. From a technical standpoint, the move wasn't a challenge to perform. Nonetheless, I could make it look insanely cool, and the cheers were deafening when I executed the move. Casper, the referee, would let us know when the match was 30 minutes in, and then I would perform the Prepare to Die DDT, and I would climb up to the top of the cage and perform the double deuce moonsault for the win. We have done thousands of matches over the years, and we would put a nice show together for the fans. At least that was the plan in my eyes. Professional wrestlers receive a lot of flak from many people, but we are professionals and do what needs to be done. There is a lot of pride and loyalty in our line of work.

Casper motioned me into the Mega Cage, and the door was locked behind the three of us. Death Row pounced on me almost immediately. Just as I expected, the punches were stronger than they should have been.

The fans were enjoying it, so I didn't have a problem with it. It made them happy and made Row feel a little more manly. I spent the next few minutes taking a lot of punches and a couple of body slams. The good part about the cage match is the absence of outside work. There was much less to manage. After a few minutes, I turned the tide and began a barrage on Death Row. The crowd erupted in cheers as they watched the babyface fight back against the evil heel.

Row's determination not to sell my punches properly annoyed me, so I turned my attention to grappling. He cooperated with the holds I was trying to execute so that was appreciated. After a few minutes of attacks from me, I allowed him a reversal of a suplex, and he laid back into me for a while. We continued this song and dance for a few minutes. Then to my surprise, Row began to climb the cage. I wasn't sure what he was trying to do, but I followed his lead and ascended behind him. I used to be terrified of heights, but I had to overcome that fear in order to succeed in this business. The Mega Cage was a bit different from the cages in the old days. At the top, there was room to walk. There was a 6-foot wide scaffold that wrapped around the ring. We traded punches back and forth for a few seconds. I finally whispered to him in his ear when we locked up once.

"What's the plan up here?" I asked as stealthily as I could.

A knee placed directly into my balls was his response to that question.

I dropped to one knee and screamed in agony. "Fuck!"

Death Row laughed and turned to the crowd to taunt them and me.

Accidental nutshots are expected, but a premeditated one was a huge red flag.

"You want to stay champion, right?" Row shrugged. "You gotta take some medicine. Medicine doesn't always taste very good."

Death Row's shit talking didn't bother me too badly because my nuts felt as if they were going to explode. He pulled me up by the hair and gave me a full-blown punch to the face that knocked me backward onto my ass. I somehow stayed on the scaffold.

"What the fuck are you doing?" I growled as I checked my nose for blood.

Death Row avoided my question and pulled me to my feet

again by my hair. He was showered with boos from the crowd. I saw John Johnson out of the corner of my eye standing with his arms crossed beside the announcer's table. His face was blood red, and he looked like he would erupt lava out the top of his head at any moment.

Death Row brought his right knee into my gut, and the air left my lungs as I bent over. The bastard quickly lifted me for his power bomb finisher called "Last Will and Testament." I was expecting to get slammed on the scaffolding. I soon realized he was tossing me to the mat twenty feet down, and I would land on my head from the unavoidable rotation. I would die or be paralyzed. I watched him laugh as I fell to the mat in slow motion. I saw camera flashes and heard a deafening gasp as I plummeted to my unknown end. I closed my eyes before impact, but that impact never came. I opened my eyes again and saw I was in some sort of dark tunnel with lightning flashes surrounding me. In the distance, I could see the inside of the Staples Center through a perfect circle, but that sight became smaller and smaller as I fell into an abyss. Was this death? Was I headed to hell? Suddenly, I saw stars and night sky as I continued to fall. Then I splashed into cold water that took my breath away. I sank and began to suffocate. I snapped out of my stupor and moved my arms and legs as quickly as I could. I swam rapidly upward until my torso launched above the surface. I took a deep breath and filled my lungs with precious oxygen and scanned my surroundings.

2

W hat...the...fuck?

    I dog paddled in a pond or lake in the middle of a wooded area, God knows where. I was dead. This was the only explanation for what was going on. The next question...Am I in heaven or hell? Why am I not standing at a gate of some sort? Falling into a fucking lake after death was freaking weird. I looked back into the dark night sky to see if I saw the doorway back to the Staples Center, but it was gone. The sky was insanely beautiful. There were stars everywhere. I decided that I better get to shore before I drowned. Can I die again? I wasn't sure how this afterlife worked yet. The shore was fifty yards away from my current location. I swam slowly toward land. The trees around the lake were freaking tall. I began to hear car horns in the distance. I had to be close to a city or populated area. There are cars in heaven? Nah, that makes no sense...none of this shit makes sense.

I reached the muddy shore of the lake. It was cool and sticky to the touch as the mud squirted through my fingers. I freaking hate being dirty. Why the hell was I getting dirty in the afterlife?

Dalton Wade!
Welcome to Zorth!

A blue floating screen suddenly appeared in my vision and scared the shit out of me. I lost my balance and fell backward, back into the water.

"Jesus tapdancing Christ!" I yelled as I stood back up, dripping wet. The sound of water falling from my body plopped into the mud under my boots. At least falling in the water again had rinsed some of the mud off my clothing. I pointed my finger and tried to touch the screen. It looked like a floating holographic computer display.

"What the hell is this? What the hell is a Zorth? Is Heaven called Zorth?"

Suddenly, I heard motion in the vegetation in front of me. I tried to push the screen out of my vision, but it wasn't working, however after the fourth swipe at the screen and yelling for it to go away, the screen vanished. I let out an exhale of relief. Nonetheless, that relief was short-lived as I heard motion again...close this time.

"I can hear you. Come out. Unless your plan is to eat me, of course," I yelled as I scanned the area from side to side rapidly.

"Hello, I am Euthani. I mean you no harm," a gentle female voice spoke.

"Okay, show yourself. I will not hurt you either."

The footsteps softly approached, and a figure emerged from the darkness. I squinted to see a slender, female figure looking at me.

"Hi, please come closer."

The female slowly approached and stood in the moonlight. A gorgeous woman pierced my vision. However, there was something peculiar about this woman. She had brownish red ears and a bushy tail of the same color that swayed behind her. Her hair was long and black and blew in the breeze coming off the water. I blinked my eyes and squinted again. She had the most amazingly gorgeous, blue eyes I had ever seen. She had a black, tight leather-like suit on, and it looked like she had some sort of device on her back...a weapon perhaps. She smiled and waved at me cheerfully.

"Are you...an...angel?" I asked as I stepped closer.

"Angel? I have no clue what an angel is. Who are you, and why were you swimming in the lake at this time of night? You must be freezing," the animalistic girl replied with one eyebrow raised.

"I just assumed since I was dead, I would see angels," I shrugged.

"Dead? You are clearly not dead. You are a little...odd but definitely alive."

"Where the hell am I then? One minute I am wrestling in Los Angeles, and the next I am floating in a cold-ass lake after falling through an invisible hole in a wrestling ring."

"Los Angeles? I am not familiar with that city? Is it on Zorth, or do you hail from another planet?"

"Oh, this is the planet Zorth. I wondered what Zorth meant in the screen thingy that popped up."

Euthani's eyes suddenly widened. "You are an interfacer? I haven't met another interfacer in a while. What class are you? I'm sorry if I am prying. Shit, I don't even know your name."

"Uh, I'm Dalton Wade. It is a pleasure to meet you...Euthani. Did I say it right?"

Euthani laughed and replied. "Yes, that is perfect. It is nice to meet you as well. You never answered me. Is Los Angeles on another planet or located on Zorth?"

I scratched my head and closed my eyes for a second. "LA is located on Earth."

"I have never heard of Earth. Is it in another galaxy?"

"Umm, I don't know. Are we in the Milky Way right now?"

"Milky Way? What's that?"

"That answers my question then."

"How long have you been on Zorth?" She asked as she moved into a more relaxed stance and crossed her slender but muscular arms.

"Not long, 15 minutes maybe. I was on Earth. Then I fell from a doorway in the sky and into this lake...on a planet called Zorth."

Euthani looked upward at the sky. I could tell she was searching or the doorway I just mentioned.

"Are you okay? You must be dealing with some amnesia.

You can stay with me, and I will help you get your memory back. I can take you to a doctor."

"I don't have amnesia. I clearly remember what happened," I shook my hands. "Listen, I need clarification of what I am seeing. You have fuzzy ears and a bushy tail. Is this some kind of cosplay thing?"

"Cosplay thing? I have no clue what that means, but yes, these are my ears and tail of course. Wow, you are really fucked up. Oops, sorry for the sassy language."

I shook my head. "You are part animal?"

Euthani's eyebrow raised. "Yes, I am a fox girl. You are a human...it appears at least."

"Fox girl? Fuck, I am going crazy."

"You are weird, I will admit. But forgive me if I am being blunt, but you are hot as hell," Euthani said as she looked me up and down.

"Umm, thanks. I get that a lot," I replied, then regretted sounding like an arrogant prick. "You're jaw-droppingly gorgeous. I hope that wasn't too forward. I'll admit we don't have any fox...girls on Earth, but we definitely need some."

Euthani's cheeks reddened, and she smiled as she stared at me with her soul gazing blue eyes. "Thank you, that is nice of you to say."

"Listen, you mentioned something about me being an...interfacer earlier. Can you tell me what that is exactly?"

"Yes! They are rare. I happen to be one as well. It is a freaking blessing from the gods. You were prompted with a blue screen not long after your arrival...right?"

I nodded. "Yeah, it almost gave me a heart attack."

Euthani giggled. "I can imagine. That is your interface. It gives you access that others do not have. You can upgrade your body, skills, and gear. With the currency of mojo, you can access a database of millions of upgrades, items, weapons, clothes, and abilities that you can purchase with your mojo."

I raised my eyebrow and looked at her with a confused expression. "Mojo? How do I get that? Do I have any?"

"That's a good question. You just arrived here so I wonder if you have any mojo. You need to bring up your interface and have a look at your reserves."

"Ok, how do I do that?"

"Sometimes when an event happens, your interface will appear without you summoning it, but you will access it manually, mostly. You just need to think about it. Just concentrate on the word 'interface' in your mind. With practice, it will become second nature and a quick process. Go."

I closed my eyes and focused on the word "interface" with everything I had. Sure enough, she was right. The blue screen from earlier popped up in my vision.

"Got it. Sweet! Can you see what I am seeing?"

Euthani shook her head quickly. "No, that is something that only you can see. At the upper right corner, you should she the word 'mojo' and a number beside it. What is that number?"

I followed her direction and saw mojo. I was expecting to see zero beside it, but I was pleased to find out that I had 10,000 mojo. I had no clue if that was a lot, but I had some at the very least.

"My interface tells me that I have 10,000. Is that good?"

Euthani's eyes widened, and her mouth fell agape. "You have 10,000, and you just arrived? That's amazing. You aren't rich by any means, but you are fortunate to have those kinds of reserves without having done anything."

I nodded in approval with a splash of excitement. I had no clue what I would be able to do with this mojo, but at least I had some at my disposal.

"Ok, now what do I do with it?" I asked her.

Euthani held up her index finger and squinted her right eye. "First things first, we need to see your class and specialty. That will determine what you need to look for in the shop."

"Shop?"

"Yeah, that is the inventory of items you can purchase with your mojo. We'll get to that in a minute. Let me talk, you silly goose. Stop interrupting me," she demanded playfully. "Now you need to swipe left until you get to the 'Class and Specialty' menu. Just do that with your finger."

I nodded and pretended I was just looking at a computer touch screen. I placed my finger in the center of the glowing blue screen and swiped left. It moved just like I was swiping my finger on a tablet. I found the screen she described. Once I selected it, I saw some information appear on a screen below the heading.

"Gundertaker Level 1. What's that?" I asked as I squinted at the screen.

Her eyes widened again. "Gundertaker, holy shit that is a special class I have only read about. It is freaking awesome, Dalton. Congrats!"

I chuckled. "Thanks...I guess. What does it mean exactly?"

"The 'gun' part of the word is fairly self-explanatory. It means you are good with ranged weapons...guns especially. The 'undertaker' part of the class means you can use the dark magic of necromancy. You aren't as powerful as someone who is a full-blown necromancer, but you will be able to do a lot of cool stuff. Dude, you are freaking lucky as fuck."

"Necromancy? You mean like I can raise people from the dead?"

She clapped and did a quick hop. "Yes! Isn't that wonderful?"

"You mean I have zombies at my disposal? I don't know whether to be scared or excited."

"You should most definitely be excited. Being just a Gunner class would be amazing, but a Gundertaker is a diverse class meaning you can do multiple things. Now, scroll down and search for your specialty perk."

I nodded and moved my finger slowly. "Pure Rank Weapon Specialist."

Euthani punched me in the arm. "Wow, you are one lucky son of a bitch! No offense!"

I shrugged. "None taken, what does this mean?"

"Having any specialty perk at Pure level is almost unheard of. Some people have defensive specialties, but you have yourself a Pure offensive perk. As a Pure Rank Weapon Specialist, you can use any weapon you pick up like an expert. Meaning you will be a master of any weapon you acquire. That is fucking nuts," Euthani replied with her eyes wide.

"Wow, that sounds pretty cool, but I am not going to war. Why am I going to need this level of combat skill?"

Euthani sighed. "Zorth is a dangerous place. The city you are in right now is Osiris. The crime rate here is through the roof. Believe me, you will get plenty use out of your offensive skills."

"City? I don't see any buildings."

"That is because you are in the park, you big goofball," she punched me on the arm once more. "The trees are just really tall so you can't see the buildings, once we make our way back to Osiris, you will begin to see the city. I come out here to get away from the hustle and bustle of Osiris, not to mention the crime rate."

"Aren't you scared to be out here by yourself if things are so bad?"

"No, not really. I am an interfacer as well, and I have my trusty crossbow right here," Euthani said as she grabbed the weapon from whatever holster she had on her back. "Tah dah!"

I had never seen a crossbow in real life, only in the movies. It looked like what I had seen on TV, but it looked much sleeker and more futuristic.

"Where are the arrows....err bolts, I mean?"

"Here," she said as she held the weapon with both hands. She pressed a button on the side with her thumb, and there was a flash of green light. Much to my surprise, there was some kind of magic bolt sitting inside the firing chamber.

She pointed the crossbow at the lake and fired it three

times in the water. I was startled and excited at the same time as the glowing green arrows penetrated the water, causing three large splashes.

"Whoa, can I try?" I asked like a child eyeing a friend's new toy.

"Sure," she replied as she gave me the crossbow.

I held my palms out to stop her. "Wait, don't you need to give me a crash course?"

"Nope, just take it."

I grabbed the weapon and held it in my hands. Suddenly, I was bombarded by a few screens. One looked like a diagram of the gun, and the others looked like some instructions. As I looked at the weapon, I felt as if I knew everything about it. I held it up quickly and shot four bolts into the lake in the same spot. The bolts entered the water at the exact same point with each of the four shots. I just glared at the weapon with my mouth open.

"See? Pure Weapons Specialist along with being a Gundertaker. You are a badass," Euthani said as she slapped me on my butt cheek.

Her aggressiveness surprised me, but I liked it. I didn't give a shit if she was part fox. She was a fucking goddess. She could slap my ass anytime she wanted.

"Now, how does this necromancy thing work?"

"In order to use that, you need a dead person or animal."

"Well shit, I was looking forward to seeing that, but I'm all out of corpses."

Euthani laughed. "It's cool and a bit terrifying at the same time. I have seen a necromancer once in person. He was a nut case...wait...you hear that?"

"Hear what?" I whispered.

Euthani pointed to the tree directly in front of us. "Squirrel...twelve o'clock."

I saw a squirrel on a large branch gnawing on an acorn, I presumed. He was about twenty feet above me. "I can make a squirrel zombie?"

Euthani nodded. "Shoot him. He is small, but it shouldn't be a problem with your class and specialty. However, aim at the head otherwise you may cut him in half with the bolt, and he won't be a very useful zombie squirrel. Do it before he takes off. Now!"

I nodded and aimed the crossbow. The outline of the squirrel's body glowed green, and I aimed at its head. I squeezed the trigger, and a bolt soared from my crossbow and took his head clean off. The squirrel's corpse fell to the ground with a tiny plop.

I looked at the still glowing squirrel, and a small box appeared over his dead body.

Raise from the dead? Yes/No

"No fucking way," I muttered as I clicked "Yes."

The outline of the corpse turned from green to purple and pulsed.

Two seconds later, the headless squirrel stood to his feet as blood dribbled out of his neck stump.

"Fuck me," I murmured.

"Really? Now?" Euthani asked, perplexed.

I turned to look at her and my cheeks reddened. "Oh, no... not that. It's an expression that means 'unbelievable' in a situation like this."

Euthani giggled. "Oh, I was like...dude, you are pretty confident. Also, I thought you were turned on by a headless zombie squirrel. I am as kinky as the next fox girl, but that was a little too kinky for even me."

I shook my head as I chuckled. "Okay, okay. My bad. Now, what do I do with this thing?"

"I am not entirely sure how the undead work completely, but you should be able to tell him with your mind where to go and what to attack. These zombies can only be used for attacks or defense. What I mean is, you can't get him to vacuum your apartment."

I erupted in laughter. "Damn, girl, you are too fucking funny."

"Thank you! That is so kind of you to say. I want to be funny," the fox girl said as she hugged my arm. "Damn, you are a muscular dude. I like that. Wow," she flirted.

"You are welcome," I smirked and then squinted at the zombie squirrel.

In my head, I told him to approach me and stand three feet in front of me. If the zombie squirrel had a head, it would have lifted to look at me. I just saw its muscles stiffen as if it were a marine standing at attention. He walked over at an average rate of speed and stopped where I wanted him to.

"Fuck me," I whispered as I stared at the hideous creature.

"Oh, I get it now. A suitable expression for the current situation. An obedient, headless zombie squirrel *IS* unbelievable," Euthani interjected.

This girl was a riot. We had only known each other for a short while, but I could see myself falling in love with her. She was hot, and her personality was amazing.

I then looked at the squirrel and mentally told it to climb the tree and return to his previous location before his untimely death. The squirrel immediately went into action and did what I had instructed him to do. It stood over top of us waiting for his next command. Little blood droplets fell from the undead squirrel perched on the tree branch and sprinkled onto the green grass below the tree.

"Ok, I think I have a beginner's knowledge of necromancy. Tell me about this mojo shop."

"Yes...I enjoy shopping," Euthani squealed. "You need to go to the Mojo Shop menu in your interface, and you will access the store. Be prepared. It will overwhelm you at first, but you will learn to use it in time."

I nodded and promptly accessed the Mojo Shop menu and boom. It looked like Amazon on steroids. There were categories upon categories. There were fucking deals blinking on the side of the screen. "This is nuts. So, mojo is like...money. I basically have 10,000 dollars in my digital wallet to spend?"

Euthani shrugged. "I have no clue what a dollar is, but mojo is money more or less. You are correct."

"What do I need first? You are going to help me...right?"

"Of course, silly, you need a gun first and foremost. Guns are pricey, so you want to be frugal. You can get a lot more out of a weaker weapon than others since you are a Gundertaker, and you have a Pure Weapons Specialist perk. Do you understand?"

"Yeah, I think so. You mean since I basically have a mastery of all weapons, I can maximize the potential of even the weakest of guns. The gun will still be weak, but in my hands, I will use it as perfectly as the gun's abilities will allow."

"Yes, that is exactly what I mean. So, I would advise you to purchase a weaker weapon that will cost you less mojo so you can use it on other things. You can buy a stronger weapon later. You can also loot weapons from people you kill. However, don't just go out there and start killing people just to loot them. With the number of assholes and crime syndicates around, you will have opportunities to kill actual bad guys and loot their weapons," she paused, waiting for an answer from me.

"Right, right."

"I would advise you to purchase a simple plasma pistol and a holster for your waist. With your specialty, you will be awesome with that weapon. You can get something better later. Take a look at this," Euthani said as she pulled a pistol from a holster on her waist behind her.

"Whoa, I didn't know you had that."

"You don't know a lot about me," Euthani winked. "Buy this plasma pistol and this holster. That will get you started. It isn't a high-quality pistol, but it is just a backup weapon for me. I use my crossbow all the time or just buy what you want. It's up to you Mr. Wade."

"All right, what are they called? How am I supposed to find these items in this maze of shit?"

"Give me a sec," Euthani said as she accessed her own interface and began swiping.

Do you accept Euthani Naboo as a friend? Yes or No?

I laughed and chose "Yes."

"Oh, my gods, you added me as a friend. I am a lucky girl."

Suddenly a blinking icon caught my attention at the top of my interface. The icon looked like an envelope. I had a fucking inbox on Zorth. This was insane. I accessed the icon and two windows popped up immediately. They were links to the gun and holster in the mojo shop.

Simple Plasma Pistol — 3,000 mojo
Do you want to purchase? Yes or No?

"Shit, 3,000 mojo for a simple pistol. You weren't lying

when you said weapons were pricey," I blurted as I clicked the 'Yes' button.

Congratulations, you have purchased a Simple Plasma Pistol for 3,000 mojo! Do you want your new gun now or later?

I chose "Now," and my jaw dropped to the floor as a glowing orb flashed in front of me. It pulsed for two seconds, and then the gun I just bought appeared and it was floating in the freaking air.

"Fuck me."

Euthani covered her mouth with the back of her hand and giggled quietly. "There you go. Just grab it."

I reached out and placed my hand on the grip and pulled it toward me. "This is awesome."

The barrage of menus and burst of knowledge of the gun overwhelmed my senses. The most interesting thing I learned was that plasma weapons didn't require ammo. They ran on batteries, and my new purchase had a full one included.

"Sweet."

"Now purchase the holster, so you have somewhere to put it," the fox girl instructed.

I followed the same process as before, and the new holster was mine. I placed it against my back on the waistband of my pants. I holstered the gun, and I was ready to roll, mother-fucker. Luckily, the holster was only 500 mojo and wasn't too hard on the ole mojo wallet. My mojo balance was now at 6,500.

"What do I need to buy now --," I was cut off by a deep male voice from behind us.

"Well, lookie what we have here. Turn around...slowly."

We obliged and saw a big Caucasian man that stood a little shorter than me. He was bald and chewing on a tooth-pick, but most importantly he was pointing a pistol at my head.

3

The bald bastard whistled. "Damn, you are freaking eye candy."

"Be nice to the lady," I said emphatically.

The bald man laughed. "Lady? I am talking about you. You are a fine hunk of beef. Where are you from honey bun boy?"

My eyes grew to the size of baseballs and then morphed into a stink face. "Me? I don't roll that way, dude. You be you though, but just not with me."

"Bah, I have a feeling I can make you roll my way if you give me a chance. I can be very persuasive, darling."

"Pointing a gun in my face isn't exactly a turn on," I replied with one eyebrow raised.

I had a gun pulled on me once eight years earlier at a live show in Carson City, Nevada. We weren't in a classy venue with classy fans. I was thrown out of the ring once, and I collided with a guy and knocked him to the floor. I grabbed his hand and pulled him up to be nice. I apologized even though I didn't have to. Shit happens in these small venues if you sit ringside. The guy pulls a gun and shoves it in my face. The match ended immediately in a no contest. So, I have experience with this sort of thing. I wasn't too shaken up by this bald guy and his gun. However, I was shaken up that he was trying to pick me up and take me back home for some nookie. I am not used to being hit on by guys...especially bald and fat, sweaty bastards like this one.

"Your loss. Now, give me all your coin!"

"Don't you mean mojo?" I asked with my hands raised.

"Mojo? I ain't no interfacer. I want fucking coin!"

"Dalton, coin is another form of currency that is used by non-interfacers."

The bald man wasn't quite as confident after I made the mojo comment. "Eh, so you are an interfacer?"

Euthani smirked. "We both are."

"Fuck," muttered the bald crook.

I knew how to put an end to this unfortunate situation quickly. I looked at my zombie squirrel friend that was still perched on the branch that happened to be right over this dude's head. I mentally instructed him to jump from the tree onto his shoulder. The squirrel immediately hopped down and plopped right on his shoulder like I instructed. The bald man was startled and turned his head to see a headless squirrel with its bloody stump only a couple inches from his oily face.

"What the hell!" the bald man screamed and began swatting at the squirrel. Unfortunately, the squirrel didn't have a head, which meant he didn't have eyeballs. He wasn't the best at dodging the incoming swipes.

When the man gave all his attention to the squirrel, I grabbed my plasma pistol and squeezed the trigger firing a shot into the side of his head. The plasma bullet left an enormous gaping hole through his head, and the bald man fell to the ground like a bag of garbage.

"Holy shit, Dalton. You are freaking brilliant. Your squirrel strategy was spot on. Nice shot too!" Euthani clapped her hands and hopped up and down.

I held the plasma gun in front of my face, and the realization that I had just killed a man sunk in. The surprising thing was...I didn't care. The bald asshole was going to either kill us or kidnap us. Fuck maybe even rape my ass.

"Thanks, the zombie squirrel was in the perfect spot," I replied as I looked at the little disgusting creature sitting on the ground. "Good job little buddy...little buddy with no head."

"Das a good boy...yes you are," Euthani cooed.

I couldn't believe we were congratulating a decapitated zombie squirrel, but here we were. I turned to look at the gorgeous fox girl and holstered my plasma pistol. "So, what now? Do we hide the body?"

Euthani shook her head and waved her hand. "Nah, the public works guys will pick him up tomorrow and throw him in an incinerator or feed him to the animals at the zoo."

"Huh? You mean the police aren't going to investigate this?"

"Police?" Euthani scoffed. "What police Osiris has are in the pockets of the crime syndicates. This guy is nothing more than a piece of garbage in the park that will be removed and thrown away."

"Hmmm, Zorth gets more interesting every minute. Okay...so what do we do now?"

"Oh crap. You need a mojo extractor from the shop. I didn't think you would kill anyone so soon. Give me a second, and I will send you a link to what I have."

"A mojo extractor?"

"Ummm, yeah. You have to suck the mojo out of his heart, you big goofball," Euthani shook her head playfully as she pulled up her interface.

I turned my head to look back down at the corpse. "Well, don't you need the mojo too?"

"Everyone needs mojo, but you can have his reserves since you killed him. You need to learn anyway," Euthani said as she swiped her fingers back and forth. "All right, I am sending you a link to a portable extractor. Eventually, you will want to get one surgically installed, but you don't have the funds right now. Buy this one," she smiled and nodded.

A blue screen popped up immediately with a product page of something that looked like a big syringe.

Simple Mojo Extractor -- 1,000 mojo

I promptly clicked on the buy button, and the syringe appeared in front of me. It was about eight inches long and two inches wide. The syringe or extractor was made of steel with a digital display on the side and a red button on the top. There was a smaller blue button on the side. Euthani pointed at the blue button and motioned for me to press it. I followed her command and a thick two-inch needle popped out the bottom. The sudden appearance of the sharp needle startled me, and I almost dropped the damn thing.

"Okay...what now?" I asked as I looked at the needle more closely.

"Simple! Go stab the guy in the heart and press the red button. Do it!"

I made another stink face and knelt beside the dead guy. "Really? Just stab him in the heart?"

"That's it! Easy as pie," chirped the fox girl. "Mmm, pie would be good right now."

I suddenly had a memory of the movie Pulp Fiction. Uma Thurman overdosed on drugs, and John Travolta had to stab her heart with a syringe. My current predicament was very similar to what I was doing right now.

"Do it before we have any more visitors. You'll be fine. Trust me."

I sighed and raised the syringe. I took a deep breath and plunged it directly where I thought the heart was. I paused for a couple of seconds, and then I remembered that I needed to press the red button. I mashed it, and the syringe made a mechanical slurping sound for a few seconds before the digital display lit up. The display showed the number 5,000.

"5,000?" I muttered.

"Hey, not too bad. Now take the syringe out and mash the blue button to retract the needle. I don't want you poking anyone. Well, not yet," she winked.

"Now, how do I put the mojo in my account? I don't have to stab myself in the heart, do I?"

"Well, kinda," the fox girl shrugged and grinned.

My eyes widened, and my mouth dropped wide open. "You have got to be fucking kidding me right now."

Euthani laughed and pointed at me. "Look at your face, so funny."

"I am glad you think this is funny. I think it sucks. I can't stab myself in the heart with this thing."

"Ugh, stop whining, little whiney boy. If you look under your shirt, you will see a steel hole which serves as a port. Look now," Euthani motioned for me to pull my shirt up.

Directly over my heart, I saw a small steel circular port that looked like a jack you would plug ear buds into. "Ah well, look at that. Now what?"

Euthani did a shallow shrug. "You put the needle in there and hit the red button. Easy."

"Ugh, that is simple but highly unsanitary. Sharing needles on Earth is a bad thing. I don't want some kind of disease from this loser. Chances are pretty good he has something."

Euthani laughed and placed her hands on her hips. "Don't worry, the steel port will kill any germs, and you will only inject pure mojo. Would I tell you to do something that would hurt you? Extracting mojo from a corpse is easier. Just stab the fucker. You don't have to waste your time with the port. They're dead anyway."

"All right, here goes," I muttered as I extracted the needle, and then I slid it into the steel port over my heart. I was expecting it to hurt, but I only felt a tingle.

I pressed the red button, and a blue screen popped up. I saw my mojo number rise with the injection. There was a beep when the syringe was empty. I took it out and retracted the needle back into the steel mojo extractor. My mojo total now read 11,500.

"It's done."

"Awesome! More mojo is always fun! You can also share mojo as well. You would just extract the percentage of mojo that we agree upon, and then I would extract the rest."

"Sounds easy enough. Damn, I don't know what I would have done if you hadn't come along. I wouldn't know jack shit."

"Hmm, I don't know Jack Shit either. Is he from Osiris?" asked a perplexed Euthani.

I erupted in laughter once more and placed my hand on her shoulder. "That is just an expression."

"Oh okay, gotcha," she shook her head cheerfully. "Now, do you want to loot this fellow? I would suggest taking his plasma gun. It is an old model and worse than what you have. What you will need to do is purchase a Shop Portal Backpack."

"What the heck is that?"

"I have one, but it is in my apartment. I don't like wearing it. It doesn't go very well with my cute outfits. Anyway, you can place items in the backpack that you would like to sell. It's best if I just show you. I will send you the link for a decent one. It is a bit bigger than mine. You are a big guy, so you won't have issues with it. A bigger bag holds bigger items, of course. You can only sell what you can fit in the bag. For instance, if this fellow had a big rifle, you wouldn't be able to sell it here. You would have to go to a sell station in town. There are real expensive bags that will hold an infinite number of items. They are called Infinite Shop Portal Bags...a complicated name I know. However, they will run you like 50,000 mojo."

Boom, another blue screen popped up in my interface and startled me again. I would get used to this eventually, I assumed. It was a product page for one of those bags she was talking about.

Shop Portal Backpack -- 5,000 mojo

"Well shit, I am going to spend what I just got from killing this fool," I pouted.

"Blah, blah, you'll be okay. This is something you need to have. You can sell this guy's plasma pistol and get some mojo back. Just do it, Mr. Grumpy Pants."

I smirked at the fox girl and purchased the backpack as she instructed me to do. It was black and rather stylish as I held it in my hands. I hadn't worn a backpack since high school, so this would be a little weird.

"Now, unzip it and put that dude's gun in there and zip it back."

I did as she told me, and a screen popped up immediately upon zipping the backpack.

Do you want to sell the contents of this back for mojo? Yes or No?

I chose yes, and the backpack vibrated. Then I saw my mojo number increase by 3,000.

"I got 3,000 for the gun. Not too bad, I don't think. This brings my balance to 9,500."

I knelt to check his wallet. I rolled him over and heard brains and blood drip from his head wound. I struggled not to throw up on the ground. The guy had terrible B.O. too. I pulled out his wallet to find no type of currency anywhere. I saw his I.D.; the perp's name was Billy Bollsax. I did that guy a favor by killing him. Before standing back up, I saw a huge shark tattoo on his arm. Euthani saw me looking at it and knelt beside me.

Her beautiful blue eyes widened. "Damn, this guy is a member of the Copper Sharktooth Posse."

4

"Copper Sharktooth Posse? What is that?"

Euthani scratched the back of her head. "Remember, I have been talking about the city being overrun by crime syndicates? They are one of the worst."

"Well, it looks like we are in the clear. He appears to be by himself. Fuck'em," I shrugged.

"Be that as it may, I say we take off."

"Sure. Where are we headed? I am hoping I can go with you."

"Yes, silly. Now let's go."

I held my hand out, palm forward. "First things first. I am bringing ole' Billy Bollsax back to life...temporarily, of course."

Euthani smirked. "Of course, you are. Go ahead and get on with it."

I pumped my fist. "Yeah, buddy."

I looked at the dead ball sack.

***Do you want to raise this corpse from the dead?
Yes or No?
You now have two undead creatures under your
control. You are at your maximum capacity at
Gundertaker Level 1.***

I immediately chose yes and waited excitedly to see what would happen. I rubbed my hands together in anticipation. The green aura around the body changed from green to purple, and ball sack squirmed. He slowly rose to his feet as blood and other nasty fluids spilled from his head.

"This is so cool. Gross but cool," I said as I nodded at the fox girl with a mischievous grin.

The dynamite fox girl rolled her eyes and giggled.

Ball sack stood still and silent as blood streamed down his body. I instructed him to walk forward six steps. He immediately limped toward me like I had commanded him to do mentally. He was as slow as the Night of the Living Dead zombies. I wondered if there was any way to make him move faster. I instructed him to turn right and run. Much to my surprise, the gory sack of shit began to jog. I instructed him to rush into the enormous oak tree. He turned and jogged at the same speed until he plowed into the knobby trunk. There was a wet splat and a low volume zombie moan before ball sack Billy fell backward to the ground. The zombie immediately stood without hesitation and turned toward me as he waited for further instructions. Billy's face had caved in from the collision with the tree. The bullet hole had weakened his head enough that it had just dented in.

I chuckled at the gory sight. "This will be so freaking useful."

"Really? Are we going to be fighting oak trees in the future? You are going to use kamikaze zombies to take them out. May I suggest tying some sort of explosive to them first?"

"You are a little smart ass, aren't you? I like that. Exploding zombies isn't a bad idea, though."

"I hope that is not all you like about me."

"Yep, that is pretty much it. Sorry," I replied facetiously with a grin.

The fox girl opened her mouth and punched me in the bicep. "You are so bad."

I laughed as I rubbed my arm sarcastically.

"My interface told me that at Gundertaker Level One, I can only command two undead. How do I get to level two?"

"By using your Gundertaker skills as often as possible. The more you use them, the quicker you will rise to level two. Training will help you but killing people with your skills works best. You can buy levels in the shop as well. They will come in the form of an injection. However, those cost serious amounts of mojo."

"Okay, I have another question for my bushy-tailed beauty."

"Ah, Dalton. I try to get it nice and bushy. I am glad you like it," Euthani hugged my arm.

"Ah, yeah, you're welcome. How do I release my risen undead minions? I don't want these things just following me wherever I go," I said as I turned to look at my zombie companions. "No offense."

"Right on. You probably can get rid of them the same way you rose them. Pull up your interface and select them and see what happens."

I nodded and accessed my interface eagerly. I selected the squirrel and sure enough a little notification box popped up.

Do you relieve this undead creature? Yes or No?

I immediately pressed the yes button, and the purple aura around the squirrel turned black. The life left the little guy's body, and he plopped on his side.

The fox girl looked at me, and then back at the little squirrel corpse. She poked out her bottom lip. "Aww, that was pitiful. Thank you, little squirrel. We won't forget you!"

I will admit that it tugged at my heartstrings a bit. It was my first risen zombie, and he had saved my butthole from unauthorized entry by a large, sweaty bald man. Yesterday, if you would have told me I would be rescued from rape by a decapitated zombie squirrel, I would have had you committed. It is amazing how your life can change from one minute to the next.

The fox girl placed her palm on my chest and lightly patted. "Can I make a suggestion?"

I nodded and smiled at her beautiful face. "You can do anything you like."

Euthani swooned. "I think you should keep the bald zombie around until we get back to the city. We may run into more issues, and it would be nice to have a meat shield. Learning zombie combat would be kind of cool, too."

"I think you're right. I'll let you lead the way. After you ma'am."

She clapped and grinned. "I can't wait for you to see my apartment! I have had no guests in a while!"

"I'm glad that you're happy," I smiled.

This fox girl's enthusiasm and personality was so infectious. I just wanted to be around her and talk to her all the time. Amazingly, her outside beauty almost matched her inside majesty. I was so lucky to have found her, otherwise I would be under a tree in the fetal position not knowing what the hell was going on. I followed her down a winding path through the forest. This would have been a really cool place if it weren't for all the disgusting garbage all over the place. The bloody zombie that limped along behind us didn't help the scenery. However, this fox girl's perfect ass swayed a few feet in front of me, and it improved the scenery by a factor of ten. The bushy red tail behind her was a little odd, but I dug it. I dug it big time. What the hell was wrong with me?

"So, you come out here a lot?" I asked softly.

She spoke to me without turning her head. "Yeah, it helps clear my head, and I like to feel close to nature. I am a fox girl, you know."

I instructed ball sack to speed up some. This trek was taking entirely too long. He obliged, and we could walk at a normal pace. The wet bloody, flapping sound was followed by a light moan periodically. The moonlight pierced through the trees and created small spears of white light that blanketed the trail we were traveling. We limited our conversation to quick flirtations every few minutes and the silence was filled with the sounds of the ball sack zombie along with chirping of birds and cricket noises. The closer we got to the city, motors running, and horns honking replaced those sounds. The car motors made more of a humming noise that differed greatly from the engines on earth. They were the sounds I had heard in science fiction movies over the years. The aura over the city was more color. There were blues, pinks, purples, and white lights. As I exited the park with my two pals, it felt as if I had walked through a doorway to another dimension. The set of Blade Runner would have been a great comparison. There were no flying cars, but they certainly looked nothing like I had ever seen before. They were sleeker and more semicircular. They were covered with glowing lights, and even the wheels were illuminated. The cars zoomed and zipped by quickly. I just stopped to try and absorb my foreign surroundings.

Euthani paused when she saw me staring, eyes wide and darting side to side and up and down. While I was engrossed in my surroundings, I forgot to tell the ball sack zombie to stop along with us. We turned our heads when we heard a car screech in an attempt to stop. They were too late. Billy Bollsax went flying thirty yards down the street from the vicious impact with the car. The poor bastard's head blew completely off and bounced down the sidewalk.

Euthani and I just stood frozen as we watched the horrible event take place. The doors of the silver and blue vehicle swung upward, and two men erupted out of the car.

The fox girl elbowed me softly in my side and pointed at the raised door of the car. I squinted and saw the same shark that was on Bollsax tattoo. "Oh, shit. This could be a problem."

Euthani pulled me a few steps over, and we knelt behind a purple glowing bench.

"What the fuck did you do, man?" the passenger yelled at the driver.

"This fucker walked right out in front of me. I didn't have time to stop," the driver replied as he looked at the front of his car. "Fuck me in the goat ass! There is a damn dent, and he cracked the grill. Goddamit!"

The passenger knelt beside the body, "Well, this bloke has lost his head over the whole situation."

"You cunt, do you really think this is a time to joke with me? I just got this thing fixed two weeks ago. It isn't like I have insurance. Fuck insurance. This is coming out of my pocket. Damn idiot bastard walked right out in front of me."

"Whoa, whoa, man, we have a much bigger problem. Holy shit, do we have a problem," the passenger replied as he stood back to his feet.

"What are you jabbering about? Screw the guy! I am glad the bastard is dead. If the car hadn't killed him, I would have."

"Shut the fuck up, this is a posse member. Look at the tattoo!" the passenger roared as he pointed at the headless corpse.

"Well, who is it?"

"We need to find the head. How the hell am I supposed to know? He is a fat fuck, so it is one of our fat fuck posse guys!"

"So, it is either Billy Bollsax or that annoying Jacque Esche?" the driver asked as he jogged down the sidewalk to locate the head.

The other posse member joined him as they frantically

looked all over for the severed head. The melon had to be a demolished sight by now. It already had a huge plasma hole, and it had been caved in completely. Now, it had bounced on the concrete after the body was hit by a speeding car. Ball sack has had a rough day.

The driver lifted a bloody ball of gore from the ground. "Fuck, it looks like Billy Bollsax to me. Jacque Esche has curly black hair. This guy is bald. Hold up mate, there is a fucking plasma bullet hole through his head. What the fuck is going on? Men with bullet holes in their heads rarely walk around and into the road to get splattered by a car."

"Are you sure he has a bullet hole in his noggin? Let me see...ah yeah, bullet hole. Definitely. What a shame."

"Well, how the fuck do you explain him walking the hell around dead...dead...there is a freaking Necromancer somewhere around here. That's the only explanation that makes any sense at all."

"What the hell dude? I haven't been around a necromancer in like forever. There aren't any around Osiris that I am aware of."

"Maybe Sly will know."

The fox girl broke her silence and whispered in my ear. "Sly Swagger, he is the leader of the Copper Sharktooth Posse. He is bad news."

"Don't we need to get out of here?"

The fox girl nodded. "Yeah, my apartment is not far, just two blocks over that way."

The driver put some sort of communicator to his head. "Let me speak to Sly. Now. We have a problem!"

After twenty seconds of the driver tapping his foot on the sidewalk, he perked up. "Yeah, Sly. Sorry to bother you. We have an issue. Billy Bollsax is dead. Yeah...dead. What happened? Well, he walked in the street, and we hit him with the car. Yeah, yeah, however, he has a bullet hole in his head. He had to have been raised by a necromancer. Yeah, we'll be right there." Then the driver put the communicator back into his coat pocket.

"So, what did he say? Was he pissed at us?" asked the passenger.

The driver shrugged. "Yeah at first, but he changed his tune when I told him about the necromancer. He wants us to bring the body back to HQ. Fuck. I will get blood all in my damn trunk. Shit, man. Do you know how hard it is to get blood out of the damn carpet?"

"Ah man, can't he just send somebody with a truck or something? Shit."

"No, he said that he wants us there immediately. Give me a hand. You get his legs, and I will get the head...umm the shoulders. We'll wrap his head in his coat or something. I would prefer to not get any brain mush in my trunk. Blood is bad enough, but brains stink bad."

The men spent the next few minutes slowly moving the big corpse from the street and into the back of the car. They fussed the whole time. The passenger vomited on the side of the car when the head rolled off Bollsax chest onto the ground causing an eyeball to pop out.

After the car pulled away, we stood and began our trek to Euthani's apartment. On the way to the apartment, I thought about my last few seconds on Earth. I would have loved to have seen the reaction of everyone when I just fell through the apron into oblivion never to be seen again. This had to be one of the biggest news stories ever. A mega popular celebrity vanished into thin air in front of everyone in the Staples Center and in front of millions of PPV watchers from around the world. What are they thinking right now? How the fuck are they going to explain this? Thank God my parents were dead, and I had no contact with any other family. It would be rough to see your loved one portal through a ring to another dimension. I couldn't help but have a mischievous grin on my face as we approached Euthani's apartment building.

5

Euthani's apartment building was enormous. She mentioned that it was twenty stories high, and her apartment was on the 19th floor. It was lit up like it should have been standing on the Las Vegas strip. When we entered the lobby, it was much more normal as to what I expected an apartment building to look like. There were a lot of grey and white with green plants scattered about. The interior was darker since it was night. There were long lighting strips up and down the corners of the hallway. They glowed at this time of night, but they would brighten up considerably during the daytime, I assumed at least. We walked over to the elevators. There were two side by side which was rare for an apartment building, but with the size of this place, one elevator would be a frustrating bottleneck. The door dinged within a few seconds of Euthani pressing the button. Most people would be asleep, no doubt. The doors closed behind us and Euthani pressed the 19th button. It lit up, and the elevator rose softly. It felt like we were going much slower than we actually were. The floor numbers on the digital display were changing at a rapid rate. Suddenly, Euthani reached her arm out and pressed the Emergency Stop button. The elevator stopped quickly, but we didn't feel a strong jolt.

"Is something wrong?" I asked as I looked at the digital display over the door. It shone the number 15.

Euthani strutted over slowly and put both hands on my face and pulled me to her lips. They were soft, warm, and wet to the touch, and she smelled like cherries. It must have been some sort of lip balm or lipstick.

I pulled away for a second. "What's going on? I mean...I am not complaining. I am just surprised."

"You are an amazing man, Dalton Wade, and a powerful man. I felt an instant connection with you. This connection is making me extremely horny." She placed her hand on my dick on the outside of my pants. "It feels like you are horny as well. Your cock grows hard, does it not?"

I exhaled and nodded. "Yeah, it is definitely growing hard, but don't you want to wait until we get to your room?"

"No, I want you now," Euthani whispered as she began to kiss my neck.

While the sudden sexual proposition of the fox girl surprised me, it wasn't something that was new to me exactly. I am or was a KAW superstar. Rock stars have groupies, and professional wrestling also has no shortage of beautiful women willing to fuck the wrestlers regularly. Wrestlers knew these girls as "ring rats." They were all over the backstage of all the venues I visited. Some nights I was in the mood, and some nights I was not. Casual sex with strangers was the norm for me. Was it something I was proud of? Not really, but it was a perk of the job. A nice blow job before or after a match may ease the pain and stress enough that we won't get drunk or pop pills. Those girls were doing exactly what they wanted to do. We didn't force them to do anything. The difference with Euthani is that I cared about her and genuinely wanted to know her. I was smitten for the first time in a long time. Sex with her was definitely something I wanted to do. I was just surprised it would be this soon. Nevertheless, if she wanted it, I would happily give it to her.

She moved to the opposite side of my neck and continued to kiss it, letting out quiet moans. I lifted her head back to mine and began kissing her lips again. This time our tongues wrestled as our kisses grew more passionate. I rubbed my hands up and down her back. She unbuckled my belt and opened my pants. Her hand slid under my boxer briefs and grasped my shaft with force. I wanted it rough, and I could tell she wanted it too. I groaned, and my eyes rolled in the back of my head.

"Fuck, you are amazing," I groaned.

Euthani giggled. "You have no idea." She pulled my pants down to my ankles and got to her knees. My cock tingled and twitched in anticipation of what was coming. The fox girl put her plump red lips around my member and took my hardness in her warm, wet mouth. I felt her tongue circle my shaft as she bobbed on my throbbing dick. I saw her large, reddish-brown ears twitch as she blew me. Her tail twirled slowly behind her. This was an experience I had never had before...sex with a girl that was part animal. It was weird, but I was absolutely enthralled with this woman. She squeezed my balls with the perfect amount of pressure. The mixture of pain and pleasure was unbelievable. I ran my fingers through her soft hair and pressed her head, so she could take me deeper. After a few more bobs, I pulled her away, and she looked up at me and licked her lips. Her bright blue eyes were the most perfect eyes I had ever seen in my life. They begged me to pleasure her. She pulled a zipper down on her top, and her breasts were freed. The leather top pushed them in close to her chest, so I couldn't decipher the actual size before. She had large, perky breasts that rivaled any pair of tits I had ever seen. She promptly placed my shaft between them and begin to move up and down as she breast fucked me.

"Holy shit," I moaned as she went up and down. "I can't be the one to have all the fun."

She took her mouth off my dick. "This is fun, silly."

I lifted her to her feet and unbuttoned her pants and pulled them down. Much to my surprise, she had no panties on underneath the leather. I kissed her stomach and grabbed her ass and squeezed. She moaned, and she ran her fingers through my hair and pulled on it. A few seconds later, she pushed my head down to her pussy. She had a perfect red landing strip of hair that I ran my tongue through until I reached her dripping, wet pussy. She convulsed and screamed as I went to work with my tongue. The smell of her juices and sweet taste made me freaking crazy. She lifted her right leg and put her foot on the handrail on the wall of the elevator. I had a much more perfect view of my dessert. I inserted my left thumb into her wet vagina as I continued to lick her clit. She began to move and pull my hair. I knew that she was getting close, so I put more work in to getting her there. I wanted her to remember this orgasm for a long time. A few seconds later, she screamed and shook from her intense orgasm. I felt more of her warm cum stream down my chin.

"Oh gods, thank you. That was amazing. Oh, fuck," she whispered out of breath.

I stood and turned her around. She groaned and grabbed the handrail tight with both hands. Her tail rubbed my chest, which drove me insane with pleasure. I grabbed the base of her soft, bushy tail as I inserted my throbbing cock into her drenched pussy. She jerked and moaned in ecstasy as she felt me penetrate her. I used her tail to pull me deep inside her. She seemed to enjoy incorporating her tail into my thrusting. I began to thrust harder and harder while I pulled her tail.

"Oh, fuck, Dalton. I am going to come again. Fuck me harder and fill me with your seed."

I followed her demands, and my dick traveled in and out of her vagina deep, hard, and fast. After a few seconds of the pounding, her pussy tightened around my cock as she exploded into her second orgasm. The new tightness around my dick brought me close to the edge. I kept thrusting while her tail caressed my cheek. The slapping of our skin together became deafening with each hard thrust. I exploded into her pussy and came deep inside of her. I moaned, and she screamed. I slowed my thrusting down to a crawl as I finished putting all my warm seed inside of her.

"Fuck, Euthani. I have been around Earth and had my share of women, but I can safely say you have taken first place. Holy shit, you are incredible. Thank you."

She lifted up and pressed her back against my torso. She grabbed my cheek and turned her head for a kiss.

"I was concerned you would think less of me. We just met after all, but I just couldn't help myself. You are unlike any man I have ever met, and I have a need you."

I exhaled and wiped the sweat from my brow as I pulled my cock out of her. "You are definitely unlike any woman I have ever met, and I want to know more about you. You are special."

She smiled and tears filled her eyes. She kept them from spilling over, but they were there. We promptly put our clothes back on, and she disengaged the emergency stop to continue our climb to the 19th floor.

When the door opened, a hallway with the same decor from the lobby met us. We kind of just melted out of the elevator door and drifted to her apartment. We felt completely satisfied. I was exhausted and wanted to plop down and sleep. Hopefully, she would let me sleep with her. She stopped at door 1979 and placed her eye in front of a retinal scanner. There was a quick scan with a beep before the door opened, and we walked in. The lighting automatically turned on as the fox girl entered, and she sauntered down the hallway. I watched her perfect ass bounce and daydreamed of our sex in the elevator.

"Love in an elevator, livin' it up while you're goin' down" by Aerosmith began playing in my head as I followed her. She immediately turned into a bedroom.

She began removing her clothes again, and my eyes grew wide. "I am going to take a shower, silly. That's my bed, I hope you plan to lie with me. I won't bite."

I chuckled. "I was hoping you would invite me. I am beat, and I am not ready to be away from you yet."

She winked and smiled as her leather outfit fell to the floor. She strutted to her bathroom in all her goddamn glory, and I just stood there watching with my mouth wide open. She snapped her fingers, and the water in her shower turned on. I thought that was fucking cool as hell.

"Dalton?"

"Yeah, what's up?"

"I don't know where my manners are. Would you like to join me?"

"Umm, yeah."

It took only a few seconds before I had removed all my clothing and eagerly walked to the shower. The shower head was on the opposite wall, and she had her back turned toward me as she washed her hair.

"Damn," I whispered to myself.

I slowly opened the glass door and entered. Steam from the scorching water filled the enclosed space.

She handed me a bottle of shampoo. "Can you do me a favor and wash my tail for me? My ass too?"

"Yeah, I can certainly do that," I replied, trying to hide my excitement. However, I don't think I succeeded.

I squirted the white creamy shampoo on my right hand and began rubbing both hands together. I placed my hands on her tail and lathered the reddish-brown fur until it looked like I had covered it with snow. She periodically let out low groans as I completed the task for her. I squeezed out more shampoo and began rubbing her ass cheeks. I washed each cheek completely and slowly so I could savor the experience. I boldly washed her ass crack, and she seemed to enjoy when my fingers touched her asshole gently. She began to rub her bushy tail between my legs and my cock was back at attention. I turned her around and placed my hands under her thighs and lifted her onto my dick. I pressed her against the wall and began thrusting again. The smell of her shampooed hair was intoxicating. She yelped and licked my nose.

"Fuck me harder, Dalton. I know you want to."

"Yeah, that is an understatement," I whispered as I followed her lewd command.

We went at it hard for a few minutes, and she came once more and pulled my head backward by my long, blonde hair. She bit my chin as I thrust. I only lasted a few seconds more before spilling more seed inside her warm pussy. I almost hyperventilated, and my body convulsed violently from the release.

"Holy fuck, that was better than the first," I panted.

"Well, I hoped you would want to do it one more time before we retired for the night. Thank you."

"Damn, you make me crazy. You are an awesome girl, inside and out. I am so glad we met."

"Me too, Dalton," she whispered as she kissed my lips

once more. I slowly lifted her off my dick and lowered her gently to the floor. We finished washing our bodies and made our way back to the bed. She slipped on a t-shirt, and I put my boxer briefs back on. We sank into the mattress, and she laid her head on my chest as we drifted off to sleep in seconds.

Two hours later, I heard a slam at the door and then another. We both lifted in the bed quickly to determine what the hell was going on. Seeing Euthani rise assured me I wasn't dreaming, and that noise was reality.

"Let's get dressed!" I exclaimed.

6

I don't think I had ever put on clothes as fast as I did at that moment. I took out my plasma pistol and readied it for battle, and Euthani did the same with her crossbow.

"OPEN UP! WE NEED TO TALK TO YOU, EUTHANI NABOO!" screamed a deep voice followed by another slam on the door.

Euthani covered her mouth to suppress a laugh.

"What is funny about this situation if you don't mind me asking?" I asked with an eyebrow raised.

"I'm sorry, he rhymed, and it tickled me a bit."

We stood behind a wall and I peeked around the corner to see the door rattle from another loud knock.

"What do you want?" I yelled.

"Oh, you must be the man in the camera. Perfect."

"What the fuck are you talking about?"

"Did you really think you would get away with killing a

posse member?" asked the deep voice. I also noticed a peculiar growl sound when he spoke. I didn't know what that meant.

"Euthani, how the hell do they know that we killed that guy and where you live? The guys that hit ball sack didn't see us."

I could tell the fox girl was in deep thought. Then she delivered a calculated response. "Cameras. There are a few police cameras left in service. They are controlled by the syndicates. Evidently, the posse has control over the ones in that area. Cameras like those have facial recognition capabilities, so I am guessing that is how they found me."

"Don't you need some kind of criminal record in the system to show up on a system like that?"

"Yeah, I do have a little criminal record. Do we really have to talk about this now?"

I was surprised. I had a hard time seeing Euthani committing any crimes, but now was not the time to ask questions.

"Last chance. Open the door, or we blast it open. We should have already done that, but everyone says I am the nice one. I fucking hate that label."

"Ugh, we are kinda fucked. That is the only door out of here. Going out on the window is out. We are nineteen floors up, for God's sake."

"Actually, they are the ones that are kinda fucked. They should have just blasted in the door initially while we slept, but no...this fucktard gives us warning they are here and time to get our gear. Let them come in, and we blast them."

She was absolutely right. I had to get in the soldier mind-set. I had the weapon skills with my class, but I was still a pro wrestler right now. I had to push that to the side and embrace who I was now.

I held my right hand at a 90-degree angle beside my mouth and yelled. "Listen dipshits, you are welcome to come right on in. We aren't going out there."

"Your funeral, asshole!"

A gun blast sounded and popped the center of the door, and then they shot at the door handle. Neither gunshot caused penetration.

"Geez, what kind of door do you have?"

The fox girl shrugged. "I don't know. They installed them last year. Yay for me, I guess."

Another gunshot rang out and dented the door inward. "That door isn't going to hold much longer. We need a plan," I said with my back to the wall. "Stay here."

I sprinted to the cabinet near the door and pushed it quickly in front of the doorway. This shit is what they do in the movies, maybe it will help. I could hear mumbling in the hallway from several people. I moved closer to the door, but I made sure I stood outside of harm's way. I could tell they were fussing at each other about a plan. If I had to guess, there were four posse members in the hallway. I would bet good money that two of them were the guys from the street. It sounded just like them, albeit muffled by a wall. Euthani peeked around the corner of the wall and looked at me, clearly wanting some sort of direction. I just waved for her to go back into cover. This shit was all new to me. I have played some shooter video games and paintball a few years ago. I have watched a lot of action movies my entire life as well. These three things were my only training. Nonetheless, I was a Gundertaker, and I was supposed to be a badass. I had to work on getting some of my swagger back from my old life. I was fucking Dalton Wade, The Cooler!

Two more blasts hit the door and dented it in even further. It would not hold much longer. Hell, it was an act of God that it had lasted this long with the amount of punishment it was receiving. I need to find out about the manufacturer. I am sure I'll be in the market for some sort of living space soon. What the hell was I doing? Four gangsters were here to kill me, and I am thinking about buying an apartment.

"Hey Dalton," Euthani whispered in my ear.

I almost jumped out of my skin. I had no clue she had snuck up behind me. "Dammit, I told you to stay over there."

The fox girl rolled her eyes. "Dalton, I appreciate all of this "save the girl, damsel in distress" thing you have going on, but I am also an interfacer and actually experienced in this world. Let me help. Otherwise, we will lie in a pool of our own blood soon."

She was right. I had no clue what I was doing. This wasn't a video game, and there were no respawns. "You're right. I'm sorry."

"No need to be sorry, I am very touched," the fox girl whispered as she kissed my cheek, and she held up her crossbow while she glared at the door.

I heard the sound of something being placed on the door and heard one perp yell "Clear!"

I grabbed the fox girl and dove on top of her as the charge exploded, knocking the door off the hinges.

My ears rang, and my vision wasn't in fine working order. I blinked a few times as I aimed my plasma pistol at the door. A posse member slowly climbed over the busted cabinet, looking straight ahead as he pointed a pistol.

Euthani wasted no time at all. She shot two plasma bolts into his torso and one into his head...well, through his head is more like it. Blood and brains splattered her pristine white walls as the body plopped to the floor. It was the passenger of the car from earlier.

"Harry!" the driver screamed from the hallway. Euthani suddenly moved forward and performed a graceful flip while she shot three more plasma bolts through the doorway into the hallway. It looked like a scene from a John Woo film.

"Fuck me!" I yelled with my eyes wide.

"Hell yeah, I like it when you talk dirty to me," she playfully said as she got back into an attack position on the opposite side of the room. "I shot one guy who was standing in the middle of the door, and he is dead. I think it was the driver guy from earlier."

"To hell with this, let's fall back," one man growled from the hallway.

"Ah, you fucking pussy!" another man exclaimed. "We have a job to do. Come back! Sly will slit your damn throat."

"Hey, put your guns away and get the hell out of here. No one else has to die," I yelled at the door.

"Fuck you, man! We ain't going nowhere until you stop breathing!"

"It looks to me like your friend abandoned you. Now you are outnumbered. Do you really think it is wise to engage us?" Euthani spoke in a surprisingly calm and peaceful voice.

"Bitch, I didn't ask you a damn thing!"

All right, I was ready to kill this bastard. This little plea for a truce was futile. What the fuck was I thinking? I am a necromancer. I laughed as I pulled up my interface and selected the corpse inside the apartment. He may have been in worse shape than Billy Bollsax, but I just needed him to be a bullet sponge long enough to take this guy out. The man's arms twitched, and one leg moved as he came back to life right in front of our eyes. Euthani smiled and gave me a thumbs up from the other side of the room. I replied with only a wink.

I commanded the undead gangster to walk through the doorway. He had some trouble traversing the debris that was once a wooden cabinet, but he succeeded and made his way into the hallway. A scream erupted from the hallway and filtered into the apartment.

"Harry! What the hell?"

I instructed him to pounce on the man.

"No, get off me, you undead fuck!"

I motioned for both of us to exit the doorway. I peeked out and saw my zombie lying on top of the perp. The zombie was attempting to bite, but his jaw wasn't working properly due to the trauma from the crossbow. I looked the other way to see an empty hallway, and I motioned for Euthani to aim her crossbow down the corridor in case the deserter returned.

I walked beside the zombie as it nipped at the gangster's face. There were a few cuts from his teeth, but he could not fight his broken jaw. I stood over the perp and pointed my pistol at his head. The man's eyes almost popped out of his head. "No please, we can work --"

My plasma round went through his head before he finished his statement. I turned and checked on Euthani. She stood with her crossbow aimed down the hallway. "You good?" I asked.

"Yeah, I'm fine. You?"

"Yeah. Do you think he will come back?"

"Doubtful. We need to keep our guard up though."

"Agreed."

"Ok, Dalton. Get some mojo. You can have these two perps. I am good. I want you to get some gear from the shop. I have a feeling the posse will come after us again. However, since you raised that fellow from the dead, you cannot extract mojo. Get what you can from the other two."

"Yes, ma'am. I like it when you order me around."

The fox girl winked with a crooked smile.

I was able to extract 12,000 mojo from the two corpses and loot a plasma pistol and a shotgun.

"Blah, these weapons aren't really an upgrade. I mean the shotgun packs a punch, but I don't really want to lug that thing around. It has seen better days, anyway. I think I will sell them to the shop. Since the shotgun is sawed off, I think I can get it to fit in the Shop Portal Backpack," I informed Euthani.

"Excellent decision. Get it done. If it doesn't fit, I have a sell station in my bedroom. I'll get us a couple bottles of water out of the fridge."

I nodded and stuffed the weapons into the backpack quickly and zipped it back up. I was able to salvage 9,000 mojo from the weapons, which was awesome. The shotgun was worth more than I had suspected. "Sweet."

"Catch!" Euthani chirped as she tossed me a water bottle. I removed the cap and drank the contents in two gulps. I hadn't realized I was so freaking thirsty.

"I feel bad about getting all this mojo. You deserve your share of it. Let's do 50/50, Okay?"

Euthani raspberried. "I will take mojo when I want mojo. Don't worry about it. Trust me, I am good."

"All right, I just wanted to clear the ole' conscience. Do I need to go shopping again?"

Suddenly, we heard a very artificial computerized voice from behind us. "Good job tonight. Very impressive."

We both turned with our guns out.

"That is not a good idea," said the robotic-sounding figure standing near the window at the end of the hallway.

"We understand math. Two against a man with no weapon are pretty good odds. Who are you?" I asked the mystery man.

I still could not get a good look at him. He stood in front of the window and the lights from the outside just made him look like a black silhouette. I saw him flip something open on his arm. He delivered two keystrokes and then vanished.

"What the fuck? Where did he go?" I asked frantically as I scanned the area in front of me.

A monotone voice broke the silence behind us. "Please

drop your guns and put your hands up and turn around slowly."

"Shit!" I whispered as I hesitantly dropped my gun to the hallway floor and raised my hands in the air. The fox girl followed suit.

As soon as we turned, we were greeted by two glistening platinum pistols. One weapon was in each of our faces.

"I am not here to hurt you," added the robotic man.

I squinted my eyes a bit to get a better look at this odd man. He wore a brown trench coat and what looked like a brown fedora or whatever Dick Tracy wore back in the day. The man was an inch taller than me, but he was slender, and he didn't appear to be all that muscular. However, he was covered by a trench coat. The parts of his body I could see were mostly metal or steel. However, his face looked to have some human flesh. It was almost like he was in the process of becoming a human but decided not to finish the process.

"Let's go inside," the metal man commanded.

I nodded and led the way into the apartment living area. I used my foot to move the shredded wooden cabinet out of the way.

"Please have a seat on the couch. Do not attempt anything stupid," the cyborg man commanded in his metallic monotone voice.

We followed his instructions and sat down slowly. We assumed taking our hands down would be fine, so we did so.

"Place your hands on your knees where I can see them. Don't try any funny business. I have no problem ending your lives right now."

"So, are you in the posse?" Euthani asked softly.

"Do not insult me. I would never associate with such filth. You did the world a favor tonight by killing these three vermin."

The anger surprised me in his voice. It was good to know that he wasn't a gang member, but who was he...or it?

"One of them got away, I am afraid," the fox girl added solemnly.

"No, I killed the pest on my way to you."

I nodded and shrugged. "Okay, are you going to tell us what you want? What is your name? Who are you with? Why are you still pointing those huge pistols at us?"

The cyborg delivered an exotic laugh as he holstered his beautiful shiny pistols.

"So, are you here to kill us? Why the hell would you want to do that if you weren't in the posse?"

"I am not here to kill you. I already stated that I was not here to hurt you," the cyborg replied.

I nodded slowly. "Okay, well then who are you?"

"I am Stranger Zero."

7

I had to admit, this Stranger Zero character was cool as hell. The way he talked, the way he moved, and the way he dressed was slick as fuck. Not to mention his platinum pistols were epic. Damn, I sounded like I had a kinky cyborg crush.

"You aren't here to kill us. So, why are you here?" asked Euthani as she crossed her slender arms.

"I would love to explain right now, but time is of the essence. We need to go. I have transport," replied Stranger Zero as he glanced out the hall window.

"Are you going to tell us you have free candy next? Jesus, your name is even Stranger...literally. It isn't the best idea to go anywhere with you," I added with an eyebrow raised.

"I do not have any...candy," Stranger Zero replied dead-pan. "You don't have a choice. Five cars have arrived, and a dozen posse trash are headed this way."

I looked out of the window to see if the cyborg was telling the truth. "Shit! He's right."

"Even if we go with you, we will run right into these guys on the way out," Euthani added with her eyes wide.

"This is not a problem," Stranger Zero replied calmly.

I sighed. "I beg to differ."

Suddenly, Stranger Zero's guns extended from his sleeves directly into his hands with a metallic zipping sound. The cyborg turned toward the window and began firing his pistols.

Boom.

Boom.

Boom.

Boom.

The entire window blew out and cool air exploded into the hallway. "What the hell are you doing?" I asked as I checked myself for glass.

He ignored me as he accessed the panel on his forearm he had used before when he cloaked. After two keystrokes, we heard a loud humming noise and saw a glow pulsing from below the window. Euthani and I stood frozen. We were completely clueless as to what would happen next. A silver and black vehicle floated beside the hole in the wall. Two doors opened and Stranger Zero jumped into the door at the front of the flying car. Euthani and I looked at each other with a lot of apprehension. She shrugged and then sprinted to the opening and leaped into the same door that Stranger Zero had entered. Suddenly, I heard the eruption of gunfire behind me. Bullets whizzed by me and slammed into the wall.

"Dalton, get your ass in the car! Now!" Euthani screamed.

I took a deep breath and ran toward my safe haven. The posse would have a perfect shot in a second or two. I dove into the open door at the back of the car. I caught a flash of the nineteen-floor drop before sliding across the backseat and slamming into the other door.

"Hold on," Stranger Zero instructed.

The doors shut quicker than they had opened. I heard bullets ding off the side of the steel, but there didn't look to be any penetration into the cabin. The car banked left, then dove at almost a 90-degree angle. My stomach felt like it was in my throat.

"Fuuuuck!" I yelled with my eyes closed. I had never been a huge roller coaster fan, and that is exactly what it felt like, but with no safety restraints over my shoulders.

We leveled off after a couple of seconds and landed on the street. We then swerved in and out of traffic as we traveled at a very high rate of speed. Stranger Zero and Euthani looked as if they were on a peaceful Sunday drive.

"Are you okay?" asked Euthani with a smile.

"Yeah, I'm a little queasy, but I'll live."

"I apologize for the sudden drop, but it was either drop or die," Stranger Zero stated in his monotone robotic voice.

"No worries, SZ...Is it all right if I just call you SZ for short?"

"That will be fine."

"SZ, that sounds cool," Euthani nodded with a grin.

The car slowed down, and SZ drove less erratically a few minutes later. I finally was able to sit straight up in the smooth leather seat and fumbled around for the seatbelt. I promptly fastened one after a few seconds of searching.

"You are wise. Seatbelts save lives," announced SZ.

"Yeah, I wear one all the time. You can't be too careful," Euthani interjected with a sweet smile.

POW!

An explosion on the right side of the car scared the shit out of me. We began to swerve back and forth on the street.

SZ calmingly broke his silence. "It appears we have blown a tire. It was damaged by a bullet, perhaps. I fear I will not regain control." SZ fastened his seat belt in one fluid motion.

A symphony of screeches and car horns filled my ears from all around us as we went wild on the freeway.

POW!

The front passenger side tire blew, and that was all she wrote. We spun around 360 degrees and went straight at a parked car on the street. The car was very low to the ground, like an exotic sports car on Earth. It served as a ramp, mostly. There was an ear-splitting crash as we contacted the parked car. We launched in the air like a motorcycle daredevil and did a corkscrew before we slammed into a parking lot. Before we hit the ground, a multitude of gigantic airbags filled the inside of the car from all directions. It felt like we were in a bouncy castle at a child's birthday party. I was shaken and dizzy from the crash, but chances were good that I would have been killed without these giant airbags.

SZ spoke first. "Are either of you injured? I am perfectly operational."

Euthani chimed in quietly. "No, I don't think so. That was intense."

"I'm good. One hell of a safety system in this thing...damn," I replied with a cough.

"Splendid. Let us evacuate. Chances are high that the posse will catch up with us," SZ informed.

I pushed my way through all the slowly deflating airbags until I found the window. I could escape with no issue. I thought I was out first, but SZ and Euthani were doing weapon checks outside the car. We heard vehicles in the distance speeding our way, and we all knew they were coming for us.

"Come now," SZ demanded as he removed a manhole cover in the middle of the street. "Down here, now."

As we made our way to the hole, SZ tossed a small brick-shaped object inside of the wreckage. "I would advise you to get down there. Quickly."

Euthani descended first, and I followed right behind her. SZ walked toward me with a robotic swagger as the car exploded behind him. It was quite an awesome sight. It looked like a stylish action scene from a Michael Bay film.

"Go, they will be here in a moment. Did the accident damage your eardrums?" asked SZ in his smooth mechanical voice.

Euthani had made it to the bottom, and I descended the ladder into the sewer at a lightning-fast rate of speed. I looked up and saw SZ on the ladder pulling the manhole cover back over top. There was a loud clang, and the light dimmed.

Euthani had the back of her hand over her nose. "Yikes, this place reeks."

"It is a sewer. It is full of human waste, which makes the odor more pungent," SZ added as his feet hit the stone floor at the bottom of the sewer.

"Eh, we knew that, but thanks for reminding us SZ," I muttered to the cyborg.

"Will they suspect that we went down here to stinky town?" I joked.

SZ looked at me and placed his head at an angle. "Stinky Town, we are still in Osiris...not Stinky Town. There is no Stinky Town on Zorth. To answer your question, there is no way to know for sure if they will follow us down. My hope is the exploded car will cause them to believe we are dead. The Copper Sharktooth Posse is a stupid syndicate led by a moron."

"What's the plan?" Euthani asked politely.

"We will continue east in the tunnels, and I will contact Astra for an extraction," the cyborg replied.

"Astra?" the fox girl asked.

"She is my friend and also a member of our group."

"What group is that exactly?" Euthani asked and waited patiently for a response.

"The Cosmic Peacekeepers. You will learn more when we reach the HQ," Stranger Zero responded.

"At least with a name like Peacekeepers, chances are pretty good that you are nice people," I said as I gave SZ a thumbs up.

"Yes, that would be correct. We are interested in doing

good for Osiris. Now, we need to continue in the event the posse learns of our whereabouts. Once we put enough distance between us and the crash, I will contact Astra for extraction. Let's move."

Euthani began following the cyborg man. The stone floor of the sewer stuck to her shoes, and she made a disgusted face. "Ugh, this is nasty. I will try not to look down."

"This environment is unsanitary. You are correct in your assessment," SZ added.

I followed the direction of SZ as he traveled the web of corridors in the sewer. "Who is Astra?"

"She is a Cosmic Peacekeeper and my close friend. Please keep the chitchat to a minimum. There are dangers in the sewers. We must be vigilant."

I nodded slowly and glanced at Euthani. "No problem, lead the way," I pretended to zip my lips.

Euthani smiled and did the same. I wondered what dangers the cyborg talked about other than stepping in a piece of shit or contracting E-Coli or some other nasty bacteria. We followed him in silence for a few minutes. The only sound was the sloshing of our feet in the wetness and the muffled sound of traffic above. SZ appeared to know where he was going. The sewer just looked like a dark and smelly labyrinth that I would get completely lost in. I grinned every time I looked at Euthani because the gorgeous fox girl continued to carry a disgusted expression on her perfect face. She tried to raise her bushy tail higher than normal to avoid getting it soiled in sewer nastiness.

We turned a corner, and SZ stopped in his tracks. His

platinum pistols ejected from his trench coat sleeves and into his hands, which was very cool, by the way. Euthani and I followed suit as we pulled our pistols from our holsters. We were much less stylish, but we were ready to fire at any threats just the same. The cyborg began punching something into his forearm display, and a bright light appeared to emit from his chest. When the light brightened our view, we saw four dark figures approaching us in the muck.

"Mire Walkers at 12 o'clock," murmured the cyborg. "Mire Walkers are easy to kill. The problem escalates as their numbers rise. Our gunfire will probably instigate more of them to attack. Watch your back."

Stranger Zero opened fire as the Mire Walkers moved faster toward us. He looked like Doc Holliday from one of my favorite films, *Tombstone*. Every shot was true, and all four of the Mire Walkers dropped into the sewage from perfectly placed headshots.

"Shit, good shooting SZ," Euthani stated with her mouth wide.

Suddenly, I felt a hand grip my ankle and a terrifying moan filled my ears. I looked down to see a Mire Walker rise from the river of sewage. It looked like a zombie that had been dunked into a pool of shit. It opened its mouth and attempted to take a chunk out of my calf muscle.

"Fuck! They're below us!" I aimed my plasma pistol at its head and squeezed the trigger before he sank his teeth into my leg. The Mire Walker's head exploded, and black matter splattered all over my pants.

"Ugh, nasty!" I exclaimed with a stink face.

I heard more moans and screeches around me.

"Focus and hit your targets. We are surrounded. Bites from Mire Walkers will cause your flesh near the bite to go necrotic within a few minutes, not to mention the trauma of the initial bite," the cyborg instructed.

"Dalton, there are fucking ten of them!" Euthani screamed.

The tunnel filled with green flashes as we open fired at the ravenous Mire Walkers. Some of our shots hit their targets, and some pierced the stone walls. They were mostly Euthani's frantic shots that missed their mark. My Gundertaker class was fucking incredible. Every shot I took were perfect headshots.

I saw a Mire Walker approach Euthani from behind and put both of its gruesome hands on her shoulders. It was moving in to bite a chunk out of her neck. She screamed in horror as she anticipated her demise. I squeezed the trigger of my gun and landed a perfect shot in the monster's temple, and black goo spurted on the nearby stone wall. Euthani breathed a sigh of relief. Stranger Zero finished taking out the rest of the Mire Walkers. The stench from the corpses caused me to empty my stomach onto the floor of the sewer.

"God, they reek. Is everyone ok?" I asked while I was bent over with my hands on my knees.

"I have no damage," replied a monotone SZ.

"I'm good, just a little shaken up. Thanks for saving me, Dalton. It almost had me."

I placed my hand on her shoulder and lightly squeezed.

"No problem, I'm not going to let anything happen to you. I promise."

The fox girl smiled warmly. "I want to hug you, but your clothes are disgusting, and you have vomit breath."

I laughed and patted her on the back. "I understand completely. I'll get that hug later."

"Question, can you extract mojo from these things?" I asked with an eyebrow raised.

"Yes," replied SZ.

Euthani's face turned into a grimace immediately. "You go ahead, I don't want to get that close to these things. Yuck!"

I looked hesitantly at all the disgusting things and shrugged. "I need mojo. I'm going in. You don't want any Stranger Zero?"

"No. I agree with the fox girl. I have no desire to extract anything from this filth."

"Well, shit. Are you guys going to think less of me if I do?"

"Yes," SZ replied coldly as he moved forward.

"You do you Dalton. Mojo is mojo," Euthani smirked.

I shrugged and began extracting. "Fuck it, I need mojo."

I went around to all the nasty creatures and extracted all the mojo they had while I covered my nose with the back of my left hand. I ended up with 8,000 mojo from the disgusting experience.

"If you are done, we need to move forward," SZ stared at something on his forearm panel.

We walked for half an hour and took out three more Mire Walkers along the way. I was beginning to wonder if the cyborg was getting lost.

"We are close. I have contacted Astra, and she will be at the exit awaiting our arrival."

"Sounds great, I hope you have a shower wherever you are taking us. I smell like shit...literally," I replied as I sniffed my shirt.

We made a left turn, and Stranger Zero spoke again. "This is the final corridor, and we will climb the ladder at the end."

Euthani and I stayed silent but nodded.

As we approached a curve in the tunnel, we smelled a new aroma. It was even more horrible than the Mire Walkers. "Oh fuck, what is that?" I asked with the inside of my elbow over my nose.

"I do not know. We must keep going," SZ motioned to keep moving.

We heard a disgusting wet, gurgling sound, and the smell was getting more pungent. After we came out of the curve, we saw a huge mound of...something. It appeared to be ten feet tall and twenty feet wide.

"What the hell is that?" I exclaimed with my eye wide.

SZ stopped in his tracks. "It is a Slime Behemoth. They are very dangerous.'

"Yeah, I figured that. What do we do?" I asked as I turned to look at Euthani.

She looked terrified at the sight. We moved closer to the

pile of slime. It didn't engage us. We could see six Mire Walkers floating inside of the Slime Behemoth.

"Is that thing...absorbing them?" Euthani asked quietly as to not alert the monster.

"Yes, it moves around the sewer all the time searching for food," replied SZ at his normal volume.

I pointed my gun at the monster and motioned for Euthani to do the same. "How do we kill it?"

Stranger Zero appeared to access his interface. He began swiping back and forth and up and down quickly. "I have confirmed my initial hypothesis. The Slime Behemoth has a core in the center. We need to penetrate the core to kill it."

The Slime Behemoth finally engaged us and began sliding to our position. It moved slowly, but it looked even larger than I initially thought. We all began firing our pistols at the mound of slime. We saw the bullets enter the body, but they didn't penetrate the Slime Behemoth very far.

"What do we do, our bullets aren't going very deep?" I asked as I backtracked with my gun still raised at the monstrosity.

Stranger Zero pulled something from his pocket and pressed a button. He threw what appeared to be a grenade of some sort. It stuck on the outside of the slime. A little light on it pulsed as the slime absorbed the sphere. SZ waited a few more seconds, and then hit some buttons on his forearm panel, and the grenade exploded. A large hole appeared in the center of the mass of goo.

Stranger Zero began firing inside the hole with both pistols at once. "Fire!"

Euthani and I moved beside the cyborg and fired our weapons into the hole he made. The Slime Behemoth let out a deep moan. Suddenly, SZ raised his arm, and he conjured a bright blue spear in his hand. He threw it into the hole before it closed back up. We saw a bright flash deep within the slime and a muffled pop. The Slime Behemoth began to squirm and then it flattened to the bottom of the sewer. It was a huge puddle of green liquid goo.

"Damn, that was awesome!" I yelled at the cyborg. "What weapon was that?"

"Laser spear," replied Euthani from beside me.

"Let's go, Astra is here. You may extract mojo from what is left of the core if you don't mind getting...sticky," SZ added as he circled around the puddle of green.

I looked at Euthani, and she just shook her head. "I'm not walking in that. You go ahead."

I smiled and shrugged. "I'm shameless when it comes to mojo."

I entered the sticky puddle slowly. The goo was deeper than I initially thought. Luckily, I still had my tall wrestling boots on. It wasn't easy to walk through. I used a lot of energy to get to the basketball sized glowing core that floated in the middle of the goo lake. It was damaged, but SZ said there would still be mojo inside. I took out my extractor and stabbed into the core. A surge of rancid stink spewed out, and I threw up again. Nonetheless, I finished the extraction process and low and behold I had gained 15,000 mojo.

"Hell yeah! That was nasty but worth it. I'm riiiiiach biiiaaatch!"

"Come on, Astra awaits," SZ commanded as he began climbing the ladder to the manhole above.

We followed immediately, and I let Euthani go first. I looked at my boots and made a stink face because I was a slimy mess. My feet slipped off the rungs a few times, but I finally reached the top and exited the hole. A large shiny vehicle that looked like a futuristic Range Rover awaited our arrival. I then saw who I assumed was Astra. My eyes widened and my heart beat faster. She leaned on the vehicle with her arms crossed. She had long green hair with horns on top of her head. The horns were a lighter shade of green than her hair. She had gold reptilian eyes that pierced my soul, and a green tail hung behind her. She wore a short burgundy dress with thigh high black boots. The way she had her arms crossed was pushing up her boobs, and they were glorious.

She walked over to Stranger Zero and gave the cyborg a warm hug. He returned her affection, which was odd to see. She patted him on the chest and smiled.

"Hi, I am Euthani, and this is Dalton. Thanks for coming!"

Astra sighed and looked us both up and down. "I hope you were worth the effort. However, if Zero sees something in you, I suppose I will...eventually. Let's go. Please try to not soil my car too badly. You can clean yourselves when you reach HQ."

Astra walked around to the driver's side of the vehicle and entered. She looked at me with disdain before she got in. SZ opened the door to the passenger's side and sat down. Euthani and I sat down slowly, but there was no way we wouldn't dirty up the car. My boots dripped goo onto the floor mats.

Astra turned to look. "Gods."

Euthani smiled uncomfortably. "I'm so sorry."

Astra took two pieces of fabric from the glove compartment in front of SZ. "Here, put these on. Not negotiable."

We place the blindfolds on, and I saw nothing but black.

"I don't know you, and we can't have you knowing the location of our HQ. It is nothing personal."

"No problem, I get it," I said with a small smile.

I heard the engine rev up, and we sped off to God knows where.

8

"I would also like to add this important tidbit of information. We have been kind enough to not tie your hands together, so we expect you to keep your blindfolds on and not remove them until you are told. If you take them off, Zero will shoot you in the face. It is as simple as that. Do I make myself clear?" Astra asked sternly.

"Yep."

"Yes."

The ride in this car was freaking flawless. The shocks were damn amazing. It felt like we were floating above the road. With the blindfold on, all I could see was darkness. I reached out my hand and grabbed Euthani's. She let out a light groan and began rubbing the top of my hand with her other hand.

"You okay?" I turned my head toward her and asked.

Why I turned my head, I don't know. It wasn't like I could see her. I heard a chuckle from Astra.

"Ha ha ha, funny...right?" I asked sarcastically.

"I'm sorry it was just hilarious to see you turn your head to look at her with that blindfold on. Carry on, don't mind me," Astra laughed.

"How long will this drive take?" I asked the green hair girl.

"Hmmm, I don't know. Do you have a hot date tonight?"

"Not that I am aware of. Are you offering?"

"You wish, Mr. Wade."

"I wasn't sure, I saw how you were staring at me with those golden eyes when I crawled out of the sewer. I'll go out with you. I don't mind."

Euthani chuckled at our exchange. "Dalton is a lot of fun."

"Oh, I am, am I?" I joked with the fox girl. "I have a question for you, Astra. I am not sure if it is considered rude since I am new to this planet, but I will ask, anyway. What are you? The green hair, the horns, the gold reptilian eyes, and the green tail got my attention when you picked us up."

"Zero, I am beginning to question your judgment. Mr. Wade isn't too bright."

"My judgment is sound. You will see. However, Dalton is odd. He wished to extract mojo from the Mire Walkers. I found that disgusting," SZ replied.

Astra sighed. "We shall see. Hopefully, they are halfway competent at least. We could use more interfacers."

"Hey, we are at least three-fourths competent. I take offense to that."

Euthani chuckled again, this time more loudly. "You are too bad."

"Are you always this corny and immature, Mr. Wade?"

"Do you always dodge questions that are asked? What are you?"

"So, you are serious that you don't know what kind of girl I am? I thought you were joking," Astra scoffed.

Euthani rolled her eyes and exhaled loudly, "Ugh, he already told you that he was not from this planet. Dalton, she is a dragon girl."

"Whoa, a dragon girl? That is...intense and kind of scary."

"Scary? What do you mean, scary?" Astra asked angrily.

"I mean nothing by it. On my planet, Earth, dragons are scary. Honestly, you seem kind of scary to me. Do you actually breathe fire?"

"Of course, I can do a lot of things with fire, dummy."

"Oh, name-calling eh? Who's the immature one now?" I aggravated. It was fun driving Astra up the wall, so to speak. I had always been a smart-ass for as long as I could remember. I loved doing this...to hot girls especially.

Astra growled and exhaled loudly.

"Okay, so you breathe fire. I like it. What other things can you do with fire? What's your class and specialty perk?"

"Now you are hurting my feelings, Dalton. You haven't asked me those things. Why don't you care about what I am?" I couldn't see Euthani, but I assumed that she had her bottom lip stuck out.

"Shit! I'm sorry. I care about those things. We have just kind of been in a whirlwind since we met. It's nice to actually talk. I wish I could see you right now. Astra...hold that thought, I will be back to you in a few minutes. Euthani, please tell me about your class and specialty."

The fox girl perked up immediately. "Okay, I forgive you. Things have been intense in more ways than one," Euthani flirted.

"Ugh, gods, I don't want to hear this," Astra sighed loudly.

I patted Euthani on the hand. "Let's pretend she isn't here; please continue."

"I am a Ranger."

"Wow, BIG surprise. I tell you. The crossbow totally didn't give that away," Astra interjected sarcastically.

"You need to be the center of attention, don't you?" I asked Astra with a grin.

"Shut up," replied the dragon girl.

I turned my attention back to Euthani. "Okay, you are a Ranger. That's awesome. What does that entail exactly?"

"It just means I am very talented with bows and cross-bows. Hence, I use a crossbow as my primary weapon."

"Neat, so you are kind of like Robin Hood," I murmured.

"Robin Hood?"

"Umm, he is a guy from my world that was great with a bow. Never mind. What is your specialty perk?"

"Acrobatics."

"Yes! That certainly explains that insane flip crossbow attack you did in the apartment."

"My jumping, climbing, and dodging abilities are unmatched by anyone who does not have the Acrobatics specialty. Also, my speed and agility are better than most since I am a fox girl."

"You are just a badass all the way around."

"Thank you, Dalton, that means a lot coming from you!"

I pointed at the dragon girl driver. "Your turn, Astra."

"It really isn't any of your business."

"Ah come on, show me yours, and I'll show you mine."

"Ugh, you are insufferable. I already know you — Gundertaker with Pure Weapon Specialist. Impressive."

"That's what they say."

Stranger Zero broke his silence. "Dalton was impressive with his accuracy in the sewer. The enemies were weak, but he landed 100% of his shots."

"Hmm, that is impressive," Astra replied sarcastically.

"SZ knows what time it is," I chirped.

"I do know what time it is. Just access your interface," Zero replied deadpan.

I laughed. "It's just an expression SZ but thank you."

The car slowed down, and we turned to our right.

"We are here. The blindfolds can be removed shortly," Astra stated.

"Yay, I don't like not being able to see you Dalton, you are so handsome," chirped Euthani.

"Blah, enough with the pathetic flirting," scoffed Astra.

I chuckled at the dragon girl. "Euthani, I think she's jealous. She thinks I am handsome too. I guarantee it."

The dragon girl ignored my latest dig at her. The car stopped, and I heard what sounded like a heavy garage door opening. After a few seconds, the car moved forward, and the door shut behind us.

"You may remove your blindfolds," Astra instructed as she opened her door.

I slipped off the black fabric and the lights inside the car stabbed my eyes from the door opening. I put my right hand in front of my eyes, and then turned my head. "Shit, that's bright."

I blinked a few times and looked over at Euthani. She winked and grinned at me. "Are you okay?"

"Yeah, you?

She nodded.

There was a knock on the glass on my side of the car. I turned to see Astra scowling at me. "Do you plan on exiting the car this evening or tomorrow?"

I knocked on the window to antagonize her before searching for the door handle. I placed my hand on everything I could see, but I could not find the door handle.

"Press this button," Euthani reached across me and mashed a button in the middle of the door.

"Thanks," I said as the door disengaged and slowly rose open.

"Are you always this helpless?" Astra asked with one eyebrow raised.

"Of course, that's part of my charm."

She giggled sarcastically and motioned for us to follow her. The chamber we were in was a large garage with three other vehicles located inside. They were similar to Astra's SUV and SZ's flying car that was a pile of scrap metal right now, and there were also four extremely cool motorcycles at the end of the garage.

"Wow, those are awesome," I said excitedly as I pointed at the motorcycles.

"Yes, they are," Astra replied unenthusiastically.

"They are night cycles. Those look to be very new and expensive," Euthani informed me.

Stranger Zero spoke up as we walked. "They are the new model. We got rid of our older ones. These are much more advanced, and we have added the Silent Ride feature."

"Silent Ride?" I asked with my eyebrow raised.

"When engaged, the nightcycle is completely silent...no engine noise or road noise," SZ replied robotically.

"I would like to see that in action. I don't understand how that is possible," I mentioned.

"Hmm, I am sure you don't understand a lot of things, Mr. Wade," Astra interjected with disdain.

I could see through Astra's bitchiness toward me. I was certain it was just an act. She liked me, but she was uncomfortable with those feelings so early. I can read these things. Astra was an exotic woman. She was gorgeous, even with the dragon features. I was getting used to the half-animal women on Zorth. Euthani was a goddess, even with the bushy ears and tail. I wondered what other types of girls there were.

We left the garage and entered a steel hallway that looked like the inside of a naval ship or bunker of some sort. I had the feeling we were underground. We passed open rooms, but I didn't have time to get a look. They were all dark. We eventually entered a large room with a lot of computers and screens.

It looked like some sort of circular control room. This room contained the first sign of life since we entered. There were two men and one woman sitting at computers. They didn't look up at us when we walked in because they were completely focused on what they were doing. I looked up to see another level above the room. There were two hallways that branched off the walkway.

A booming voice came from behind us. "Welcome to the HQ."

We all turned to see a large, muscular man standing on the second level. He had his black-gloved hands on the railing as he looked down at us. The gloves didn't cover his complete hand, but only went to his knuckle. He was wearing what looked like a soldier's uniform with large black boots appeared to weigh fifty pounds. The uniform was camouflage, but the colors were black and white. He had what looked like a black, green beret type hat on. He wore large mirror sunglasses and had a thick mustache. As I looked closer, I saw a large cigar with a glowing orange tip at the corner of his mouth. The cigar had so much girth he could not shut his mouth completely. His biceps rivalled my own, and I was sure he wasn't on steroids. Suddenly, the man just leaped over the steel rails and soared to the level we were own. It was startling and cool as hell at the same time.

The large man pulled out his cigar. "The name is Choicemaker, and I am the leader of this ragtag group of assholes called the Cosmic Peacekeepers." The man extended his hand, and I immediately grasped it, and we shook for a few seconds. Choicemaker's grip was powerful as shit. After he let go of my hand, he softly grabbed Euthani's hand and kissed the top. Euthani swooned at the old-fashioned gesture.

"Dalton. Euthani. I am glad you are here. We need all the help that we can get. The more interfacers, the better. Let me rephrase that...we need interfacers that ARE good people. Here in Osiris there aren't many good people left. Hell, this whole fucking solar system is full of dirtbags. Are you good people? Will you help us?"

"Yes, to the first question, and I will give you an 'I don't know' answer to the second question. Listen, one second, we are in Euthani's apartment, and then we are fighting the Copper Sharktooth Posse. The next thing we knew we were swept away by Stranger Zero. After that, we get in a terrifying car accident and end up in a sewer full of monsters. Now we are here, so we are trying to play catch up," I replied so quickly that I was out of breath.

"So, you say that this isn't a normal night for you?" Choicemaker asked with his eyebrows raised.

"Umm, no."

The enormous man slapped me on the arm. "I am just busting your balls, man. You need to lighten up."

I chuckled uncomfortably and looked over at Euthani. She appeared to be nervous and confused about our current situation as well.

"Well, I don't think you really have much choice in this situation. We will not force you to join the Peacekeepers, but in the end, I think you will. Your situation is dire out there right now. The posse has declared war on you two. If you go out there by yourselves, you will die sooner rather than later.

So, if you want to live, you need us," Choicemaker placed his massive hands on my right shoulder and Euthani's left to emphasize his point.

The situation frustrated me to no end. First off, I fell through a wrestling ring into another world on the other side of the universe. Second, Euthani and I are pulled into a fucking gang war soon after I arrived.

I exhaled a long breath. "You're right."

"I agree," Euthani added.

Choicemaker squeezed our shoulders and backed away. He put his cigar back into his mouth and grinned. "You guys are going to love it here. We take care of our own, and we kick ass along the way too."

9

After the decision to join the Cosmic Peacekeeper, they took us to our bunk rooms where we would live from this moment on. I expected to have a sleepless night due to all the shit going through my head, but I was wrong. I fell asleep within seconds of hitting my pillow. When I awoke, I didn't remember where I was, and it took me by surprise. Part of me believed that the night before had been a dream or that I had a concussion from my fall from the top of the Mega Cage. However, it hadn't been a dream. I was on a world called Zorth, and now lived at the Cosmic Peacekeeper HQ. I shook my head and put my clothes back on. Hopefully, there would be a laundry room somewhere around this underground base that I could use. I really didn't want to wear my wrestling gear all the time. I took a leak and my morning shit and then headed back to the control room. I was starving, and I hoped there would be some kind of breakfast foods somewhere. I stuck my head in Euthani's bunk room, but all that greeted me was an empty bed. She was already awake. I had been by her side my entire life in this world, so my stomach dropped when she wasn't there.

The control room was empty, but all the different computer screens were still up and running. There were no people monitoring them, though.

"Dalton! Good Morning!" Euthani said from downstairs. She waved at me joyfully and smiled.

My spirits lifted immediately. "Hey, you are a sight for sore eyes. I missed you last night. I'm not used to you not being by my side."

"Aww, I missed you too Dalton. You're so sweet and handsome. Come on down, there is breakfast waiting for you!"

"Sweet. I'm on my way."

I walked down a winding steel staircase, and I saw the gorgeous fox girl running toward me. She jumped into my arms and gave me a warm hug. I held her tight. I didn't want to let her go. We had only known each other for a short time, but she was the most important person in my life. She pulled back, and then came in for a quick kiss on the lips.

"Mmm, I needed that," I cooed.

"So, did I," Euthani said as she tousled my hair playfully.

"Oh, God, I can't even imagine how my hair looks right now. You look just as beautiful as ever, foxy lady."

"Dalton, you're making me blush. You're so nice to me!"

I pulled her in for another hug. "So, where is this breakfast at? I am freaking starving.

"Yay! Follow me, it looks so good, and there are new people to meet. Let's go!"

We entered a steel room with a kitchen at one end and two long tables at the other. The smell of bacon, eggs and sausage filled the room, which caused my mouth to water.

"Dalton, good morning, I think you know everyone in here. We have another monster girl on the way, Blowkos. She is an ass-kicker, but she is a medical genius. She serves as the official Peacekeeper doctor. She will help you two with something later this morning. There she is now right behind you," Choicemaker smiled and nodded at this unknown girl near the door.

I turned around and almost shit myself. A gigantic woman looked down at me and smiled. "Dalton, I presume?"

"Yeah, you must be Blowkos?" I extended my hand, and she grasped it with her massive hand.

She was tall and muscular with horns on her head. The most striking feature was her white skin with black spots scattered up and down her arms. She was bizarre but beautiful. She had a narrow whitetail that fluttered behind her, and it had a small tuft of black hair at the tip. Her eyes were large with black pupils. She wore blue jeans and black military boots. Blowkos had a white tank top that covered enormous breasts that almost spilled out the top.

She chuckled. "Are you wondering what I am?"

I nodded. "I'm sorry, I didn't mean to stare. Where I am from, we don't have monster girls, so this is all new to me. Are you a...cow girl?"

"Well, we prefer bovine girl, but yes. Do I disgust you?" Blowkos asked with a bushy black eyebrow raised.

I shook my head quickly. "No, not at all. You're gorgeous."

"Thank you, that is always nice to hear. Some people are grossed out by us bovine girls," Blowkos grabbed me by the back of my neck and pulled me in for an unexpected hug. My face plowed directly into her voluptuous rack.

Choicemaker and Astra roared in laughter from one of the tables.

"I think you guys will hit it off real fast. Blowkos is as good as they come. She has saved my ass more times than I can remember. Not only is she one hell of a doctor, but she will also fuck anyone up that picks a fight against the CP. That is Cosmic Peacekeepers for short if you are wondering," Choicemaker added.

"I figured as much," I replied with my head still pressed into tits.

"Blowkos is a beast in hand to hand combat, and her weapon of choice is a plasma mini-gun. May the gods have mercy on anyone on the other end of that thing," Choicemaker laughed and shook his head.

Blowkos blushed as she released me from her iron grip. "Choicemaker is too kind."

I was a bit disappointed by the sudden release. I was right at home between those titties.

Euthani finally broke her silence. "Hi, Blowkos. I agree with Dalton. You are beautiful, and I am Euthani."

Blowkos smiled and pulled her in for a hug. This hug was less forceful and not aimed directly at her cleavage.

"You guys are scheduled for a procedure this morning, I hear," Blowkos said with a grin.

"What kind of procedure?" I asked as I looked back and forth between the bovine girl and Choicemaker.

"We want to surgically install a mojo extractor into your arm. That way you don't have to fiddle with one of those ancient syringes. The ones we use have had an upgrade I think you will find exceptional. They refine the mojo you extract, thus giving you more for the shop. Hypothetically you could get 1,000 mojo, and then the extractor in your arm refines it, which may give you 1,500 mojo. We don't always know the improvement because it isn't set in stone with each extraction. We just know that you get more when the mojo is refined. You can thank Blowkos for designing that little feature."

"Wow, that's amazing," Euthani said with her eyes wide. "I have always dreamed of a surgical mojo extractor. So, you will do this for...free?"

"Absolutely, you are a Peacekeeper now. We take care of our own, and what is ours is yours," Choicemaker replied with a gigantic smile. He had shoved another huge cigar in the corner of his mouth. "You guys eat some breakfast, and then Blowkos will do the surgery. We want to get you up and running for training soon."

"We will put you under with anesthesia because I will have to slice into your arm. There is a lot involved, even though it may sound like a simple procedure. You will both be fine though."

I nodded nervously. "All right, we'll just have to put our

faith in you."

Astra broke her silence and sighed. "So, you don't seem to be too excited about this, Dalton. This is quite a gift to be given for free."

I glared at Astra. "I am excited about it, but I am just a little nervous about the anesthesia part."

Astra scoffed and continued to eat her eggs.

"You must excuse Astra as she is infatuated with me. She wanted to fuck last night, and I turned her down. She is a little pissed at the rejection," I said as I looked around the room.

Euthani laughed, but Choicemaker, Blowkos, and Stranger Zero stared at Astra in shock.

"You are so full of shit," Astra screamed as she stood up. Her eyes transformed into orange fire and smoke billowed from her mouth. She conjured a ball of violent fire in her palm and prepared to throw it at me. Choicemaker grabbed her forearm, and she fell out of her rage. Her eyes went back to normal, and the fireball dissipated.

"Whoa, whoa. Shit!" I yelled as held my hands in front of me. "I'm just kidding."

"You do not kid with Astra," Stranger Zero interjected as he sat there with no food in front of him.

"Astra, please don't kill our new recruit," added Choicemaker with a grin as he turned toward me. "You have some balls, Dalton. I'll give you that."

"He may lose his testicles if he keeps alienating Astra," said a monotone Stranger Zero.

"You are correct, Zero. I will roast them and feed them to

him on a plate," Astra said as she held her fist out. SZ lightly placed his against hers, which was odd to see.

I chuckled awkwardly and pointed to the empty table. "Maybe I need to sit over there this morning."

"I think that would be a good idea," Euthani agreed.

After breakfast, we followed Blowkos to her lab on the other side of the complex. She stood three inches taller than me, and her arms were the same size as mine. The bovine girl's ass was legendary in those skin-tight blue jeans. I stared at her bouncing cheeks the whole way to the lab. Euthani elbowed me in the side when she saw where my gaze was.

"I see what you are doing. You aren't even trying to hide it. You are so bad," Euthani whispered.

"I have a nice ass," Blowkos interjected.

My cheeks reddened. "Yeah, you most certainly do. Sorry about the staring."

"Don't be, it makes a girl feel good to be wanted by a handsome man," Blowkos flirted.

"Would you two like to be alone?" Euthani joked.

I chuckled uncomfortably. "I'm good."

"There is always time later for that sort of thing, my fox friend."

"I think you have a new pal, Dalton," Euthani winked.

"All right, this conversation is taking an odd turn right now. Let's get our minds on this surgery."

The bovine girl turned and extended her arms from her

sides. "We're here. Please lay on whatever table you like. I can do both of you at the same time."

"That's what she said..." I chuckled as I looked at the floor.

Euthani looked at me, perplexed. "Yeah, she did say it. Did you hit your head this morning?"

"Never mind."

We both laid on the surgical tables with a bit of hesitation. Blowkos attached electrodes and hooked us up to some monitors. She inserted an IV and began administering some fluid into the opposite arm. The fluid burned a bit as it initially entered the vein.

"What is that?" I asked as I stared at the bag that hung above the table.

"It's a mixture of different things. Your anesthesia is one of them, so will get sleepy soon. When you wake up, you will have a mojo refiner and extractor in your arm. You will love it."

"How long is the recovery?" Euthani asked from the table opposite of mine.

"You will need to rest your arm for the next 24 hours, and then you will be ready to go. We'll train you to use it right afterward. You will do a lot of sleeping today because of this anesthesia.

"Sounds good," I said with a nod as my eyes became very heavy. I blinked and then I succumbed to the medicine and fell asleep.

10

M y eyes were dry, and my vision was cloudy. I blinked aggressively to get some moisture flowing so I could see.

Where was I?

"Dalton, wake up sleepy head. You've been out all day and night. I was beginning to think you were never going to wake up. You sassy boy, you," Blowkos said as she rubbed my left arm lightly.

My eyes moistened, and I adjusted to the light in the lab. I saw the bovine girl sitting beside me looking at a monitor that showed my vital signs and other shit that I wasn't familiar with.

I began to lift myself to a sitting position and was stopped by Blowkos.

"Hold it right there. You aren't ready to get up yet. I don't even have your IV out, so just lay back down and relax. Let me take care of you."

I exhaled and nodded. I laid back down on the table like the cow girl had instructed me to. I would have laid down regardless due to my sudden dizziness.

Light footsteps entered the lab. "Dalton, you're awake! I'm so glad, you have been out a while."

Euthani, the bombshell fox girl, dashed beside me and placed my hand in hers.

"Hey, how...are you?" I asked while I continued to blink for more moisture. Euthani was a woman that I wanted to see without obstruction.

"I'm fine. Everything went just fine. I woke up about eight hours ago. I was getting so worried about you. Here look at my arm, you can hardly tell anything was done. All you see is the tip of this titanium cylinder here on the top of my forearm at my wrist. If you look at my arm from the side, you can see that the cylinder is raised up some. It is a little sore, but it isn't too bad. Watch this," Euthani demanded. She held her right arm where I could see it, and a needle the size of a pencil shot out of the cylinder that she spoke of. "This is why the cylinder is raised. You don't want to stab yourself with the extractor."

The titanium needle was almost ten inches long. The device reminded me of Wolverine from the X-Men shooting out his adamantium claws.

"What did you press to make it eject from the cylinder?" I squinted at her arm.

Euthani smiled, and her eyes narrowed in excitement. "All you do is tell it to come out with your brain. Isn't that awesome?" Euthani made a stabbing motion with her new device and smiled. "See, you just stab this right in the dead person's heart, and it takes their mojo right out. Well, at least that is what I think it does. I haven't exactly used it yet since there are no dead guys lying around," Euthani stuck her plump bottom lip out.

"That's definitely cool," I replied as I raised my forearm to look at my own device. I brought my augmented forearm in front of my face for a closer look, and I touched the cylinder with the index finger of my left hand. I cringed as I moved my left hand too close, and I almost jerked out my IV. "Ah, shit I'm sorry."

"Let's remove that for you," Blowkos laid my arm back down on the surgical table and occluded the vein above the IV with her index finger and middle finger. She then slid the catheter right out of my arm and smiled when she placed a band-aid. "All done."

I thanked her and directed my attention back to the extractor. "Alright so, I just get my brain to tell the extractor to work?"

"You first need to bend your wrist a bit, so your hand is pointing downward. If you don't do that, the needle will not eject for safety purposes. Now, bend your wrist and tell the device what to do," Blowkos said as she stood over me and pointed at my arm.

When I bent my wrist, it felt like something happened inside the device that opened it, or it at least felt like it opened. The feeling was very faint, but I felt something. I looked briefly at Euthani as she looked on in anticipation.

I told the needle to eject and boom it worked perfectly.

The needle shot out of the cylinder so fast. I touched the tip of the titanium needle with the tip of my index finger. The tip of the needle was sharp, and I pulled my finger away and looked at it. I expected to see some dark blood ooze from a hole, but I had not broken the skin.

"Can this be used as a weapon as well?" I raised my eyebrow at the bovine girl doctor.

"Yes, but I would only use it as a last resort. It is for extracting mojo, not killing people. However, if you get in a bind and need to stab someone in their eye socket, it will work like a champ. Now retract the needle for me."

I looked at the needle and willed it to return inside my arm. I nodded my head as the command left my brain. Swoosh...click...the needle returned to the titanium cylinder in my arm. "Sweet."

"When you insert the needle into one of your victims, you will have to tell the device to begin extracting the mojo. It doesn't begin automatically. Once the mojo starts entering your device, your interface will pop up. You will see that there is a mojo extraction menu now, and you will see the percentage rise as the mojo enters. If you are sharing mojo with a partner, you will mentally stop the extraction at the agreed-upon percentage and retract your needle. Then the other party can extract the percentage they are supposed to receive. Once you have extracted the mojo and retracted your needle back into your arm, the mojo gained will be calculated. During this calculation, the refinement modifier will play a role in the mojo amount received for shop use. Does this all make sense to you?"

Euthani and I both nodded hesitantly.

"Excellent! I think you two will enjoy these surgical extractors. They are much more convenient, and the refining feature helps to maximize your earnings."

"I can't wait to try it out. We need to go kill something or someone," I said sarcastically.

The cow girl chuckled. "As a Cosmic Peacekeeper, you will have ample opportunity to use this device. There is no shortage of scum in the galaxy." Blowkos turned the lab equipment off and began walking to the lab entrance. "All right, you should be okay to do some light training. Choicemaker would like you to go see Stranger Zero in the armory. I can take you there now."

11

"They're all yours Zero. Go easy on them since they just had surgery," Blowkos directed the cyborg with a smile.

Zero scoffed. "I have adjusted the training to accommodate them while they are in recovery. The two of them should not have a lot of issues with today's firearm training. They are a Gundertaker and Ranger after all. Thank you, Blowkos for bringing them to me."

As Blowkos walked out of the firing range, she placed her hand on my shoulder and whispered into my ear. "You be sure to let me know if he works you too...hard." The bovine girl made sure that one of her giant breasts touched my arm. She turned her head as she continued, and her long black hair caressed my face. I was enamored with the lavender scent that swooped into my nostrils.

My face reddened as she continued to the hallway, and I

felt a tingle below my waist. Euthani shook her head and chuckled. I wondered why the fox girl didn't act jealous of the other women. Blowkos didn't hide her lust for me, and Astra was interested as well even though she acted like she was not. I would take down her defenses in the very near future. I wondered if monogamy was just not a thing here on Zorth.

My attention returned to Stranger Zero, and the gun range that we stood in. There were four guns spaced apart on the platform in front of us. I was shocked by the size of the range with the HQ being an underground complex as it was at least 50 yards to the back wall.

"If you are able to stop daydreaming of Blowkos, I would like you to approach the table here," SZ said as he motioned with his right hand to come forward.

"Pssssh, we were just waiting on you Zero. Our bad," I smirked and looked at Euthani. "After you, my lady."

She curtseyed and swayed her hips as she walked to the gun table.

The long black steel table had a plasma pistol, a plasma rifle, a shotgun, and a crossbow.

"Nice!" I barked as I looked at the beautiful weaponry.

"I have a plasma pistol right here," I added as I unholstered my weapon and placed it on the table.

"I know that. I was with you last night. Do you remember?" SZ asked in his monotone robotic voice.

"Yeah, I just meant that I could use mine since it is what I am used to."

"Dalton, you are a Gundertaker with Pure Weapons Specialist as your perk. You will be a master of each of these.

Nonetheless, you will find that our plasma pistol here is much higher quality than your ancient relic."

"Well, maybe it was the only weapon I could afford at the time, and I did pretty damn good with it. You have said so yourself."

"Do you always make things difficult? This is a more advanced weapon, and you would be a moron not to use it. Are you a moron?"

"Nope, I'll bite, give me the damn thing," I scoffed as I reached for the weapon. Zero extended his arm quickly and grabbed my wrist.

"I have not given you instructions yet. Please do not touch the firearms until I tell you to do so," SZ demanded before releasing my wrist.

"Dalton be the nice guy that I know that you can be," Euthani whispered.

I nodded and smiled at SZ. "I'm sorry, please continue."

"Yes, as you can see here are four of our most popular firearms. We have the 69x Plasma Pistol, the Cobra Plasma Rife, the Hellstorm Plasma Shotgun, and the Raven Crossbow."

Euthani clapped lightly and chirped. "Oh, my gods, I have only dreamed of using one of these."

I looked at her beautiful face and spirit and grinned. She was an amazing creature. I just loved seeing her happy, and I would do everything in my power to keep her happy.

"Euthani, I suspect you will be highly skilled with the crossbow. You are a Ranger and have used one for years.

However, I am sure you will need more practice and training with the other weapons you see."

"Dalton, you should need very little help, but I am convinced that even a Pure Weapons Specialist can benefit from practice," the cyborg added as he crossed his part flesh part machine arms.

"I agree. Now, who's first," I replied with excitement.

"As you said earlier, ladies first. I also think it would be discouraging for her to see you go first with your elite skill. Please choose your weapon to use first."

She nodded and reached for the Raven Crossbow that beckoned her. Once it was in her hands, her beautiful blue eyes lit up like a child on Christmas morning.

"The Raven has a stealth plasma bolt mode. When activated, the bolt will be the color of the environment. For instance, the bolt would be black outside at night, and the bolt would be white light during the day. Then there are green and red to choose from when you need to be seen by your party," Euthani smiled and pressed a button on the side.

I was startled by a sudden shout from SZ. "Lights off in firing range."

All the lights in the range went out, and it was almost pitch dark.

Suddenly, we heard a sharp buzz, and I saw a green glowing bolt in the firing chamber. The pulse from the plasma lit the room. "Now, I will switch to stealth mode." There was a faint beep, and the green was gone.

"Did you cut the crossbow off?" I asked as I squinted at the weapon.

"Nope," Euthani whispered, and I heard one of the target mannequins explode. "Stealth mode...waah laah!"

"Holy shit, it's silent too?" I asked with my eyes wide.

"Did I not mention that? Yes, it is silent. It is also very awesome," the fox girl replied in the darkness.

"Lights on in firing range," SZ announced as illumination filled the room. It caused a brief surge of pain in our eyes.

"Very good, Euthani. Now we have a hologram target system in place. I will activate it, and you may use your crossbow. They are holograms, but they do detect when they are hit."

"Engage Target Hologram System!" SZ shouted once more.

We heard a buzz that turned into a soft hum. The hologram of a man in a soldier uniform ran from the side into the middle of the room and hid behind some artificial cover. He stood up for a moment and began firing hologram bullets. It was cool as shit. I couldn't wait to play with this thing.

Euthani noticed the hologram's foot outside of cover, and she fired a red plasma bolt right through it. The hologram screamed and stood to his feet. Euthani took the opportunity to fire another bolt right between his eyes. The hologram vanished after that perfect headshot. Afterward, several hologram soldiers and a large crab monster appeared, and she took them down with flying colors. The crab monster took a little longer because she hadn't fought a crab monster before obviously. Her crossbow was smooth as silk when she squeezed the trigger. She continued her target practice with the other three weapons. She struggled with the shotgun. She wasn't used to dealing with a lot of recoil when she fired a weapon. She had an okay performance with the plasma rifle and pistol. She was disappointed with her performance, but I was able to build her back up. She did fine, but she just wanted to make a stronger first impression in front of the emotionless cyborg. "Acceptable job, Euthani. Your crossbow skills are unmatched, but you need to work with the other weapons." SZ turned his attention toward me after he nodded at the fox girl. "Your turn Dalton, start with the pistol. The holograms will be more challenging since you are a Pure Weapon Specialist, but ultimately you shouldn't have a great deal of trouble."

The cyborg backed away and motioned to the range. I lifted the pistol, and I was bombarded by every piece of information available about this weapon. All of it seemed to download into my brain immediately, and I felt one with the firearm. It felt like a body part I had lived with all my life. SZ was correct. The 69x was a much more advanced weapon, the rate of fire especially. I liked the new sights on the muzzle as well. A soldier ran from the left of the room, one from the right, and one from the wall at the back of the range. I went into beast mode. Not literally, but I've always liked that expression. I squeezed off three shots and placed headshots in the hologram victims with ease. Stranger Zero said nothing. He just continued to glare at the range. The next attack consisted of five holograms running in extremely fast from five different directions.

Boom.

Boom.

Boom.

Boom.

Boom.

The same thing happened as before. They were all toast. The big difference in this situation was that they didn't fight back.

"Shit, Dalton, that's fucking sick," Euthani yelled.

"The hologram targets cannot contract a sickness. However, that was a very impressive display of your Pure Weapon Specialist skillset," SZ added with a mechanical voice. "Use the plasma rifle now."

I lifted the Cobra Plasma Rifle slowly to eye level. "Whoa ha ha, nice!" I turned to Euthani with a nod and crooked grin. She playfully rolled her eyes and smiled.

SZ didn't say another word before two crab monsters showed themselves with a soldier on top of each of them. It was a hilarious sight, and I chuckled. I pressed the stock against my shoulder and looked down the sights and found one of the men on top. I squeezed the trigger. I had the weapon in semi-automatic mode, and I nailed him in the chest twice and once in the head. I did the same with the other soldier. It was now time to take out the crab creatures. I switched the Cobra to automatic mode and opened fire on the closest crab to my position. The hologram simulated armor on top of the crab, so I had to aim lower in order to hit the kill spot. The final crab creature leaped, and I had a clear shot to the underbelly. After five bullets in succession, the hologram was defeated.

"Well done, Dalton," Stranger Zero complimented.

"Thanks, it was fun. I felt like I was back at the arcades when I was younger."

"These simulations are a good way to get acquainted with weapons, but actual firefights are much more stressful. Your performance while plasma bullets zip by your skull is a much different experience."

"Yeah, we got a taste of that last night, didn't we?" I raised my eyebrow at the cyborg.

"A small taste at best," the cyborg scoffed and motioned to the shotgun.

My experience with the shotgun was much the same as the pistol and the rifle. I showboated a bit, which Zero didn't find amusing at all. I took the shotgun and hurdled over the table into the range. I took out the targets with ease from close range.

Stranger Zero slowly walked up to me and got directly into my face. "Dalton, if you go into the hot area again like a buffoon, I will kill you myself. We don't tolerate idiocy."

"I'm sorry man, back on Earth, it was my job to showboat and get a crowd going. It's a part of me, but I'll work on it. Are we cool?" I patted the cyborg on the shoulder and then laid the shotgun back on the table.

"I am not cool. The temperature is a constant 73 degrees Fahrenheit. My body regulates temperature much differently than you or Euthani. If you are cool, put on more appropriate attire or speak with Choicemaker."

I grinned and looked over at a laughing Euthani. "It's just an expression, SZ. It means I hope you aren't angry with me."

"In that case, yes, we are...cool," SZ replied slowly deep in thought.

The next stop of the day was the garage. There was another side that we didn't see on our way into the facility. This served as a gym. There were several exercise machines and weights. There was a square platform that looked to be used for mortal combat. We heard some grunts and heaves coming from the corner of the gym. Choicemaker was shirtless, wearing sunglasses, and bench pressing an ungodly amount of weight without a spotter.

"You need a spot man?" I asked as I walked over.

"Rawr! I'm done!" the muscle man yelled as he placed the bar back on the rack like a rag doll. "Nothing like a good work out! Eh, Dalton?"

"In my former life, weightlifting was a very close friend of mine. How much were you pressing?"

"Bah, I have been a pussy this week. That was 600 pounds. I got to get back at it harder. I am losing muscle mass."

"Holy shit. 600 pounds? Are you on anything? I know that is kind of personal. No judgment from me."

"On something? You mean some kind of drug or enhancer?" Choicemaker pulled the cigar out of his mouth. I immediately regretted asking the question thinking I had pissed him off. My first day as a Cosmic Peacekeeper, and I have pissed the boss off.

"No, this is all nat-chu-raal. My class is strength-based," he replied as he wiped the sweat off his brow with his shirt.

"What kind of class?" I crossed my arms.

"Berserker," Choicemaker said proudly as he placed the cigar back into his mouth.

"Berserker? What is that? Sorry, I am new here...remember."

Choicemaker laughed and patted me on the side of my arm. "No worries, Dalton. I'm here to answer any questions that you have. I am a beast in hand to hand combat. I have a core inside of me that will charge when I am in a fight. Once it is full, I can activate the core and go into a frenzy where I am stronger, faster, and harder to damage. It is as simple as that my friend."

"That is intense. What is your specialty perk?"

"Charismatic Strategist."

"Really?"

"Yep, really. I can lead and inspire people. I can motivate people to do things they may not want to do. I am rather difficult not to like, not to mention insanely handsome. I am also a master at analyzing situations and problems. I can determine the best plan of action to accomplish my desired outcome. See, I am perfect for this job."

"That's amazing, sir," Euthani said softly.

"Bah, let's stop this sir business right now. This isn't the military. Just call me Choicemaker or just Maker for short. It's up to you. It's your...choice," Choicemaker chuckled at his own pun.

"SZ gave us a good introduction on how to handle some

firearms. What have you got for us?" I asked as I crossed my bulky arms.

"Cutting right to the chase. I like that. Well, you have experience in hand to hand combat, so I figured we would spar for a bit. I want to see what you got. You are a pretty big guy yourself, and you could probably give me a run for my money. I won't go into berserk mode, so don't worry about that."

My stomach dropped a bit for two reasons. One reason is this guy was huge and had an affinity for fighting. Not to mention he was an excellent strategist. Second is that I haven't fought in a real fight in a very long time. All the matches I have participated in were a product of detailed planning. I wasn't scared by any means, but I didn't want to be embarrassed on my first day.

"Yeah, I'm game if you are."

Choicemaker clapped his hands together. "All right let's go! No gloves, full contact...right?"

I cringed mildly. "Sure. Go hard or go home."

Choicemaker pumped his fist in the air. "That is what I love to hear, go hard or go home! I haven't heard that one before, but I fucking love it. I'm going to use that one."

My heart began to pump due to apprehension, but there was a bit of excitement mixed in there. I took off my shirt and dropped to the floor for ten push-ups to get the blood flowing and my muscles up and running.

"Be careful, Dalton. You look good, so I hope he doesn't hurt your pretty face. Please protect it for me...okay?" Euthani asked with a wink.

"You got it," I replied as I saw Astra, Blowkos, and Stranger Zero enter the gym for the show.

"Dalton, I hope you have a last will and testament. You are going up against the best. It's kind of reckless if I'm going to be perfectly honest," Astra said with an evil grin as she approached.

"Ummm, Blowkos...is it okay for him to fight since he just had that extractor implanted?" Euthani asked with mild concern.

"He'll be fine. It is titanium, so it won't break," the tall beautiful bovine girl replied as she looked at my bare chest and bit her bottom lip.

"Good luck, Dalton. However, Pure Weapons Specialist does not apply to your fists," SZ added.

"I figured as much, but thanks for letting me know for sure," I replied sarcastically.

Choicemaker roared from the mat. "Yo, stop with the chit chat. Let's get down to fucking brass tacks! Show me what you got, Dalton. Don't hold back."

I stepped on the mat with my chin up and chest out. "You don't hold back either."

"Nah, I'll have to hold back a little, otherwise you may be hospitalized or worse after our sparring session. The berserk mode is savage. Believe me, when that core is activated, you don't want to be my opponent."

I sighed. "All right, fair enough. What are the rules?"

"Ummm, we usually do knockout or submission?"

"Shit, okay," I said as I raised my fists.

Maker did the same and then held his hand up. "Fuck, I

almost forgot." He ran off the mat and put his sunglasses and cigar against the wall. He had huge brown eyes and a small scar beside his right eye.

"Are you going to ask me on a date?" Choicemaker joked when he caught me looking at his face.

"I hadn't thought about it, but now that you have asked...," I replied sarcastically.

"Tell us when Zero," Choicemaker shouted.

Zero perked up and walked quickly to the side of the mat. "Are you two ready for battle?"

We both nodded at the cyborg and he said, "Fight!"

Maker lunged forward immediately and swung a haymaker. I dove to the floor and somersaulted. He would have taken my head clean the fuck off. One thing you had to know in wrestling was how to properly take a fall. Performing the quick somersault on the mat was something I had been working on for years. I had perfected it to where I would be able to stand quickly after the rotation.

"Nice one, Dalton."

Maker walked over and threw a few jabs and a right hook. I was mostly able to stay out of their way. One of the jabs grazed my cheek, but I hadn't taken a big hit yet. Nonetheless, he had not either.

Astra screamed from the sidelines. "Are you going to attack him Dalton or just stand there like a limp dick?"

I chuckled as I winked at her which was a mistake. The loss of focus resulted in a hook to my right cheek. The force behind the punch was insanely strong. My vision went away in my right eye for a few seconds which freaked me the fuck out, but I didn't go down surprisingly. That was a monster punch. I shook my head to try and get some of my bearings back. I decided to take a risk that I thought would surprise him. I dove directly into his stomach and lifted him. I pivoted to my left and slammed him on the mat flat on to his back. He began to cough as the air escaped his lungs from the impact. I pushed my upper body up and punched him directly in the middle of his face. I was greeted by the loud snap and crack of the man's nose. Blood began to gush from the smashed nose immediately. I stood up in horror. "Fuck, man, I'm sorry."

Maker took advantage of my lack of focus and weakness to do a quick leg sweep. He swept both of my legs so fucking hard that I landed on my head instead of my back. I thanked God that I was able to move my limbs after I smashed into the mat at that awkward angle. I rolled over onto my stomach and placed both hands on the back of my head in agony.

"You give up?" asked Choicemaker softly.

"Fuck no," I barked as I pushed myself to my feet. I was woozy, but Choicemaker gave me a chance to get straight before he attacked.

"I like that, Dalton."

Choicemaker did a spinning heel kick that shocked the hell out of me. The speed at which he launched the attack was incredible for such a large man. I was able to lift my right arm up to block the impact to the side of my face that would have done me in for sure. The back of Choicemaker's foot slammed into my new titanium mojo extractor, and it hurt like freaking hell. The impact sent a shockwave from the extractor down my arm bones to my chest. I quickly forgot that sensation as I felt Choicemaker's mammoth fist slam me in the gut. Then his left hand slammed into my gut again from a different angle. The pain and loss of air in my lungs were insane. I felt my breakfast rising to my throat as well. The Charismatic Strategist finished me off with a powerful uppercut that I only felt for a second and then I saw black.

I woke up in Blowkos lab on the surgery table again. I was greeted by a sharp pain in my gut from the punches, and my face hurt severely from the gargantuan uppercut from the Berserker.

"Hey Dalton, I didn't expect to see you back so soon," Blowkos said as she shone a penlight in my eyes to check for dilation. "You took quite the uppercut. You soared through the air directly after Choicemaker's fist smashed into your jaw.

I tried to speak, but I was shocked to find out that my jaw wasn't moving. I tried again and again, but it wouldn't move.

Blowkos placed her hand on my forehead. "Calm down, I'm right here. Your jaw has been wired shut for the time being. There was a break which is the reason for the drastic measure."

I shrugged angrily at the gorgeous cow girl.

"Believe me, no one feels more terrible than Choicemaker. Here is a piece of paper and a pencil if you want to communicate. Let me know right away if you need some pain medication.

How long will it be wired shut?

"A couple of days."

How is that possible? My jaw is fucking broken!

"After I scanned your head and found the exact location of the break, I injected medical-grade nanobots into the crack. They went to work immediately, and they will have you good as new very soon. That is the main reason I wired your jaw together so tight was for the nanobots. If the break had room to move, you would constantly undo what the nanobots are doing. You will be healed soon, and your jaw will be stronger from the work done by the nanobots. You broke Choicemaker's nose, so I had to inject him with nanobots too. So, you aren't alone in your pain."

I just gave a quick thumbs up and a wink to the cow girl. I couldn't be angry with Choicemaker. He was a fucking berserker and benching 600 pounds. I told him to not take it easy. I was more motivated to get better at hand to hand combat. Guns weren't going to be an option all the time.

How the hell was I going to eat?

12

I moved my jaw slowly after the wire had been removed. My jaw had been wired shut for 26 hours, and it was a relief to open my mouth again. It was a strange, scary situation to have your mouth locked up and immobile. I expected a lot of pain, but there was absolutely zero, which freaked me out a bit. I began to open and close my mouth normally without any issues. I tentatively touched my face with two fingers determined to search for some sort of pain spot.

"You good?" asked Blowkos as she tossed the wire in the trash can.

"Yeah, too good."

"How can you be too good?" the bovine girl asked with a grin.

After she turned toward me, my eyes immediately fell to her ample cleavage spilling out of her tank top. I didn't care if she saw me. She was into me anyway, and she had been flirting like crazy since we met.

"Dalton? Come in, Mr. Wade. I'm up here," Blowkos laughed as she pinched my chin and lifted.

"You caught me. I'm sorry...maybe."

"Feel free to look at my breasts whenever you like. I look at your ass and bulge in your crotch regularly, so it's only fair."

I laughed and shook my head as I looked at my crotch. "You know these are still my wrestling pants, so the bulge is a little more pronounced."

I immediately realized that sounded bad. "I mean, the goods are still impressive. Don't get me wrong. Fuck."

"I have no doubt your cock is nice. I hope to take it for a ride at some point," Blowkos winked.

"Goddamn, you are direct. I like it. No bullshit."

"Life is too short. We should say what we mean. I want to fuck you at some point. Do you want to fuck me?"

I opened my mouth, but it took a couple of seconds for the words to come out. "Ah, yeah. I would love to take you up on that."

"Good, Euthani said you are quite the lover, and she enjoyed your skills very much."

I coughed in surprise. "Oh, you two have talked about that?"

"Of course, we have. Do you not talk about women with your guy friends?"

"Yeah, I guess."

"So, what's the problem?"

"No problem. Glad she gave me a good review."

"It sounded pretty wild. She said you fucked her in the elevator and then you fucked her again in the shower just minutes later. That is great stamina."

"I aim to please. However, when you have an ass like Euthani, it doesn't take a lot to get you going again," I replied as I had a flashback of water streaming down her ass in the shower.

"She is a pretty fox girl. All fox girls I have met have been drop dead gorgeous."

"You are drop-dead gorgeous too. You are my first bovine girl. It's awesome that the first one I met is the hottest one."

"You're making me blush, Dalton."

Her white skin reddened from my compliment and caused her to look at the floor for a moment.

"It's just the truth," I shrugged and smirked.

"Bovine girls are not seen that way, usually at least not on Zorth."

"I ain't from Zorth, and you are a goddess. Don't believe anything different. The people here don't know what the hell they are talking about," I scoffed.

How anyone could deny this woman's beauty was beyond me. I couldn't wrap my head around it. She smiled and looked like she was going to burst into tears at any moment.

She looked into my eyes warmly. "Do you mind if I give you a hug?"

"No, I'm always up for a hug from a gorgeous woman. Bring it on in."

Blowkos hugged me more tenderly than I expected. I could tell she appreciated my comments about her appearance. She did make sure she pressed me into her breasts which was fine by me. I was startled by two other arms wrapping around my waist from behind.

"I am sorry if I startled you. This hug looked so nice, and I wanted in," Euthani whispered over my shoulder.

"The more the merrier," Blowkos cooed.

I felt things beginning to happen downstairs. As much as I enjoyed our group embrace, I knew I was going to poke Blowkos with a huge boner momentarily. Threesomes were nothing new to me. Ring rats were willing to do most everything for me, but these girls were on another level of beautiful.

"Ladies, don't we have somewhere we need to be?"

"Don't you like having the arms of two women around you? Breasts pressed in the front and the back doesn't appeal to you?" the bovine girl asked sarcastically.

"Umm, yeah, that is the problem. I am liking it too much. Well, a certain part of my body is becoming more rigid if you know what I'm saying."

Suddenly, I felt the fox girl's hand slide down from my waist to grab my bulging member.

"This part of you?" Euthani whispered while she bit my ear lobe.

"It has been a long time Dalton. This needs to happen now, or I am going to explode," Blowkos begged as she kissed my forehead.

"I'm game for damn sure, but the others could show up any minute," I said with an eyebrow raised.

Euthani began to unzip my pants. "The others are out in the city doing something, so they won't be back anytime soon."

Blowkos placed her hands at the bottom of my shirt and pulled it off in one motion.

She purred at the sight of my muscular torso and rubbed my chest as she put her lips on mine. The kiss was soft at first and then it gradually became more violent. Euthani put her hand inside of my boxer briefs and grabbed my shaft. She squeezed it hard and began to stroke it slowly while she kissed my back. I almost sunk my teeth into Blowkos' bottom lip as I was overcome by the sensation. I took off the bovine girl's shit, but the collar got hooked onto one of her horns and dangled.

"Bovine girl problems," she laughed as she threw the shirt across the room.

Blowkos was taller than I was, so I was able to plunge my face into her giant breasts easily. I squeezed her left nipple causing her to moan in ecstasy and placed my mouth onto her pink right nipple and began to suck. I was gentle, but then she grabbed the back of my head and pushed me closer. That was my signal that she wanted more, and I started sucking more forcefully. I twirled my tongue around her nipple with each suck. I then removed my left hand from squeezing her nipple and slid it downward. She began to shudder from the pleasure and anticipation of my hand reaching her pussy. Euthani had stopped stroking and began to squeeze my balls as she squeezed my ass cheek with her right hand.

"My gods, you are solid muscle. You make me so fucking hot, Dalton," Euthani muttered as she began to breathe faster.

My hand went through a soft patch of hair, and then reached Blowkos' pussy. I pressed my index fingertip against the bean.

"Fuck, Dalton, don't stop."

After a few more seconds of playing with her bean, I slid my middle finger into her sopping wet pussy. She gasped and squirmed violently. I pushed my finger into the warm wet tunnel deep to her cervix.

I turned my head toward Euthani. "Kiss me."

To my surprise, she had taken her clothes and underwear off while I was distracted by Blowkos. She looked at me with her beautiful blue eyes and nodded. Our tongues wrestled with each other as I continued to finger the bovine girl in front of me. The fox girl pressed her breasts against my back. The warmth of her body was invigorating.

I eyed the hospital bed at the other side of the room. "Let's go over there. Ladies first. I want to admire you from behind."

Blowkos began to remove her pants and panties at the same time. I stood there in awe of her perfect body. Euthani and Blowkos walked beside one another in front of me. I didn't follow right away. I chose to stare at their round asses as they bounced and swayed in almost perfect unison. Their tails spun and fluttered as they strutted.

Blowkos looked at me over her shoulder. Her eyes were filled with hunger for what was about to happen. "How do you want us, Dalton? You are in charge."

"I want you on your back with your legs spread and Euthani on all fours."

Euthani moaned and purred. "Your wish is our command."

They both did exactly what I told them to do. The sight in front of me was almost too much for me to process. They were incredibly beautiful, and they wanted me with everything inside them, as did I.

"Dalton, what are you waiting for? We need you so bad," Blowkos begged as she bit her

bottom lip. She began rubbing her pussy.

Euthani groaned in agreement.

"Fuck her first, Dalton, I have had you already, I like to watch anyway."

"Please, listen to her Dalton. Fuck me!" the bovine girl demanded.

Euthani rubbed the inside off Blowkos thigh which made her longing more vicious.

I put the tip of my dick in her pussy causing her to quiver and gasp.

"Keep going."

I slowly pushed in further and further until I was completely submerged. I paused for a few seconds and looked her in the eyes. I placed both hands on her heaving breasts and squeezed.

Her eyes rolled in the back of her head as I began to thrust slowly and then I picked up speed. The slapping of our skin echoed in the room. Euthani began to rub my ass as I fucked Blowkos hard and fast. I looked over and winked at the fox girl. She bit her bottom lip and winked back. She wanted me, but she was thoroughly enjoying the show.

"Dalton, I am going to come. Go deeper."

"You want it, you got it. I thrust as deep as humanly possible as she teetered on edge. I felt her pussy walls contract and tighten around my cock as she came. She tried to scream but nothing came out. Her breath had literally been taken away.

"My turn," Euthani purred.

I took my dick out of the bovine girl, and she gasped once more.

Blowkos rolled to her side and propped her head on her hand. "Mmm, carry on, gods you are hot Euthani." The fox girl winked and kissed the air.

Euthani grabbed my dripping dick and took it into her mouth. She moaned as she cleaned off our mixed juices. Her tongue twirled around my shaft as she slid up and down. After a minute of ecstasy, I slowly pulled her head from my dick. Her tight lips coming off over the head of my dick made a popping sound. I stood behind her and admired her perfectly formed ass and watched her reddish-brown tail flutter back and forth in anticipation. Her cum began to drip from her clit onto the sheets. The smell of her juices filled my flared nostrils. I closed my eyes and enjoyed the aroma for a few seconds.

"Fuck, you smell good."

She looked into my eyes with lust and ravenous hunger. "Stop teasing me Dalton and stick your dick deep inside my pussy."

I smiled and followed her command. I rubbed the head of my dick in her juices causing her to moan. She was so wet that my dick slid in with absolutely no friction or resistance. This time I didn't start slow, and I began to pound her hard immediately. I fucked her so hard I was giving my balls concussions. I slapped her ass and caused both girls to gasp. It didn't take long for the fox girl to scream in ecstasy from a powerful orgasm. Blowkos laid in the same position while she bit her index finger and watched the scene like we were a good movie on TV. The orgasm from Euthani had brought me to the edge, and I was going to fall over soon.

"Come inside of her, Dalton," Euthani whispered.

"Are you sure? I'm almost there and was going to fill you."

"Yes, I am sure. I want to watch."

Blowkos laid down on her back and spread her legs wide open. I pulled my dick out of the fox girl and crawled on top of Blowkos. She grabbed my shaft and guided me into her wet vagina.

"God this feels freaking fantastic. You girls are fucking amazing."

"Please fill me with your seed, Dalton."

My member felt like it was going to explode. The fox girl slapped my ass cheek extremely hard. It was a little weird, but I liked it. As I reached my orgasm, I grabbed Blowkos' tits, probably too hard, but I had lost control.

I groaned and fucked her as deep as I could. I came deep within her tunnel, and to my surprise, she came again as well.

"Holy fuck. That was amazing," I said as I rolled off her onto my back between the two monster girls. They both laid their heads on my shoulders and placed their hands on my chest. All three of us were completely satisfied from the wild sexual experience.

"Thank you for including me Euthani and Dalton. It was very fun, and I needed that release.

"You are welcome and thank you for including me as well.

Shit, sex with two goddesses is something most men never get to experience."

"I had quite a good time as well. We must do that again," Euthani purred as she patted my large pecs.

"Is coming inside you girls going to be a problem?" I raised an eyebrow.

"No silly, only a fox man can get a fox girl pregnant. The same with any monster girl," Euthani grinned.

"Well, that's a relief," I replied with a yawn.

"Relief? You don't want us to have your babies?" asked Blowkos sarcastically.

I grinned and looked at the bovine girl. "No, it's nothing personal. I just have no desire to have a Dalton, Jr at this point in my life."

"Fair enough, they would be very cute children though," Blowkos replied with a smile.

"If your DNA is involved, I would agree with you. Alright, as much as I have enjoyed our time together this morning, I think I need to hit the weight room. I thought I was a beast, but Choicemaker proved that I have a long way to go."

"You are a beast, Dalton," Blowkos cooed. "However, you must understand, Choicemaker's class and specialization make him a behemoth. You will never match his strength and mortal combat abilities. On the other side of the coin, Choicemaker will never match your skills with firearms."

"And good looks," Euthani interjected with a giggle.

I smirked at Euthani. "Be that as it may, this physique doesn't just come naturally."

"I would not advise you to spar with Choicemaker

anytime soon. I was apprehensive when he asked you to do it because I had a feeling you would come away with a significant injury."

"Luckily, this world has those nano things. I can't believe I healed so fast. Another question for you, do the nano things just die after they are done and float around in my body?"

"No, they will cover what they fixed and make you stronger. Your jaw will be much more difficult to break now. If there are any nanobots that do not meld with the others, they will exit your body in your urine."

I nodded and pushed myself up.

I spent a couple of hours in the weight room working on each area of my body. I found that I was stronger on Zorth. I wasn't sure why that was, but it was. There were several pieces of equipment that I had to get instruction from Euthani on how to use. Once she told me, it made perfect sense. Each piece of equipment was much more advanced than anything I had ever used on Earth. The machine's targeted specific areas effectively and efficiently.

Afterward, I took a shower, and I headed to the firing range again. The group was back from wherever they went, and Stranger Zero followed me to the range. He supplied me with different firearms to use and sure enough I was able to master them all immediately. As cool and kick ass as Stranger Zero was, he couldn't hide his fascination at my skills with the guns. I imagined that he wasn't used to others being better than he was.

"Well, aren't you special," the dragon girl, Astra, mocked from the doorway.

I turned to see a drop-dead gorgeous monster girl with an eyebrow raised. She was into me. She just didn't want to give me the satisfaction...yet.

"Good morning, Astra. You look well," I grinned.

The dragon girl crossed her arms. "May I suggest something to you? Your outfit looks ridiculous. That may be the way your world dresses, but here it looks funny. You need to access the shop and buy you some new clothes. I would be happy to help you as I am tired of seeing that thing you have on. I already have something in mind. I will send you the links. I am sure you are not proficient with the store yet as you aren't proficient with most things."

"Sure," I shrugged.

Astra sighed and began swiping through her interface. "No, No, that won't do, No...Yes!"

I received a notification from her. I had to add her as a friend first and then I was met by a barrage of windows. A pair of leather pants and a gray shirt that was threaded with titanium was first. It looked rather shiny, but I would trust her judgement. She then sent me a pair of boots that were bad ass. They had a blade that ejected from the tip. She sent a link to a pair of gloves with titanium knuckles and it then she sent me some black sunglasses with night vision capabilities. Lastly, she sent me a long black leather trench coat. I placed all the items on the table in the armory and smiled hesitantly. This was certainly not my normal style of clothing, but I had no clue how people dressed, and I didn't want to look like a dork.

All in all, this stuff cost me a whopping 25,000 mojo, which killed my mojo reserves. "Fuck, this shit is expensive."

"Ha, this is low tier stuff, Dalton. However, it will serve you well right now. You will look much more normal, and it will provide you protection. The titanium shirt will stop most projectiles, and your trench coat will stop you from being burned alive. Your pants are fireproof as well and should protect you from small, bladed weapons. The boots offer the small blades, and the titanium knuckles in your gloves will crack heads. The sunglasses will add night vision and a small amount of protection from foreign objects. I'll turn my back as you get dressed," Astra instructed as she turned around showing her round ass and green tail.

I looked at Stranger Zero and twirled my index finger. "Can you turn around? I don't really like cyborgs looking at my naked body. No offense."

"None taken. I will turn around. I will say that Astra has made excellent selections. Carry on."

I slowly removed my wrestling attire and put on the titanium threaded shirt. I was expecting it to be rigid and uncomfortable. However, I was wrong. It was flexible and soft. It was almost impossible to believe that this was bulletproof. After I was done, I accessed my interface and clicked on my profile. I saw a hologram of what I looked like. Astra did good, this outfit looked fucking epic. I looked like a bulky Neo from The Matrix series.

"How do I look?"

Astra and Stranger Zero turned around quickly. Astra's eyes were wide as she looked me up and down. "Umm, it works, I guess."

The cyborg nodded. "Splendid. Astra is a genius."

Astra grabbed SZ's arm and hugged it tight. "Aww, thank you."

"So, are you two...a couple?"

"Of course, we are two people which is defined as a couple. You ask obvious questions," Stranger Zero replied with his emotionless robotic voice.

Astra laughed and shook her head. "No, he means...are we lovers."

"Absolutely not. I am a cyborg. I do not have lovers."

"I didn't know how things worked on Zorth. You guys seemed really attached to one another."

"Zero is my best friend. We have been through a lot together. He has my back, and I have his. Isn't that right?" Astra asked as she patted the cyborg on the arm.

"Yes, I like Astra very much. She would qualify as a close friend. I do like her more than everyone else I have had contact with."

"I get it. You guys are ride or die...that's an expression," I said as I looked at SZ. I knew he wouldn't know what I was talking about.

"That is a good way to describe it if I am understanding that correctly," Astra smiled. "Let's go have lunch."

Astra let go of Zero's arm and walked out of the room toward the dining area.

"You first," I motioned for Zero to go on ahead.

"I do not eat food, so I am not in a hurry to get there."

I shrugged and walked past the cyborg and then turned back. "So, do you charge yourself at the end of the day? Do you plug yourself into something?"

"No, my core will operate for 100 years before I will need a replacement. I will receive maintenance every 25 years."

"How old are you?"

"I am a new model. I was only created ten years ago."

"Cool, it's a pleasure to know you."

"You as well."

When I entered the dining area, I was met with gasps from Euthani and Blowkos.

"Doesn't he look spectacular?" Astra said with pride.

"Gods, you look even more insanely hot than before," Blowkos replied with her eyes almost bulging out of her skull.

"You did very well Astra...gods," Euthani added in a stupor.

"Damn son, you do clean up well. I am not hitting on you, so don't get too excited. I'm just saying," Choicemaker laughed as he shoveled a spoonful of food into his mouth.

13

We ate our lunch in relative silence, but my curiosity was getting the best of me. I was interested in what Choicemaker, Stranger Zero, and Astra had done earlier in the morning while I was having my amazing threesome with the two monster girls.

I finished off my bottle of water and placed the empty bottle back on the table. "Choicemaker, where were you guys this morning?"

Before he could get a word out Astra interjected. "Aren't we being nosy?"

I just looked at her and raised an eyebrow.

"Well, funny you should ask, Dalton. The next item on the docket will include two packages that we acquired while we were out today. They are gifts to you."

Astra tried to chuckle without others noticing, but it was obvious to everyone.

"Gifts? What gifts?" I asked with a smirk.

Choicemaker tossed his dish in the sink with too much force, and it shattered. "Fuck! That is the second one this week."

"Maybe you should try laying the dish in the sink next time," Blowkos said sarcastically.

"Bah, it is a manufacturer's defect. Fuck'em," Choicemaker scoffed.

"Wrong, you tossed the dish in the sink with too much velocity. That is the reason for the breakage. You need to be more careful. That is the twelfth dish you have destroyed this year. Are you under the assumption that dishes grow on trees?" asked Stranger Zero.

"Are we really doing this? Arguing over some broken dishes?" Astra rolled her eyes.

"Exactly fuck'em!" Choicemaker slammed his fist on the counter causing Blowkos' dirty dish to fall to the floor and shatter.

"Damn those jackleg manufacturers," I added with a grin.

"Exactly right, those things should be able to take a fall like that. We are going with disposable plates from now on. Blowkos...put that on the grocery list! Everyone get your asses to the firing range!" Choicemaker demanded as he stomped out of the dining hall.

Choicemaker's demeanor was hard to decipher at times. This was an instance where I couldn't tell if he was really excited or angry.

"Astra, what are these gifts?" I asked as I took my dish to the sink.

"You'll just have to wait and see," Astra smirked. "Zero, you need to keep your mouth shut. I want to see the look on his face when he sees what we brought him."

"Okay, Astra," Stranger Zero gave the dragon girl a thumbs up and looked at me. "I will not reveal the gifts, so do not ask me in the future."

Blowkos laughed. "Dalton, these two are tight and very loyal to one another."

"I can see that. Let's go and see what these mystery items are."

"I love presents!" Euthani chirped.

All of us entered the firing range to find Choicemaker standing with his gigantic arms crossed inside the actual fire zone. He wasn't behind the gun table. As I approached, my eyes were drawn to a couple of large black bags on the floor in front of him at his feet.

I stopped in my tracks and squinted at the two bags. "Are those...body bags? With actual bodies inside?"

Astra busted out in laughter. "There it is. That's the face I wanted to see."

"Why the fuck do I need dead bodies, and where did you get the dead bodies?"

"We went down to the public works department. These were a couple of fresh ones found on the street last night. Don't worry, they are just a couple of gangbanger thugs, so it's no big loss. They were fixing to go in the incinerator, and I told them we would take the stiffs off their hands. They agreed because the fuckers stink when they burn up in that incinerator."

"Okay, that's the where part of the equation...now I would like to know the why," I said as I walked within a few feet of the black bags.

"Duh...you are a Gundertaker. I want to see your necromancy skill in action brother. I didn't have any dead bodies here, so I had to go get some. Waah laah," Choicemaker motioned like a magician at the bags.

Astra continued to laugh. "Your face keeps getting better and better."

"Couldn't this have waited after my food had a chance to settle?"

Astra spoke again sarcastically. "You are part necromancer, and you are grossed out by a corpse? You suck as a necromancer. Maybe you should be a bunnymancer and control cute furry bunnies...living bunnies."

"Fuck you, dragon girl," I growled at her. "Open the damn bags, and I'll tell them to eat your ass and not in a good way either."

Choicemaker erupted in laughter. "Oh brother, I see what you did there. Funny shit, man." Choicemaker shook his head and knelt beside the corpses. He unzipped each of them and covered his nose. "Fuck dudes, these things are ripe already. They were just killed last night. We should have done this outside."

The cloud of rotting flesh aroma made its way to all of our nostrils and caused us to gag.

141

"Stop gagging, Dalton. This is your specialty," Astra said with the back of her hand over her nose.

"I think we all need to learn to suck it up considering I am a member of this team now. Don't you think?" I said as I took my hand down from my nose.

"Darn tootin', Dalton, let's get close and sniff these bastards," Choicemaker put his nose a few inches away from the bodies and inhaled. The berserker stood up and backed away. "Alright, that was a bad idea. Don't do that."

He walked over to the trash can beside the gun table and violently emptied his stomach into the container while we watched in disgust. He wiped his mouth and walked back over to his previous position.

All of us stood there with wide eyes. We wanted to laugh, but we didn't want to embarrass him more than he already was.

Maker put his hands on his hips. "Sorry about that, team. That stench got the best of me. Anyway, moving right along. Dalton, you need to raise these guys up from the dead, so get to it."

"All right, that will be easy enough," I said as I pulled up my interface. I saw the highlighted corpses on the floor and chose to raise them. At Gundertaker Level One, two undead were all that I could control right now. The black bags began to shake, and moans began to echo in the firing range. Choicemaker was startled by the sudden movement and backed away a few steps. There was a chorus of gasps from everyone that stood beside me. Each corpse raised into a sitting position. They both had black jackets on with white bloody shirts underneath. The one on the left had a bullet hole in the center of his head, and the other had two holes in his chest. Thick blood oozed out of the bullet holes of each corpse like jelly out of a donut.

"Uuuugh, that's fucking nasty," Astra muttered followed by a dry heave.

A few moans continued from the undead as they pushed themselves to their feet. Their arms dangled down beside them, and they both leaned to their left. They were upright and waiting for their next command.

"Damn, that is cool brother. Gross as all hell but cool," Choicemaker nodded.

"Excellent," Stranger Zero approved.

"You still got it. Good job!" Euthani hugged my arm.

"Looks like you got a rise out of us and them today," Blowkos murmured.

Euthani and I looked at the bovine girl and chuckled. "That was bad, but funny bad," Euthani said.

"I don't get it," Astra scoffed.

"Never mind, it's just an...INSIDE...joke between the three of us," I winked at Euthani and Blowkos.

"Ok, that was just bad," Euthani smiled and shook her head.

"Come on, it was funny, right?" I asked with my hands raised a bit.

"No, it was pretty bad, Dalton. We still love you though," Blowkos replied with a grin.

"Is anyone going to fill us in?" Astra asked with her arms crossed as she leaned on her right leg.

"Well, I filled these two in earlier," Dalton added with a chuckle.

"Stop, just stop...I just can't," Euthani laughed to the point of tears.

Astra sighed heavily in frustration.

"I think these odd statements are puns, bad puns," Stranger Zero said to his aggravated dragon girl buddy.

Choicemaker finally chimed in loudly. "If you clowns can get a hold of yourselves, we can focus on these walking stink sticks in front of me. I didn't stink up my transport for nothing."

"You're right Maker, we're sorry," Blowkos replied. "Please continue, Dalton. We need to un-dead-stand your powers."

"Fuck!" Choicemaker yelled.

Euthani and I exploded in laughter.

Stranger Zero looked at a confused Astra. "That was a humorous pun unlike the ones from Dalton."

"Dalton is just bad at everything," Astra scoffed.

Suddenly, we heard piercing gunfire echo in the large room. Choicemaker had a plasma pistol raised, and we could see steam rise from the end of the barrel. "Shut the fuck up. Dalton, do your thing."

I mentally instructed both zombies to turn toward Choicemaker and walk. They began to wobble and limp slowly toward the huge man.

"There we go," Choicemaker nodded and gave me a thumbs up. He began to back up as the zombies closed in.

I instructed the zombies to begin jogging which startled

Choicemaker, and he began to move quicker. He lost his balance and fell on his ass.

"Shit! They're gonna get me!"

I instructed the zombies to stop right over top of him and then I prepared myself to get yelled at.

"Ha ha, awesome brother! You could have made them eat me, right?"

I was shocked by his excitement. I expected him to be furious. "Yep, that's right."

Choicemaker rolled to his right and stood. "Yikes, they almost dropped some kind of goo on me. I don't think I got any on me. That shit won't come out in the wash," Choicemaker scanned his pants for droplets. "Now, can you make them fight each other?"

I shrugged. "I don't see why not."

I instructed the chest wound Charlie to grab the other by the neck. The head wound Harry didn't make any attempt to resist Charlie's attack. Charlie pulled him in for what looked like a kiss and sunk his teeth deep into the middle of Harry's face. The zombie growled and ripped a huge hunk of nose and cheeks into his maw. Charlie began to chew the rancid meat, and then he swallowed the rotting chunks. He went in for Harry's neck next. Charlie's teeth plunged into the side of his neck, and he bit down and tore an enormous hunk of skin, meat, and blood vessels into his mouth. I assumed he would continue to attack until I stopped him.

"Fuck, Dalton. You can do it. Now stop. This is nasty," screamed Astra with her head turned and eyes closed.

Before the zombie took another chunk out of Harry, I

instructed him to stop and back away. Gore and congealed blood oozed out of the new wounds. Jell-O like blood and burgundy flesh dangled from the attacker's maw and dripped on to the floor. The plopping sounds echoed in the long room.

"Splendid," Stranger Zero complimented.

"Wow, can you imagine how cool it will be when you could raise more than two?" Euthani chirped as she performed a barrage of light claps.

"Yeah, it would be useful. That's for damn sure," I nodded at the fox girl before I turned to Choicemaker. "Have you seen enough?"

"Almost, but I want to see one more thing," Choicemaker replied as he laid a pistol on the floor. "Get one of them to pick up the pistol."

"No, that's stupid," scathed Astra.

"Do it, Dalton," Choicemaker replied sternly.

"You got it," I said as I instructed Charlie to walk to the gun on the floor. I told him to pick it up and hold it in his hand.

The zombie limped over slowly to the gun and bent over. He extended his hand and lost his balance falling to the floor. There was a disgusting wet splat when he made contact and then we saw fluid pool under his body. The zombie's abdomen had burst from the fall. It began to drag itself to the gun leaving a gory mess behind him. The zombie's intestines spilled to the floor in a disgusting pile. The zombie finally grabbed the grip on the gun and held it. It stopped and waited for instruction. I then told it or what was left of it to stand to its feet. As it struggled to stand, more entrails spilled to the floor. The stomach-churning stench from the gruesome scene blanketed the room. I raised my arm and put my nose in the inside of my elbow. Astra stomped out of the room as she made a horrible gagging sound.

After a few moments of struggle, the zombie was able to stand. He stood even more awkward than before due to his guts that now hung from his body. He still held the gun, but he wasn't holding it properly. He was a zombie so that made sense that he wouldn't know how to hold a gun correctly. I attempted to instruct him on how to hold it properly, but I was interrupted by a notification from my interface.

A Gundertaker Level One cannot direct his undead companions to fire weaponry. You must reach Gundertaker Level Two to instruct undead companions to use small weapons such as pistols, knives, and clubs.

"Oh snap, when I reach Gundertaker Level Two, I will be able to get them to use pistols and knives. Kickass."

"Yeah, brother!" Choicemaker exclaimed.

14

The next few hours consisted of gun training and weightlifting. The zombie practice was cut short due to the terrible shape the undead bodies were in. They were making a terrible mess all over the floor, and they were stinking up the entire complex. I went into my interface and disengaged my control of the bodies. Choicemaker and Stranger Zero took them out to a nearby dumpster and tossed them in. Maker said it was trash day, and they would take care of Harry and Charlie soon enough.

"Dalton, Euthani, Blowkos...come to the control room. We need to have a team meeting. Zama and Fiji have arrived from their mission. Let's go," Choicemaker yelled from the other side of the gym out of sight.

"Zama? Fiji?" I asked as I placed my 100-pound dumbbells back on the rack. Euthani's ears perked up at the names as well. I thought we had met the whole team.

"You don't know about Zama and Fiji?" Blowkos asked with a surprised look on her pale white face.

I chuckled. "If I did, I wouldn't have asked you."

Euthani walked up beside me and hugged my arm. "Eek, you are sweaty."

"I'm sorry, it comes with the territory, I'm afraid. A lot of blood, sweat, and tears go into constructing the body you see here."

"You are such a dork. I will get that hug later when you shower...deal?" the fox girl asked as she threw me a towel to wipe off the excess sweat.

"Deal."

Blowkos exhaled with frustration. "Do you want to know about them, or are you going to eye fuck each other for the rest of the night?"

Euthani winked at me with a cute smile. "Sorry, Blowkos. We are all ears, see?" The fox girl moved her ears like they were dancing on top of her head and then she giggled.

"The puns are strong in you little one," I sarcastically punched Euthani on the arm.

"Ugh, I give up," Blowkos huffed and began to walk past us. I grabbed her wrist and kissed her on the cheek. She reddened and grinned at the gesture.

"Please continue. We'll be good, I promise," I told her.

"Zama and Fiji are the only other members of the Cosmic Peacekeepers. Choicemaker sent them on an undercover mission a week ago. They worked on getting intelligence from the Copper Sharktooth Posse, and they were to return to tonight and tell us what they had learned. Choicemaker wants to rid Osiris of the posse."

"Funny, he never mentioned them before. Let's not keep them waiting," I replied as I threw the white towel over my shoulder and began to walk toward the control room. I stopped a few steps into the trip. "I guess these are monster girls as well?"

"Of course, Zama is a lamia, and Fiji is a bunny girl."

"Lamia, what the hell is a lamia?" I asked as I scratched the back of my head.

Blowkos chuckled and passed me. "You'll have to see for yourself."

I turned to Euthani. "Do you know what a lamia is?"

"Yes, however, this will be the first one I have met. She will be interesting. I love making new friends," Euthani chirped as she sped by me.

I was getting no answers, but I would get them soon enough. When I entered the control room, I saw everyone but the lamia. I recognized the bunny girl because she looked like a bunny. She had long white fluffy ears with bright green eyes, and she had a button nose with freckles scattered across her face. She had human skin much like Euthani and Astra and wore a pink tube top looking thing that held in beautiful round breasts. They looked to be larger than what you would expect for her body size, but I wasn't complaining. She had what looked like black boy shorts on that showed off her beautiful human-like legs all the way to some white sneakers. She smiled at me and skipped over. She extended her hand, and I grasped it without too much force.

"You must be Dalton. I have heard a lot about you," Fiji said softly.

"I wish I could say the same. I only heard about you a few minutes ago, but it is certainly nice to meet you as well. You are my first bunny girl," I grinned, and she nodded.

"Do I look like you thought I would look?"

"Umm, kinda. I was expecting more fur though. This is going to sound a little forward, but I am going to ask anyway. Do you have the fuzzy white tail?"

Fiji laughed and turned around. She had a white tail just like I had imagined. It looked like white cotton and was the size of a softball. She lifted her butt and looked at me over her shoulder. The boy shorts she had on were very short. Her butt cheeks hung out the bottom of them like Daisy Duke's shorts did from one of my favorite shows from the 80's, The Dukes of Hazzard. She even jiggled her ass as a bonus. I quickly ignored the tail to watch the bouncing ass cheeks.

"You like?" Fiji asked flirtatiously.

I nodded once. "Most definitely."

"You want to touch it?"

"Ummm, excuse me?"

"My tail silly, do you want to touch it?"

"I would like that very much if that is okay with you."

"Well, I asked," she smirked as she turned her tail to me again.

I slowly reached out and touched her tail with my fingertips before I palmed it. It was as soft as it looked. She moaned and shook her ass checks some more. Each cheek lightly slapped against my hand.

Damn, this bunny girl is flirting with me big time in front of everyone.

Suddenly, I felt something large wrap around my thighs and waist. I looked down and saw what looked like a fucking anaconda but bigger.

"Holy fucking shit!" I screamed as I attempted to move the snake off me, but it was futile. The snake squeezed harder before relaxing and unwrapping from my body.

Laughter erupted from around the room, and I turned quickly to look for the big ass snake that had just been wrapped around me. My eyes widened when I saw a figure that was human above the waist and a big ass snake below the waist. My jaw dropped to the floor. Snakes had always scared the shit out of me. From the waist up, this girl was drop-dead gorgeous. She had long red hair that went down to her waist, and big yellow reptilian eyes which were very similar to Astra's. She had on what looked like a steel bikini top. I assumed it was something similar to the shirt I had with the titanium threading.

"Dalton, everyone thought it would be funny for me to grab you from behind. I am sorry if I scared you," Zama hissed.

I gulped and shook my head. "It's ok, I have just had a fear of snakes all my life. Seeing you is a shock to the system. It's nothing personal. No offense."

"None taken, I tend to cause fear with my appearance."

I held out my hands in front of me. "You're beautiful."

Zama slithered in one spot and blushed. "Thank you."

"Ugh, why does every woman here blush around this big buffoon," Astra scoffed.

"Big Buffoon? You got the big right," I smirked at the dragon girl and winked.

"Ugh, you are soooo annoying," Astra replied as she crossed her arms over her mountainous chest. The tops of her tits spilled over just a bit, which looked very nice.

"Now, you are staring at my boobs! Have you no shame, human?"

I shrugged. "Not a lot...no."

Choicemaker's voice thundered over the room suddenly. "Okay, okay, kiddies you can play later. We have work to do. Well, half of you have work to do."

"Why just half?" Astra scoffed.

Choicemaker chewed on his huge glowing cigar. "Well, some of us have to stay here. Everyone can't go on the mission. Can I please continue?"

Astra sighed and turned her head, but she didn't reply in words.

I raised my hand to get Choicemaker's attention away from the pissy dragon girl. "What do you have for us?"

Maker nodded and removed the cigar from the corner of his mouth. "Fiji and Zama have done one hell of a job getting intel on the posse. Fiji snuck in last night and mapped out their HQ. She also got a count of how many baddies are there. She even has the key code to get into the building. They went above and beyond. A few of you are going there tonight to exterminate the vermin from the face of Zorth. They have been a menace for a long time, but they are beginning to prey more on the innocent for no reason at all other than evil. They have set fires to random apartment buildings, kidnapped women, and forced them into the sex trade. We need to stop these thugs. That fucking Sly Swagger is the biggest piece of shit you will ever see. If we take him out, the posse will dissolve."

"I agree with your plan. The posse is a vile gang that should be stopped," Stranger Zero replied.

"I want in," I interjected as I stepped forward.

"If he goes, I go," Euthani added as she stood beside me. I looked at her and smiled. I didn't deserve her loyalty.

"I hoped you would say that Dalton. It's time to get your feet wet. Wet with the blood of these motherfuckers."

"I wish to go as well. I have a score to settle with these gangsters," Zero said.

Astra stepped beside the cyborg. "I am going wherever he goes."

Choicemaker slammed his fist against the table. "Hell yes, this is what I am talking about. You guys are going, and the rest of us are staying behind and monitoring the assault from vest cameras. However, I am going to send Fiji to hang out in the building across the street as a lookout. She is to stay put and let you know if anyone is entering the building. She is not to engage unless the shit hits the fan. Are we clear, Fiji?"

"Yes, perfectly," the bunny girl replied with a confident nod.

"Good, I am going to send the layout that they brought me to your interfaces. You will get some vest cams from Blowkos and me. Zama and she will monitor from the control room.

Zero, get Dalton and Euthani proper weapons and make sure batteries are full and you have spares."

"I will go now," Zero said as he turned toward the armory.

"Zama get them the layout and put it on the system here as well. They need to get going."

"We're going tonight...like right now?" I asked with my eyebrows raised.

"Is that a problem? It's late, so they are going to be tired and drunk. It's the perfect time," Choicemaker replied sternly.

My cheeks reddened and I shook my head. "No problem, just clarifying."

Choicemaker placed the cigar back in the corner of his mouth and nodded at me.

I received a notification in the corner of my vision. I pulled up my interface and accessed the notification from Zama. Suddenly, a 3d holographic map appeared right in front of my eyes. I was able to zoom in and out, and I could turn it in all directions. "Cool toy."

"The map is pretty self-explanatory. Do you understand, Dalton?" asked the lamia.

"Yeah, I think so. You guys are awesome for getting this for us."

The bunny girl grinned and clapped. "You are so welcome, Dalton!"

Fiji reminded me so much of Euthani. Their personalities were very similar, and they were both full of positive energy. They were such a joy to be around, and they weren't hard to look at either.

A few minutes later, Stranger Zero returned with our

weaponry. "This is for you Euthani. A Helsing 666 Caliber plasma crossbow, I hope this will suffice. There is a full charge, and this unit has stealth mode as well. Take these spare batteries."

"Oh, my gods, it will so suffice," Euthani replied bursting with excitement.

"Take these, Dalton," Stranger Zero said as he handed me two shiny pistols.

I held them in my hands, and I was filled with knowledge. I was bombarded by information windows and diagrams showing everything about the weapons.

"Grulke Industries LOF 2000 plasma hand cannons...whoa," I murmured as I stared in awe.

"Those are like my own. They are a generation behind, but they are still great weapons."

"Thanks, sick as fuck."

"You are sick? You will need to sit out this mission as you will put the team in danger," Zero replied matter of factly.

"Nope, that's another expression. Add that to your database," I said as I holstered my new pistols and patted him on the back afterward.

"Added."

"Are you three ready to go? Are you sure you don't want to back out Dalton? We'll understand," Astra walked up behind us.

"No, I think I'll be just fine. I may show you a thing or two. I am sure you would love that," I winked at the dragon girl.

Stranger Zero fidgeted with one of his platinum pistols

and returned it under his sleeve with that cool contraption he had.

"I got to get me those things you have in your sleeves," I told the cyborg.

He ignored my statement and looked at his buddy Astra. "Are you armed?"

"I have a backup pistol...yes."

"Back up? What is your primary?" I asked with a stink face.

She glared at me and her eyes began to turn a violent orange. She opened her mouth, and I saw a glow in her throat. She then raised her arms with her palms up, and a fire orb the size of a baseball appeared out of thin air on each hand. Then I saw movement behind her. Two wings extended from her back and stretched outward. They were both four feet in length and looked exactly how a dragon wing looked in the movies and tv shows. It was fucking awesome. She flapped the wings and rose all the way to the ceiling in the control room. She descended to the floor with her glowing eyes still locked on mine. After she landed, all the fire, she conjured vanished, and she returned to normal. "I use a pistol as a backup weapon. As you can see, I am well equipped to handle tonight's mission."

"I can see that. That was awesome. Congrats on being a super cool dragon girl."

I was very happy that Astra was on our side tonight. Going up against a fire breathing dragon girl would be extremely intimidating.

"Ok guys, are you good to go? Time's wasting," interjected Choicemaker.

"We are ready," Stranger Zero replied robotically.

"Alright, you four take the two new nightcycles. Fiji has already left on hers. She wanted to get into position before you guys got there," Choicemaker replied as he chewed on his cigar.

As we walked to the garage, my heart pounded in my chest. It was from excitement for the most part. I was afraid somewhat but not as much as I expected. My gun skills and necromancy skill really gave me confidence. I did things that not many people in the galaxy did. Hell, there may be no one in the galaxy with pure weapon specialty and necromancy. I was a fucking Gundertaker, and I was going to kill some gangsters tonight. These sons of bitches deserved what they were going to get from us...the fucking Cosmic Peacekeepers. It felt great to belong to something that was real. I had been an actor for a very long time while I was wrestling. I was now a soldier...a warrior in the wild, wild west.

Stranger Zero straddled one of the nightcycles and Astra straddled the other one.

The cyborg looked back at Euthani and I. "You will not drive. You are not familiar with the operations."

"You'll get no argument from me," I replied as I looked at Euthani. "If you don't mind, I would rather ride behind Astra. It will look kind of odd for me to ride behind a cyborg."

Euthani giggled and hopped on the nightcycle with Zero.

"So, I guess that means you are going to ride with me. How did I get so lucky?" Astra asked sarcastically.

"You are pretty lucky," I replied as I straddled the cycle behind her. "You know, if you slide back a few inches, you might feel something you may like."

"Ugh, you are such an asshole. Hold on, if you fall off, I am not going to stop," Astra replied perturbed.

"I think I'll manage just fine," I whispered as I wrapped my arms around her waist. The dragon girl shuddered from my touch.

"You keep your hands right there, or I will set you on fire."

"I believe you. You don't have to worry about me because I plan on being a perfect gentleman on our date night. Where are you taking me? I could go for a good juicy steak."

"Ugh, shut up and hold on."

"Don't we need helmets?" I asked as I looked around the nightcycle.

"Helmets? Are you a pussy? No, we don't need helmets. Do you want to look like an idiot?" Astra scoffed.

"Well, I was just thinking about how it would really suck to crack my head open on our first date. I don't know how good a driver you are."

"I'm an excellent driver I will have you know, Mr. Wade."

The garage door slowly opened, and Zero and Euthani sped out of the door like a bat out of hell. Astra pressed a button, and the nightcycle began to vibrate and buzz softly. The wheels lit up in neon blue as Astra began to rev the engine of the nightcycle. It certainly did not sound like a Harley Davidson. It made more of an electronic zipping sound. Suddenly, my head flew backward as the dragon girl took off like a dragster and out of the complex. We were going fast, but it felt like we were flying. It was such a smooth ride much like the car on the way here had been. I felt the cool wind soar through my long blonde hair, and it felt amazing. A few of Astra's green strands of hair tickled my nose as the wind flowed through her beautiful hair. She smelled of jasmine and vanilla. I closed my eyes and inhaled her scent ravenously.

"Are you fucking smelling my hair?" Astra asked loudly.

"No, I am not. It is just blowing in my face. Nice shampoo choice, though. I've smelled better, but your hair smells okay."

"Just okay? My hair smells wonderful. I just had a shower two hours ago."

"Just kidding, your hair smells terrific. It makes me wonder what the rest of your body smells like," I said sarcastically.

I felt an elbow hit me in the gut...hard. "Fuck, I am just kidding. Do you want to take me out of commission before we even start the mission?"

"You are riding with Zero on the way back if I don't kill you first."

"Nah, you would miss me too much."

I was rewarded with another elbow to the gut. This time it took my breath away but not in a good way. "Ok, fuck. I'm going to shut up now. Just try not to kill us on the way there."

Astra gripped the throttle on the nightcycle and pulled backward to speed up.

15

Both nightcycles swerved through the sparse traffic on our way to the HQ of the Copper Sharktooth Posse. I was mentally preparing myself for battle. My heart was pounding, and adrenaline pumped through my veins. My breathing increased substantially, and my eyes were dry from keeping them wide open during our speedy trek downtown. Conversation between Astra and I had stopped a couple of minutes after we had left. I wanted her to have full attention on the road as fast as she was driving. We even passed Stranger Zero on the way there. I had the feeling that Astra was a very competitive dragon girl in everything that she did. We traveled through a luminescent section of the city that looked prosperous, but we soon entered the slums. Shitty buildings, garbage, and wrecked cars lined the side of the streets. We zipped past three corpses. Two of which were on the sidewalk, and we had to swerve to miss the third corpse in the middle of the street.

Suddenly, Astra and SZ cut the lights on the nightcycles and pulled up on the sidewalk beside a ratty building. The windows were smashed out, and some of the windows were covered with wooden planks. The stench was terrible. There had to be another corpse around somewhere that we hadn't seen.

"We're here. There is the HQ across the street," Astra said as she pointed to a building that showed some life. There were lights on, and it appeared to be in decent shape from the outside.

Stranger Zero approached from behind. "Fiji is on the third floor of this establishment. We will meet up with her and then make our assault. Let's not waste any more time."

As we walked toward the open door, I looked back at the bikes. "Don't we need to hide them? This isn't exactly the best part of town. Don't you think someone will steal them?"

"If they are stolen, they have a tracker on them. We will find them and kill the thief dumb enough to take them," Stranger Zero replied in his monotone robotic voice.

"Okay, lead the way," I motioned for us to continue.

We entered an open door that had been kicked in at some point. We dashed up the staircase until we reached the third floor. The beautiful bunny girl awaited us with a smile and wave.

"Hey guys, glad you could make it," Fiji said sarcastically

"Let's take a look at the posse HQ and determine our best course of action," Stranger Zero replied.

We walked over to a large window that overlooked the building perfectly. There was no sign of life anywhere on the outside. We could see some movement through the windows and hear the muffled sound of music coming from the second floor of the three-story building.

"What's the plan?" I asked as I peered out the window.

Stranger Zero was swiping and motioning like he was moving the holographic map. He ignored me for a couple of moments.

Euthani was nervous, I could tell. She hadn't spoken since we arrived, and she was hugging herself with her arms. I put my arm around her to give her some comfort and a reminder that I was there with her. I wasn't going to let anything happen to my fox girl. She looked up at me and smiled in appreciation of my compassionate gesture.

"Since I arrived, two men have entered the building from the front door. There is a retinal scanner," the bunny girl stated.

"Look, there is someone walking to the door right now. Is there anyone with him?" Astra asked as she pointed at a man in the leather jacket and jeans. He walked slowly looking at the sidewalk with his hands in his pocket.

Stranger Zero looked at Euthani and motioned for her to approach. "Euthani, use your crossbow and shoot him straight through the neck. I will remove his eye to use with the retinal scanner. That will make our breach rather easy. Now, before he gets inside."

Euthani nodded nervously, but she equipped her crossbow. She raised it and looked through the sight at her target.

She held her breath and squeezed the trigger. The plasma bolt soared into the night and went straight through the man's neck decapitating him. Blood erupted like a geyser from the stump, and his head bounced twice as it hit the pavement.

"Fucking A! Nice shot!" I patted her on the back.

"That was impressive accuracy. Let us go quickly before he is found by anyone. We will enter without an issue. Fiji does not have any cameras marked on the map, so we should be good there," SZ replied.

All three of us sprinted down the stairs to the first floor and out the door. Our night cycles were in the same spot so yay for us. Euthani's confidence had skyrocketed after her perfect kill, and I was happy for her.

"Mojo extraction will be completed after we are finished. Do not stop in the middle of our assault. Are we clear?" Stranger Zero asked as he looked at each of us in the eye, but he paused for a couple of moments when he reached my eyes.

"No problem, it's your world boss," I held my hands up.

Stranger Zero nodded, and we crouch-walked across the street to the dead gangster. His head had bounced fifteen feet away, and it was looking straight at us. A large rat had already made its way to the severed head. He was licking the blood and nibbling on the dangling meat.

"Yuck," Astra whispered.

"Since the head has been removed from the torso, I will take his entire head to the scanner. That will prevent damaging the eyes during removal. Let's go," Stranger Zero replied as he grabbed the oily brown hair of the head and picked it up. He swatted the nasty rat away that still had its teeth sunk into a flap of skin. Blood dripped to the ground leaving a small puddle. As he walked toward the front door, he left a trail of red. The music from the inside of the building became clearer, and we heard loud voices from the second floor. The door was made of steel and had no window. There was only a small square glowing retinal scanner above the doorknob. The cyborg held the head upward with a hand on each ear. He put the right eye in front of the red screen, and a beam of light shaped like a small cone scanned the eye of the man. The screen turned green, and we heard the door unlock. SZ grabbed the knob and entered the building slowly. He held his index finger in front of his mouth instructing us to be quiet as he went in first with Astra behind him and me then Euthani. We all had our guns in hand except for the dragon girl. The floor was a mess. There was trash scattered everywhere, and clothing was strewn about. We heard snoring from a couch in the corner of the room. Stranger Zero told us to hold our position while he cloaked. He wasn't completely invisible because we knew where to look, but to an unknowing party, he would be unseen. His cloaking ability looked just like the alien in the movie Predator. It was cool as fuck.

A couple of moments later we saw blood spurt from the sleeping man's neck, and the fluid splattered on the wall behind the couch. SZ uncloaked and wiped off a big ass knife and sheathed it. He turned and looked around the room for others, but there were none. There was an elevator, but we chose the staircase. The lighting was shitty due to many bulbs being out, but that worked to our advantage. We slowly traversed the steps to the platform in front of the door with a large sign displaying the number two. The rock music was loud, and we heard a lot of commotion from the inside. These guys were partying, things were about to get ugly. It would have been much easier to just kill them all in their sleep, but it was what it was. I wanted some target practice with live assholes.

Astra broke her silence with a whisper. "Watch out for any civilians. I am willing to bet they have some women here. Some may be members of the posse, but only fire at them if they attack.

"Place your weapons on silent mode. They should have that option," Zero instructed.

"Gotcha," I replied as flipped a small lever on the side of each pistol.

"Astra stay in the back and avoid firing if you can. I would like a silent assault if possible," Zero requested.

"Fuck, I don't get to have any fun? You assholes better share the mojo. I got you Zero, let's do this," Astra replied hesitantly.

Zero nodded and unlatched the door. There was a low volume click, and the hinges squealed. The music was loud enough that they wouldn't be able to hear it. Zero went into the hallway and squatted beside the wall and motioned for us to enter. There was a large room at the end of the hallway where the partying was taking place. No one had seen any of us, so we had the advantage. We crouch-walked slowly down the hallway. Zero held up ten fingers and then held one hand to show five more fingers to tell the crew that there were fifteen gangsters.

"Any of those civilians?" Astra whispered from behind the pack.

Stranger zero nodded and held up two fingers and whispered, "Women not part of the fifteen."

"Do they look like willing participants or prisoners?" I muttered.

Zero shook his head.

"Okay, we need to make sure we don't kill them in this gunfight," Astra added.

Suddenly, a door opened behind us. We turned to see a man exiting the room buckling his belt. That must have been a bathroom. Euthani wasted no time and shot a plasma bolt directly into his heart when he saw us. The only sound made was the dead weight plop onto the floor.

"Fuck, two kills already Euthani, you are a damn boss," I muttered.

She winked and moved her hips like a hula dancer. We had almost forgotten about the fifteen deadly gangsters a few feet away from us.

"Astra, you stay here and cover our backs in case anyone else comes out of the shitter or a bedroom," I demanded.

She nodded in agreement, surprisingly. I expected a snide comment about me telling her what to do. Stranger Zero motioned toward the full room, and we walked behind him slowly. The men were making a human woman dance on a table in her bra and panties. She was crying and shivering in fear. I gritted my teeth and tightened my hands around the grips of my pistols.

"Dance, girl, dance!" a gangster yelled at the terrified

blonde on the table. "You better fucking dance, or we will kill you like a damn rat."

"Okay, I'm sorry, please don't hurt me," she pleaded and began to move more.

"Now, that's more like it. Your sister over there is doing alright. You need to follow her lead," the man chuckled and put a cigarette in his mouth.

The other lady was in the corner of the room standing on another table. She had been forced to remove her bra, but she did have on her panties. She had more of a crowd around her screaming and grabbing at her while she danced awkwardly. Suddenly, one of the men hopped on the table and grabbed her breasts. The woman screamed and tried to push him away.

"Come on now, I know you like it. Be still!" the man exclaimed as he slapped her in the face.

I had seen enough. I lifted my right pistol and fired a shot across the room. The plasma round went through the side of his skull and out the other. Blood and brains splattered on the wall, and his corpse fell off the table to the floor.

"Get down, girls!" I screamed at the half-naked women. The men in the room spun around in shock. They saw all of us enter the room armed to the teeth ready for war. The captive women dove onto the floor and rolled under the tables that they were on seconds before. That was quick thinking on their part.

"They're under the tables. Watch your fire!" I yelled at the team as I squeezed off another round into the neck of a gangster near the other dead one. The crook grabbed his throat, but it was futile. He was done. Blood gushed through the cracks of his fingers down to his chest, and he fell backward on top of the other dead guy. I suddenly saw an orange glow envelop us from the rear. Another gangster had come out of a room down the hall, and the dragon girl incinerated him with a stream of vicious fire from her mouth.

Stranger Zero began shooting at the gangsters alongside Euthani who launched plasma bolts into the flesh of the posse. These guys had no clue what was happening. One minute they were partying, and the next a crew of badasses had walked in their house to kill them. A man made it to his pistol on a table, and as he lifted the gun to shoot us, Zero had launched off the back of the couch in what looked like slow motion. Zero began alternating fire with each pistol as he flew. The man took six plasma rounds to the chest before Zero landed on the ground. I turned to fire another shot at an escaping gangster. Little did he know there was a dragon girl waiting down the hall he fled to. Two fire orbs were launched from the hands of Astra, and they engulfed the man in a hurricane of flames. He wailed in agony and attempted to roll around on the floor to put the fire out, but it was too late. He stopped moving quickly as the fire went out. I was shocked that the fire would just extinguish itself. I knew I would need to ask her questions later about that ability.

"Behind you!" Euthani screamed in my direction. I turned quickly to find a man lunging for my midsection for a takedown. I couldn't get my guns up before the guy's right shoulder plowed into my rib cage. We both went straight to the floor. I tried to return the air that had escaped from my lungs. I landed on what was left of a coffee table, and it hurt like a bitch. Luckily, I hadn't been impaled, thank God for the armor I had purchased. He straddled me and punched me in the face twice. One of the punches only grazed my cheek, but I felt warm liquid streaming down my cheek, so I knew he had cut it with his knuckles. I punched him as hard as I could in the liver with my titanium knuckle glove. The man erupted in screams of pain and suffering. Anytime you are hit in the liver you are fucked momentarily at the very least. This gave me time to grab one of the pistols I had dropped, and I placed the barrel under his chin and squeezed the trigger. The top of his skull shattered into dozens of pieces. Blood and brain matter erupted toward the ceiling like a gore volcano. The pressure from the plasma round had blown both eyes out of his sockets. I pulled his torso on top of me for a second to protect me from the falling gore. I pushed him off me and jumped to my feet. The firefight was over, and we had won.

"Everyone alright?" I asked as I touched my cheek with my index and middle finger.

Everyone replied that they were okay and had no injuries.

"Gods, Dalton. Are you okay?" Euthani leaped over a dead body and put her hand on my cheek.

"It's fine. It's just a scratch. Don't worry about me. I am glad you are okay," I replied with a kiss to her forehead.

Stranger Zero placed his finger to his ear. "Yes, thank you for letting me know."

"Was that Fiji? What's wrong?" Astra asked out of breath.

"Fiji states that two more vehicles have arrived. Six more men are headed into the building."

We heard commotion from the 3rd floor as well as commotion from the six men entering the lobby on the first floor. I didn't think they would be stupid enough to take the elevator, so I began running to the door to the stairwell.

Stranger Zero followed behind me. "Cover us, Euthani and Astra. I have a plan for the six that are coming up."

Stranger Zero pushed passed me and took a circular device out of his brown trench coat. He mashed a button on the top that caused a small red light to blink on top. He quickly tossed it against the wall beside the flight of stairs to the 2nd floor. The door downstairs slammed opened with a tremendous force and smashed the wall. I counted six men, and they were in single file as they headed up the stairs. They were close to one another as they reached the stairs to the second floor. Zero pressed a button on a remote as he slammed the door shut. A millisecond later there was a deafening explosion that shook the building.

"What the fuck was that?" I asked with my eyes as wide as they would go.

"A simple remote mine," Zero replied as he opened the door. It was a truly macabre scene. The mine appeared to have killed all six of the men. Body parts and blood decorated the stairwell, and the air smelled metallic and like cooked meat which was overloading my smell receptors."

"Are the stairs still standing? What the fuck?" I asked with my eyes wide.

"It looks like they are. I still advise you to be careful when you descend later because the stairs may collapse."

I turned to look in the other direction. I saw Astra and

Euthani glare at the stairs on the other side of the room. I thought it was weird that there was another stairwell. I figured that this might have been a two-story apartment, and the other staircase went directly to the second floor. I had a feeling we would find Sly Swagger waiting for us.

"Hold up, I am going to make a couple of friends," I said as I quickly pulled up my interface.

Astra scowled at me and placed her hands on her hips. "Friends? What the hell are you talking about?"

I ignored her rant and selected two corpses to raise from the dead. I chose a couple that weren't torn up so bad. I mainly wanted them as bullet sponges. The two dead bloody corpses I selected squirmed and slowly raised to their feet in front of us.

"Oh, I get it now," Astra replied as she watched my necromancy skills in action.

The zombies moaned and blood dripped from the gunshot wounds. Their faces and heads were intact. They just had a multitude of gaping chest wounds. They stood still and awaited instructions from their Gundertaker master.

"I'm hoping these guys can walk up steps. We'll soon find out," I added as I instructed them forward to the dark stairwell. I found that I was able to instruct them with more detail than just "move forward" or "attack." This was a gamechanger. I told them to grab the handrail for support and slowly move up the steps carefully. I was shocked to see them following my mental instructions perfectly even though their feet were wobbly, and they slipped a little. Nonetheless, they were doing a fine job of walking up steps. The main cause of slippage was the blood that dripped out of the first undead's wounds onto the floor.

Stranger Zero stepped beside me and smiled. "Splendid. Is there a cool-down period between raises?"

"What do you mean?"

"When these zombies are destroyed, can you raise more, or do you have to wait a certain length of time?"

"I am not sure. None of my minions have been taken out by others...only me."

Stranger Zero nodded and turned to the girls. "We need to go. Hopefully, it takes a few moments for the gangsters to realize they are zombies."

I dashed to the steps and followed my undead compadres. They were slow, but they were doing a good job traversing the steps. I was able to hear some commotion and voices from upstairs. The muffled conversations were frantic and loud. Obviously, panic had set in. My zombies entered the doorway to the third floor. I was curious to see what was going to happen, so I peeked around the corner. I am not sure what experience the gangsters have had with zombies.

"Sphinxtor, what the fuck is going on down there? You hurt? I see blood," a man said from a kneeling position behind the couch.

"Well, answer me goddammit! Fuck you, I'll ask Testeez...what the hell is going on?"

For the first time since arriving on the 3rd floor, moans slowly rolled out of the zombie's mouths.

"I can't hear you. Fuck, you guys are bleeding bad. Were you shot?"

By my count, there were six people out in the open on the third floor, and the others stood quietly with their weapons equipped. I instructed Sphinxtor, the zombie, to attack the first guy. All of us would charge in when the chaos exploded.

None of the men realized that their friends were undead zombies. "Sphinxtor, are you high? What the fuck are you on? You looked completely fucked."

The zombie just fell right on top of the kneeling gunman and began to bite into his face. "Help! He's fucking biting me."

I instructed Testeez to walk past the first guy and continue to the next one a few feet away. The man ran toward his friend who was now a snack for Sphinxtor. He stopped in his tracks when he saw that Testeez looked to be in the same state as Sphinxtor. He quickly pointed his gun at Testeez. "Back up! Get the fuck back! I don't know what the hell is wrong with you guys, but I will kill you if you don't back the fuck up!"

Testeez continued his march toward the gunman without pause. Suddenly, the gunman squeezed the trigger and shot the zombie in the chest. The round went through and blew a volleyball-sized hole in his back. The zombie stumbled but kept moving forward. The terrified gunman let go two more rounds into his chest and blew two more huge holes out his back. I was able to see completely through him now. "Fuck me! What are you?"

The man moved backward and lost his balance. He fell hard to the floor, and his head bounced off the concrete. The others in the room began firing everything they had. They knew their friends were dead, and they were scared shitless. Testeez fell on his victim before he had his head blown off. He took a chunk out of the unconscious man's neck before the top of his skull exploded from gunfire. He went limp and plopped on top of his prey. Two men ran up to the first gunman who looked like spaghetti now. Sphinxtor the zombie hadn't looked up since he began feasting on the thug.

"Holy shit! Die!" the posse thug said as he fired several shots in the back of Sphinxtor. These losers hadn't put it together that you need to take the head out, or they don't permanently die. He kept chowing down while getting shot repeatedly.

"Die, what the fuck are you?" he screamed as he continued shooting rounds into the torso of the zombie.

I pulled up my interface and selected the fresh dead man behind the two thugs and selected "Raise". The dead zombie began to wiggle as the new zombie came alive. He pushed the body off him and struggled to get to his feet. Sphinxtor was finally down for the count after the dumbasses got the idea to shoot him in the head. Little did they know that another living corpse was behind them. The zombie sunk his teeth into one of the men and grabbed the neck of the other. They both screamed in horror and agony. I was shocked at the strength of the zombie as I saw his fingers plunge into the neck of the man like it was a piece of pie. Several other posse gangsters stood dumbfounded as they watched the carnage unfold. After they snapped out of their stupor, they began to walk toward the remaining zombie and fire rounds upon rounds into the monster.

I turned my head back to the team. "Let's go. There are four of them. Give'em hell. I will raise two more zombies."

Stranger Zero, Euthani, and Astra zoomed past me and opened fire. The thugs didn't know what had hit them. They were showered with rounds and bolts before they even realized what was happening. Astra didn't need to use any fire. Zero and Euthani took the men out before Astra had a chance to light them up. The dragon girl stuck her lip out in disappointment.

"Can you guys actually miss once and a while? I like to have fun too."

Euthani dashed over to Astra and hugged her. "I am sorry, Astra. You can have the next one okay?"

Something rare happened. Astra smiled. "Damn, Euthani you made the ice queen smile."

"Shut up, Dalton. Don't you have some necromancy to do?" Astra scoffed and flashed her orange fire eyes at me.

I rolled my eyes and raised two of the bodies that were in the best shape. I wanted them to be able to take some punishment before going down. Suddenly a man sprinted from behind a table toward a door on the other side of the room.

Stranger Zero dashed over couches and chairs to shoot the man in the calf muscle. He screamed as he fell to the floor while grabbing his shredded leg. Zero knelt beside the injured man and grabbed him by his black hair with his left hand. He pulled him face to face to him and said, "Where is Sly Swagger? Tell me now!"

"Fuck you, robo-faggot, I ain't got to tell you shit."

Zero punched him in the face hard with his right fist. "Tell me now!"

The man spit blood in the face of the cyborg, and he punched him again. I heard a crunch from one of the bones in his face and heard teeth clatter onto the floor.

"Zero, hold up. I got an idea." I said as I instructed my zombie to go to their location and wait for my instructions.

The thug's eyes grew wide as he saw bloody walking corpses slithering over to him to do God knows what. They both stood over top of him on opposite sides. They moaned and growled as they looked at the fresh meat lying on the floor just waiting to be devoured. I instructed them to kneel beside him and wait.

"Get away from me! Get these things away from me!"

"Tell us where Swagger is," I demanded with my muscular arms crossed.

I instructed the zombie on the left to grab the perp's hand and lift it to his mouth. He bit off the man's index finger. The crunch was stomach-churning as the zombie began to chew the finger. The thug wailed in agony as blood squirted from the stump.

"I don't know where he is!"

I told the other zombie to grab his nuts and squeeze. The man's eyes almost popped out of his head as the zombie crushed his scrotum with ease.

"Alright, alright. He has locked himself in the vault through that door down the hallway!"

"What is the code to enter?" Zero asked.

The man hesitated to divulge that information. So, the zombie snapped another finger off with his teeth.

"Fuck, fuck! 6969! Get these things away from me!"

Astra walked over and kicked the man in the face. "6969? Can you idiots be any more disgusting?"

"Move the hell away, you dragon bitch!"

"What did you call me?" Astra growled, and her eyes burned orange with fire.

"Bitch! You are a fucking bitch!"

Astra placed her hand on the guy's head, and it began to glow orange and red. The man started screaming as his skull began to cook at the hands of Astra the scorned dragon girl. "Am I a bitch now?"

The man convulsed as his head cooked in front of our eyes. The smell of burnt hair and human flesh was nasty. After a couple of moments, the man's head was burned to a crisp, and it was as black as a piece of popcorn that had been in the microwave too long.

"Shit, Astra. Remind me to never call you a bitch," I scratched the back of my head as I shook it.

"Yuck, do any of you have any hand sanitizer?" Astra said as she looked at her hand and made a yuck face.

Euthani smiled and raised her hand. "I do, I do." The fox girl reached in her pouch and pulled out a container of crystal-clear sanitizer. She held it over the dragon girl's hand and squirted twice. Then Astra rubbed her hands together vigorously.

"Thank you, Euthani. You are quickly becoming one of my favorite people."

"Oh really? That is so wonderful. You are so awesome!" the fox girl exclaimed as she hugged Astra again.

Astra smiled until she saw me look at her which caused her eyes to narrow. "What are you staring at?"

"Mmm, nothing," I smirked.

"We are wasting time. Let's go," Stranger Zero interjected as he headed toward the door.

"You heard the man...cyborg...let's go."

We snuck down a dimly lit hallway and took a right. We reached a steel door with a glowing blue keypad. This wasn't a bank quality vault, but it looked impressive for a shitty street gang's hideout.

"Swagger! It's over." I yelled as my zombie companions finally caught up to us. I had forgotten that I hadn't inactivated them yet, so they gave me a scare.

"There is no point in yelling. He can't hear you inside that vault," Stranger Zero added.

"Well let's key in the ingenious and highly cryptic code that we were given," Astra scoffed as she placed her finger on the keypad.

Stranger Zero put his hand on hers. "We will unlock it. Get behind the undead for cover."

"Thank you, but I don't need cover. I am going to open the door and torch his ass."

"We got this Astra. Listen to Zero," I interjected.

"Did I ask for your opinion, Dalton?" She asked as she quickly punched 6969 into the pad. The vault door quickly unlatched and opened. She had her hands out in front of her and her mouth open ready to blast Swagger to oblivion.

What we didn't know was that there were other gang members in there with him. A plasma bullet plowed into Astra's arm and spun her around. Stranger Zero leapt in front of her to shield her from the barrage of incoming bullets. Plasma rounds blanketed Zero's back, and he fell on top of Astra covering her body. I directed my zombies to dash into the room to soak up some bullets. Screams echoed inside of the vault from the horror of seeing their zombie friends waltzing toward them to take a huge bite out of them. I heard dozens of little splats and thuds from the plasma rounds penetrating the flesh of the zombies. I rolled on the floor and fired at the five guys from between the legs of the zombies. They had no cover or hope to avoid my blazing rounds that sped toward their exposed bodies. Bullets cut through their legs, and they fell to the floor. What was left of the zombies pounced on two of the men, and I took out the other three with shots to the head.

Cowering in the corner of the vault was a man with a white tank top, leather pants, and a cowboy hat. He had several gold chains around his neck and sunglasses on. This had to be Sly Swagger. He turned his head and held his hands up.

"I give up. I won't be any trouble. I don't have a weapon. Don't kill me. I will give you whatever you want just tell me your price. It doesn't matter how much it is, I will get it to you," Swagger begged.

"No thanks," I said nonchalantly as I raised my Grulke Industries LOF Plasma Hand Cannon and blew Sly's brains all over the steel wall of the vault.

"Dalton!" Euthani screamed from behind me. "Come quick!"

I spun quickly to find a bleeding Astra cradling the head of Stranger Zero. She was in a state of shock as tears streamed down her face.

"Fuck!" I exclaimed as I checked on Astra first. It appeared to be just a flesh wound on her right upper arm. "Euthani, see if you can get the bleeding stopped."

She nodded as she pulled out something that looked like a small tube of toothpaste. "This is a nanobot ointment that Blowkos gave me. I will put some in the wound."

I nodded as I knelt beside the still cyborg. I suddenly heard Choicemaker in my ear communicator. I had forgotten that we had vest cameras on, and they were watching from HQ.

"Dalton, he may still be alive. These cyborgs are tough sons of a bitches. He probably just shut himself down due to his injuries."

"This is Blowkos, open his mouth. There should be a blinking light under his tongue. If that is still blinking, he is alive."

"Gotcha," I muttered as I opened the cyborg's mouth and lifted his tongue. There was a faint light blinking under the skin under his tongue. I held the vest camera close so Blowkos could see for herself.

"Okay, he is alive, but barely. Choicemaker and I are on our way now. We will be flying the cyberblade. We'll be there in a few minutes. Is Astra hurt?"

"She got shot in the arm. Euthani has squirted some of

that ointment you gave her into her wound. Astra is in more shock over Zero, I think. She isn't talking."

"Hold tight...we will be there very soon," Blowkos yelled into the receiver and then the sound cut off.

"Astra, they are on their way. Zero is alive. They're coming on something called a cyberblade, whatever the fuck that is."

"It is an aircraft with rotating blades on the top," Euthani interjected.

"Oh, a helicopter," I replied.

"Helicopter? I have no idea," the fox girl shook her head.

"Never mind, how is her arm looking?"

"The nanobots appear to be working. The bleeding has stopped at least," she replied as she rubbed Astra's head.

I knelt directly in front of her. "Astra, are you alright? Are you hurt anywhere else other than your arm?"

"He saved me. Those bullets were meant for me. He told me to step away, but I didn't listen. Now...now...he's dead," Astra cried.

"No, no. He isn't dead." I said as I placed my hands on her cheeks. "He is alive. They're coming to get him right now."

"Gods, what has happened!" Fiji screamed as she jogged down the hallway. I had forgotten she was even in the area. Choicemaker must have told her about Zero.

"Zero is in pretty bad shape but alive. Help is on the way," I replied.

She placed her hands over her mouth and tears filled her eyes. "Can I do anything?"

"Let us know when the cyberblade gets here," I nodded.

"You got it," the bunny girl replied as she turned to run back in the other direction. She was out of my sight in almost an instant.

"He isn't dead?" Astra whispered.

"No, my friend. He is very alive," the fox girl kissed her on the forehead.

"Dalton, they are landing now!" Fiji popped her head around the corner.

My eyes widened, and I shook my head in disbelief. "Shit, Blowkos wasn't lying when she said they would be here very soon."

16

Euthani, Fiji, and I watched the navy blue cyberblade lift off with the injured Stranger Zero. The cyberblade was very similar to a helicopter on Earth just much sleeker and quieter. The aircraft had the glowing lights that was adorned on most vehicles I have seen since I arrived on Zorth. Astra stayed by Zero's side and held the cyborg's hand. Blowkos sat on the other side of him in the nightblade as she worked on her patient. I hoped he would be okay, but things were looking very grim now. He had twelve gunshot wounds. Some were in the fleshy parts of him, and the others impacted his mechanical sections. Nanobots were hard at work on his flesh wounds, and they would be done in three to four hours. The bullet wound that put his life in danger was the one that damaged his core. Blowkos didn't waste any time going into more details before they took off.

We stayed behind for the next two hours extracting mojo

from all the dead bodies. Euthani and I shared the mojo. Fiji only requested 5% of the extractions. All in all, I ended up with 40,000 mojo from extraction and weapon sales to the shop. I couldn't complain. It would have been a happier occasion had the cyborg not been severely injured in the assault. Our next task would be returning the nightcycles to the HQ. Fiji had her own to return so that left Euthani and I in charge of the other two. We had not been assigned access to the cycles, so Fiji had to use her fingerprint to turn them on.

"Just sit on the cycle and get ready to hold on. You won't have to drive it. I will activate the auto drive, and the AI will return you to the HQ," Fiji informed us as we mounted our cycles.

I raised an eyebrow and shook my head. "This world never ceases to amaze me. Okay, what do we do?"

"Nightcycle. Authorization code 3050...return to HQ," Fiji said to the bike.

"Yes, Fiji. It will be done. Hold on tight to avoid injury and/or death," the night cycle replied robotically.

"Well that sounds scary," I said as the bike began to move off the sidewalk and back onto the street. I turned my head to see Euthani behind me with her eyes closed and teeth smashed together.

We gradually picked up speed until the bike reached 70 miles per hour. It was exciting and terrifying at the same time, being out of control was a polarizing experience. The cool night air zipped through my hair as we swerved in and out of traffic. I imagined being pulled over by the police for erratic driving wasn't high on their list of priorities. I periodically looked behind me to make sure Euthani was still attached to the bike. She had opened her eyes, and I think she was becoming more comfortable with the ride. After a half hour of travel, the bike pulled off the freeway and turned down a small side street and then onto a smaller paved path. This would be the first time seeing the complex from the outside. I didn't turn and look when we had left earlier. I was too busy trying not to die. The land was flat, but the path began to descend below the ground. All I could see was the steel doorway, which opened as we reached within twenty yards. The bike slowed to prevent a decapitation thankfully. The complex was completely underground, I expected that there would be structures above ground, but I was wrong. The bike came to a stop, and Euthani arrived a few seconds afterward.

"You have arrived. Have a good night," the robotic AI said.

I had no clue if I needed to reply. "Uh, thanks I guess."

There was no reply from the nightcycle. I dismounted, and I was embraced by the fox girl immediately.

"Thank the gods we survived the raid and the terrifying trip back here."

"Yeah, it was a wild night. Really crazy," I replied as I moved my neck around to loosen the tense muscles.

Everyone was huddled around the unconscious cyborg. Astra's eyes were bloodshot from her heavy sobbing. Wires were all over the place. They were attached to him and attached to several monitors listing all kinds of information that I didn't understand. Everyone looked at us as we entered the infirmary. I noticed that the cyborg's chest had been opened to reveal a shiny sphere. Blowkos had two attachments that appeared to be powering the device.

Choicemaker walked over and extended his giant hand. I grasped it, and he shook it firmly. "Great job out there. You guys alright?"

I nodded. "Yeah, we're good. How's Zero?"

Choicemaker motioned to Blowkos to come over. "I'm gonna let her talk to you because I don't want to tell you wrong."

"He's alive, but his core has been damaged. It is working enough to keep him alive but in a cybernetic coma like you see here. He won't wake up until his core is repaired or replaced."

I crossed my arms and nodded. "Okay, what do we need to do to make that happen?"

"We can't," Choicemaker added with a heavy exhale.

Blowkos tilted her head to the side. "It can be done, but right now, it is impossible."

Astra stood and walked over. She was clearly exhausted mentally and physically from the night's events. "Please just spit it out for the sake of the gods. Zero must be fixed. Whatever I have to do to make that happen, I will do it."

"Zero has a hakrium core. Hakrium is a very rare element that is not available on Zorth or anywhere in this star system. If I had the element, I would be able to fix him no problem. The core was pierced by gunfire, and the element was released. Without the element to put back in his core, he will just be a vegetable."

I nodded and glanced at Astra. "So, the fix is simple, but getting what we need to fix it is difficult?"

"Yes, that's a good way to put it," Blowkos replied with a nod.

Choicemaker took his cigar out of his mouth. "It's more than difficult. It's impossible unless we get the proper starship. I don't have one. We can't afford something like that, nor have we really needed one until now."

Blowkos held her hand up to add to Choicemaker's thought. "Stranger Zero's home planet is Seon 8. It is the only known planet in the galaxy that has a hakrium mine, so that is the only place to get it. The problem is getting there. It is in another star system and that will require a warp drive to travel there."

"Isn't there a transport service or something that can take us there?" Euthani asked.

"Commercial transports do not leave the star system. Only certain people have the ability to travel out of the system...obscenely rich people or syndicates that have stolen ships," Choicemaker replied with a sigh.

"What about Emberlynn? Would she help us?" asked Astra as she wiped her nose with a tissue.

Choicemaker shrugged and exhaled. "It's worth a shot, but you know I am not her favorite person. If I ask her, the answer will be no."

"Emberlynn?" Euthani asked.

Astra sniffed and looked at the fox girl. "She is Choice-maker's ex-lover. They were together for 5 years until they split because Choicemaker wanted to start the Peacekeepers and do some good on Zorth."

Choicemaker chuckled. "She wasn't exactly on the up and up, and she was into some things that I wasn't too keen on."

Astra leaned forward toward me. "Oh yeah, she is a vampire. We forgot to add that little tidbit of information."

My eyes grew wide, and my mouth parted. "Vampire? Oh really..."

Choicemaker shrugged. "Yep, a vampire and a damn hot one at that. Most vampire women are insanely beautiful. Her coven was off the chain."

"Coven?" Euthani inquired.

"Yep, vampires live in covens. She is the matriarch of the Shadow Scourge. They are a large coven in the city of Helios. The big reason we split was the fact that I didn't want her to turn me. She wanted me to be a vampire like her and rule alongside her. Even though the Scourge didn't go apeshit and suck the blood of everyone in sight, they still did evil shit that I just didn't want to be a part of. Vampires must feed, or they die, it's just the way of the beast. While I was there, I was able to convince her to use livestock or hunt for animals. Hell, I even advocated they steal blood from the hospitals and blood banks. I'm not proud of that, but I loved her. Still do and probably always will. The coven became restless and sick of the animal diet, so they pushed for human blood and other bipedal intelligent species like our lady friends here. She ultimately gave in, and I told her I was out. That was three years ago, and I haven't seen her since. I hear they have gotten into other "unlawful" ventures since then and became a major player in Helios. They are thriving no doubt and most definitely have multiple starships. They had one when I was there, and they weren't pulling in millions in coin like they are now. She said they bought that one, but I think they stole it from somebody. Be that as it may, Astra is correct, Emberlynn is our best shot at hitching a ride on an interstellar starship."

"I'll go, and I'll convince her. I'm sure we can work something out," Astra said with a more hopeful tone than before.

"I'll go too," Euthani added with a smile.

I chuckled and put my arm around the fox girl. "I go wherever this girl goes. However, I was going to volunteer anyway, but she beat me to it. Zero, is a good dude and anything I can do to help him I will be happy to do."

"Thank you," Astra replied softly with a small smile. This surprised me quite a bit. I was expecting a lot of resistance from the dragon girl, but I was wrong.

"All right sounds good. I think you three will get the job done. We'll take care of Zero, so you don't have to worry about that. You just worry about taking care of yourselves."

Zama slithered over to our small huddle. "I will be happy to go with you as well."

Choicemaker placed his arm around the snake woman and smiled. "I need everyone else here. I hope that we took out all the posse, but there is a chance that they had some away from HQ. I need folks here in case we must conduct more business. Fiji tossed three remote cameras around the place. We will keep an eye out for any posse members returning. If we see any, we will kill them. If you'll excuse me, I need to go get something to help these three on their journey. Be right back."

Choicemaker walked out of the lab and headed toward the bunk area of the complex. I took a closer look at the cyborg on the hospital bed and patted him on his steel hand. "We got you bud. Hang tight."

"Thank you two for going with me. I'm sorry for being such a salty bitch. New people scare me a little," Astra smiled and embraced Euthani warmly.

It was nice to see this side of Astra. I knew it was there, and the bitchiness was a facade. I was shocked as she let go of Euthani and hugged me. It was nice to have the dragon girl in my arms. It wasn't the time for foolishness, but damn her hair smelled great. Feeling her breasts pressed against my chest was welcome too. Our hug lingered longer than her embrace with Euthani.

Choicemaker returned to the lab with something in his hand. "I'm going to mark on your map where their HQ is, however, you won't just be able to just waltz in that place, and if they did let you they, would be sucking your blood within moments. Show them this. Emberlynn will talk to you then." Maker held up a black chain with a large pentagram pendant dangling. It was beautiful and creepy at the same time.

Astra took the necklace and looked at it closely. "What's the significance?"

"This was a gift from Emberlynn years ago. It is a couple of thousand years old. There were a lot of vampires in the coven that were pissed that a mortal was given the relic. You show them this, and they will take you to Emberlynn. You already know this, but I will tell you anyway. Watch what you say and how you act. You will be in a den full of blood thirsty vampires. Dalton will look especially tasty since he is 100 percent human. Human blood is a vampire's favorite. Fox girls and dragon girls are enticing, but nowhere near as enticing as humans. No offense."

"Dalton is rather tasty," Euthani smirked.

Astra chuckled and quickly looked into my eyes.

"So, Maker, are we taking the bikes or what?" I asked nonchalantly.

Astra laughed. "No, silly, Helios is across the desert. It is close to 2,000 miles west of here. We'll take the Zorthtrack as the trip will take 10 hours, and the train travels 200 miles per hour. There are faster ones, but none of the 1,000 mile per hour trains come through Osiris and cross the desert. The track isn't optimal for that fast of a train, and the desert has dangers that can cause problems from time to time."

"What kind of dangers?" I raised an eyebrow.

"Bandits, night wraiths, sand covered tracks, those are the main things," Astra replied nonchalantly. "The 1,000 mile per hour super trains cost billions in coin, so they can't risk those through the desert."

"We can't just take the nightblade?" Euthani asked softly.

Choicemaker broke his silence and removed the large cigar from the corner of his mouth. "Nah, it doesn't hold enough fuel. Another reason is the night wraiths would take us down at some point, or a sandstorm would fuck up the turbines, and we would go crash in the night. The Zorthtrack is the only way unless you want to travel 5,000 miles north and pay a shit ton of money to ride the super train another 7,000 miles to get there. Don't worry these things don't happen on the Zorthtrack but every now and again. It's the only option right now, anyway, so do it for Zero's sake."

"Absolutely, anything for my friend," Astra replied with tears in her eyes again.

"When do we head out?" I asked with a yawn.

Zama, the lamia, spoke from behind us at the entryway to the lab. "I just booked 3 tickets for the next departure in 30 minutes."

After a short trip, we were dropped off by Choicemaker and Zama. We entered the train station and were surprised at the amount of people inside at this hour. The train had not even arrived yet, and we were to depart in only fifteen minutes. It looked like trains on Zorth were late just like the ones on Earth. We were all very tired, but we had 10 hours to rest on our way to Helios. The three of us were very anxious to pass out in the bunk room that Zama was nice enough to reserve. We spent the next ten minutes deep in small talk. I did my best to perk Astra up a bit, and it worked, or she acted like it did. I was pleased that she was becoming more comfortable around me. I was a pleasure to be around, I thought. We heard an almost deafening humming sound approach the station. The train had arrived, and there was no choo-choo. It was just an odd humming noise. The train was floating over the track like the maglev trains on Earth. It amazed me how similar

Zorth was to Earth in many ways. There were marks on the side of the train that caught my eye immediately.

"Are those...claw marks?" I asked as I pointed.

Astra nodded. "Those are indeed night wraith claw marks. I wouldn't worry, that could have been from months ago. They don't look all that fresh. Let's get to our bunk room. I'm going to die if I don't get to sleep soon."

The inside was very bright with a neon blue hue. Humans and different species of bipedal creatures sat in the seats. Everyone minded their own business for the most part. Euthani and Astra got a few looks from interested males and females, but they didn't attempt to make conversation. I assumed they knew the women were with me. The lizard man conductor led us to our room. All three of us plopped onto the thin mattresses and heard a knock at the door just as we gotten comfortable. A human woman motioned to the cart of food she had.

"This is part of your package, sir. I am going to leave this here with you. When you are done, please push the cart in the hallway, and I will get it later. Enjoy," the waitress said with a smile.

"Oh, my gods, that smells good. Is that meat and cheese?" Euthani asked as she sat up quickly in her bed.

"Yeah, I'm not sure what kind of meat that is, but it is indeed meat. This looks like some water, and here is some wine. We are going first class, ladies," I replied with an approving nod.

"Thank...you...Zama," Astra interjected as she grabbed a slab of juicy meat and shoved it in her mouth. "I'm sorry for the bad manners, but I didn't realize how hungry I was until this little blessing rolled in. This is wonderful. I love venison."

I put some meat and cheese on Euthani's plate and handed it to her along with a glass of wine.

She grasped the plate and smiled. "Thank you."

"Aww, look at Dalton, the gentleman. You two make a great couple," Astra said with a wink.

"Couple? I don't think we consider ourselves that, but I do care a great deal for this fox girl. I care for you too."

"Blowkos too, we had quite the threesome in the lab," Euthani said with a mouthful of cheese.

Astra almost choked on the food she was swallowing. "All three of you...fucked?"

"Yes, it was amazing. You should give Dalton a go soon. You will see," Euthani grinned while I poured her a glass of red wine.

"Well, thanks...I guess," Astra said awkwardly as the train began to leave the station.

I had ridden on trains a few times in my life, and they were loud and rough. This train was the complete opposite on both counts. The ride was silky smooth, and the outside noise was almost non-existent. We spent the next hour eating and talking when Astra looked out of the window.

"We are entering the desert now. There will be nothingness for the next nine hours."

I walked over beside her and peeked out of the window. There was nothing but sand and darkness in my field of vision.

"Choicemaker mentioned bandits. How do bandits

survive way the hell out here, and how do they hi-jack a train traveling 200 miles per hour?" I asked with an eyebrow raised.

Astra belched out of the blue. Her cheeks turned bright red; the belch had been unintended. "Fuck, Excuse me."

"Hey, we're all friends here. Feel free to belch, fart...masturbate," Euthani chuckled.

"Damn, I think the fox girl is a little tipsy. She isn't usually this sassy."

"I think I have been very sassy during our three sexual episodes. Don't you think?" Euthani asked.

"That's not exactly what I meant, but I would agree that you were a bad girl during those times."

"Gods, I am right here. I don't want to hear about your sexual experiences right now if you don't mind," Astra stuck her tongue out at the both of us. "Getting back to Dalton's question about the bandits, I have no idea how they live out here or how they hi-jack a fast train. I think the night wraiths and sandy tracks are the biggest issues."

"We're floating on the track so why does the sand matter?" I asked with a yawn.

"Because it covers the magnets, and the train won't stay on the track. Duh. A little bit of sand won't bother anything, but there are very bad sandstorms out here that will dump a lot on the track," Astra replied with a head shake.

"Yeah, that was a dumb question. I've never been a science guy though. Eh, I have never been any kind of guy. I graduated high school and jumped into the wrestling business."

"What is the "wrestling business?" Astra did air quotes.

"It's hard to explain here. I was a warrior that was paid money to fight people in arenas."

I left out the part about the matches being scripted and some of the moves were not as realistic as they seemed. I didn't want to try and explain all that to them. Plus, it would make them feel better to know they were with a warrior with experience.

Astra nodded and shrugged. She didn't ask any more questions, so my response had been a good one. However, I think it had something to do with her exhaustion. She was barely able to hold her reptilian eyes open.

"You two, go to sleep. That's an order, even though I have no authority," I smirked at the gorgeous but exhausted monster girls.

There were four bunk beds in the small room. Euthani slept on the bunk directly over me and Astra slept on the lower bunk on the opposite side. As we closed our eyes, I could hear the light hum of the train as it cut through the night air across the dark desert. There were tingles on the window from the grains of sand that bounced off as we traveled through the desert. Within seconds, the girls fell asleep. Euthani slept silently, but Astra had a very low snore. It was more adorable than annoying. I was sure she would be petrified knowing she snored in front of us. Both women looked like fucking angels as they slept with the faint moonlight on their faces. A few moments later, I was out for the count myself, and I drifted off into a deep sleep.

An alarm pierced the silence in the cabin, and all three of us sat up quickly. For me, it was too quickly, because I slammed my forehead into the bunk above me. I touched my forehead expecting to see blood, but there was none yet. The girls were already off the bunk and standing on the floor.

"What the fuck? Fire alarm?" I asked as I rubbed my forehead.

"Maybe...I don't know," Astra put both hands on the top of her head.

"Are you okay, Dalton? You hit your head really hard," Euthani walked over closer to get a better look at my forehead. "No blood but you have a knot or goose egg I have heard before."

"I'm all right," I replied as I stood and flipped the light switch. Suddenly, a voice came through the intercom instead of the alarm.

Attention passengers, we are under attack by a small pack of night wraiths. Please grab a coat or blanket and move to the hallways. Move away from all windows and cover yourself with anything you may have. Please stay still and calm. You will be updated when we have more information.

We heard the ear-piercing screech of one of these things as it zoomed by our window.

"Hallway?"

Both girls nodded and grabbed the blankets from the beds. The hallway was filled with terrified people. Some were shivering under a covering, and others had nothing but panic covering their faces.

Euthani immediately handed her blanket to a little cat girl

crying on the floor. "Here you go sweetie, cover your head. This will be over soon."

More screeches erupted from the flying beasts, but this time there was scraping sounds from their claws on the steel outside. The sound made my teeth rattle.

"What do you know about these things? How big are they? They are fucking loud; I know that much!" I yelled at Astra.

Astra raised her shoulders. "They are large. I would say their bodies are the size of the night cycles, and their wingspan is twenty feet. Their talons are razor sharp."

"How about their teeth?" I asked as I looked down the hallway.

"They are reptilian looking creatures whose heads are like a beast known as a crocodile. Their mouths are large and full of teeth. Night wraiths are terrifying creatures and killing machines."

"How long do you think they will fuck with the train? Are they looking for food or are they just pissed we are in their territory?"

"Probably the latter," Astra replied.

All the sudden, I heard glass shatter at the end of the hallway. When I saw what caused the crash, my blood ran cold. An onyx black night wraith stuck its giant killing machine head into the train and let out a scream that had to have given me some sort of eardrum damage. It quickly squeezed the rest of its body inside and grabbed a cowering man by the head with its giant mouth. The creature bit down hard and the crunch was stomach churning. Blood spewed from the body in several places. He was still screaming but it was muffled due to his head being deep in the night wraith's throat. The creature flipped its head back and swallowed the man whole. I finally snapped out of my shock as the wraith began prancing down the hallway headed to its next victim. I pulled out my hand cannons and squeezed off two rounds that hit the creature in the shoulders. There were a lot of bystanders, so I had to make sure I was accurate with my shots. Thank God for my Pure Weapon Specialist perk. Green blood began to spurt from the two wounds and covered the walls of the hallway. The creature screeched and lunged forward and began walking faster toward me. I shot it once in the head with my right-hand cannon then shot it in the throat with my left-hand cannon. These two shots were fatal ones. The creature stopped in its tracks and fell against the outside wall.

"Good work, Dalton. These fucking things were even bigger than I thought," Astra stated.

"Everyone run down to his end of the hallway away from the window and this thing," I screamed through my hands cupped around my mouth. After the last person past me, I walked closer to the creature.

"What are you doing, Dalton?" Euthani asked as she scanned her environment with her crossbow.

"I got an idea. Stand back," I said while waving my hand at them to not come any closer. I pulled up my interface to see if I would be able to raise the night wraith.

"Shit, I know what he is going to do. Stand back," Astra grabbed Euthani's arm.

Before Euthani could ask what, she was talking about, the night wraith began to push itself to its feet.

"Good boy, good boy. Now, I need you to go back outside and kill the other wraiths."

The wraith made a small honk sound and turned back down the hallway. It left a trail of green blood with each step it took. The night wraith did exactly what I said and pushed his way through the window back into the air. I had my fingers crossed that he could take one of the other ones out at least. I didn't even know how many there were.

"Shit, I need to get on top of this train. I need to see what we are dealing with."

"Are you nuts?" Astra asked. "Not only are their fucking flying monsters, but this train is traveling 200 miles per hour. You will get blown off. It cannot be done."

I heard a crash in another car and screams from passengers. Another night wraith had entered the train, and we weren't there to stop it. A symphony of screams filled the night along with the screech of the invader. "Fuck, let's go," I instructed as I began jogging down the hallway toward the carnage. Another crash sounded from the same area which caused another explosion of horrible screeches. As we approached the door to the next car, we stopped suddenly to process the scene. It looked like a huge tank of blood had exploded in the car. It was something out of a horror film. The lights in the car went out and then began to flicker. It was a terrifying strobe light effect. The movement of the living passengers looked like slow motion.

"Stay back here," I muttered to the girls. I grabbed the

latch to the door and opened it slowly as I entered the blood scene. My heart pounded in my chest, and my breathing grew more rapid. An elderly woman was crawling toward me screaming as I got closer, she raised her hand for me. I grabbed it and began to slide her in the other direction. I thought she was way too light, and I looked at her again and realized I was pulling a torso. There was nothing below the waist but entrails dragging the floor. Her eyes rolled back, and all I saw was the whites of her eyes. She was gone. I slid what was left of her body to the side of the car and proceeded forward. I passed a dozen bloody corpses that were ripped to shreds. More screeches soared by the side of the car along with the blood-curdling sound of razor talons mutilating the steel tube. As my attention was turned toward the wraiths outside, I was charged by the wraith responsible for the massacre. It looked like a giant winged crocodile lunging for me. I held up both pistols and began firing as fast as I could. Most of the rounds hit their mark, but some made glowing holes in the hull of the train car. I dove forward to slide under the flying wraith. I slid in gore as the talon of the wraith scraped the back of my thigh. I screamed in agony and immediately flipped on my back to look where the bastard was. It began its turn to make another attack. I fired multiple rounds that ripped through its head, neck, and torso. I probably shot 12 rounds before I stopped because I began to panic that I may have hit a passenger or my girls. I had to be smarter with my shots. However, had I not fired like a madman, I would be headless or in the belly of a monster right now. I pulled up my interface to raise this wraith, but I received a message.

Unable to Raise, the brain of the corpse is no longer intact.

"Fuck!" I yelled as I closed my screens in frustration. I wondered if my zombie wraith had any luck before he was undoubtedly killed. I ran over to the window and decided I have no more fucks to give and looked out. I fully embraced the possibility that I may get ripped out of the train at any moment. I put my sunglasses on and activated the night vision capability. I saw my zombie wraith chasing another wraith. After a couple of seconds, my zombie grabbed the head of the wraith and squeezed hard and yanked upward tearing the brain directly out of the skull. The wraith let out a scream of triumph only to be cut short by another wraith that sideswiped him and took him to the ground out of my vision. I began to scan the sky for others, but I thought the one that killed my zombie was the last of this pack... at least I hoped so. The wraith launched back into the sky after killing my minion buddy. It screeched and then landed right on top of the train out of my sight. I needed to end this. I thought the motherfucker was just chilling up there coming up with another plan of action, and I needed to get him before he decided on something.

I ran to the end of the car and opened the emergency exit. I found a steel ladder outside of the door. I took a deep breath and grasped the wrung and pulled myself upward. Luckily, the ladder was between the cars, so I wasn't affected by the vicious wind. I climbed to the roof of the car and peeked over with my night vision sunglasses. The night wraith was crouched with its talons buried in the steel holding him on the roof. I saw a pool of blood under him. The last wraith was injured, how bad he was injured I didn't know. I would have to make my shot from this position. There was no way I would be able to get on the roof as I would be blown off immediately. I took one pistol out of the holster, but I left the other one holstered. I had to use my left hand to hold me on the ladder. I raised the gun and almost lost it due to the 200 mile per hour winds. It was now or never, so I squeezed off five shots that all landed into the body of the nightwraith. Its talons lost their grip on the steel and let go. The night wraith used any reserves that he had for one final attack. It screeched as it dove toward my head with its mouth open and talons ready to rip into me.

"Bye, bye," I muttered to myself as I began to shoot at the rapidly approaching flying creature. A final screech pierced my ears, and he went down on top of the train and slid off to the ground that zipped by rapidly. I holstered my pistol and began my descent of the ladder back to the inside of the train. Euthani and Astra were waiting for me at the bloody doorway. They opened the door and breathed a huge sigh of relief. "Thank the gods you are okay. You are crazy, do you know that?" Euthani asked as she jumped into my arms.

Astra smiled and shook her head. "I will have to agree with the fox girl. You are nuts."

"Are we there yet?" I asked as I squeezed Euthani tighter.

"Oh, I hope so. This hasn't been a lot of fun, and I think I am fine with never using the Zorthtrack train again.

"Me too," I said as I saw what looked like medical personnel rush by to help anyone that needed them.

"I hoped I was able to save some of these people," I whispered to myself.

"Of course, you did. You and your zombie wraith took them all out. Dozens more would have died otherwise. You're a hero," Astra replied warmly.

"Hero? I don't know about all that, but I'll take that from you," I opened my right arm to make room for the dragon girl. I expected her to hesitate, but she looked excited and jumped into my arm. I squeezed both beautiful monster girls tight and kissed each of them on the forehead still expecting to get my dick burned off by Astra.

"What do you say we try and get a little sleep?" I asked with a yawn.

"I second that Dalton," Euthani yawned too.

We walked hand in hand through the bloody carnage on our way back to our rooms. When we reached our cars, there were techs covering the broken window with something that looked like metal plywood. The only casualty in our car was the man that got swallowed whole by the wraith I had used as a zombie minion. This is a crazy life I live. I thought it was crazy back on Earth, but that was nothing compared to what I was a part of now. This time when I plopped on the mattress, both women squeezed onto the mattress on both sides of me. I smiled and kissed them on the foreheads once more.

"Good night, Dalton, thank you," Astra whispered.

We fell asleep in seconds.

17

The rest of the night was uneventful, and we were able to get some much-needed sleep. I woke up earlier than the ladies and left them in the bunk room to sit in the viewing car with the glass ceiling. Surprisingly in the attack, this roof didn't get even a crack. I engaged with a bit of small talk with the conductor, and he told me that the glass was stronger than the steel tube we were in. The damage and carnage were taken care of overnight, and it was like nothing had happened. I wanted to do something for the women, so I went shopping in the mojo store. I looked through the jewelry and found a category for ballistic jewelry. There was no way in hell I could avoid clicking on that. The category was full of different kinds of jewelry, but they had shield capabilities. This was perfect, something beautiful and useful. My eyes were drawn to a necklace with a Star with a blue gem in the middle. It wasn't a pentagram because it wasn't encased in a circle. I was no jewelry guru, but I thought the necklace was beautiful.

The cool thing about this necklace was its shield capability. You pressed the blue crystal, and you were surrounded by a forcefield for thirty seconds. The forcefield was strong enough to deflect most gunfire, but large caliber ammo would just be slowed down. Blade attacks would be deflected as well. More expensive models gave you more time, but I just wanted to give them a little something to make them smile. Each necklace was 20,000 mojo so they weren't cheap by any means. This was kind of a cheesy gesture, but I liked making women smile. This would also give the ladies more survivability which was important to me.

I purchased both and dangled the necklaces in front of me. They looked even better in person. I put the necklaces in my coat pocket and made my way back to the cabin. The conductor told me we would arrive in 15 minutes. I slowly opened the door, but both girls were still fast asleep and as beautiful as ever. I didn't have the heart to wake them, so I just laid down on the other bunk and rested my eyes.

I felt a warm moist kiss on my forehead. "Dalton, it's time to get up. We're here," Euthani smiled warmly at me and tousled my hair.

"Why did you move over there? You don't like being sandwiched by two attractive women?" Astra asked sarcastically.

"Well, you were snoring right in my ear, and I just couldn't take it anymore."

"You're a lying bastard. I don't snore."

"Yeah you do, but it's adorable. I do love being the bologna in a hot monster girl sandwich, but I woke up early and took a walk. No big deal. I didn't want to wake you."

"Thank you for that, Dalton. You are so good to us," the fox girl cooed.

"You two are important to me, and I take care of what is important," I smiled and motioned for them both to hug me.

Euthani eagerly jumped into my arms. Astra still showed some apprehension, but she slowly came over and joined in. It felt good to have both goddesses in my arms. I was a lucky guy. I was used to having women whenever I wanted, but I sincerely cared for these two. It warmed my heart but terrified me at the same time. Zorth was a dangerous place. We were attacked by flying monsters last night, and we were headed to a den of vampires. The thought of not being able to protect them scared me.

"Dalton? Are you okay?" Euthani asked as she rubbed my chest.

"Yeah, I'm good. I just went off into la-la land for a bit," I replied as I rubbed their backs softly. "Listen, I got you guys something this morning from the mojo shop."

"You got us something?" Euthani asked with a grin.

"I did."

"Me too?" Astra asked with an eyebrow raised.

"Yeah."

Astra's cheeks reddened as she looked at Euthani and smiled.

I pulled both star necklaces out of my coat pocket and handed them to each girl simultaneously. Both monster girls' eyes widened at the unexpected gift.

"It's beautiful. I can't believe you got me a necklace. Thank you so much!" Euthani squeaked as she put the chain around her neck and then she held the pendant where she could stare at its beauty.

"This is too much Dalton," Astra said as she stared into my eyes.

"Nope, I insist. I also have a selfish reason for getting you these," I replied with a grin.

Euthani crossed her arms and mashed her boobs together revealing ample cleavage that I was always glad to look at. "What is this reason?"

"These are ballistic necklaces? Am I right?" Astra replied.

I smiled wide and gave a corny thumbs up gesture. "Yes, that is my selfish reason. I want you to be safer, so I wanted you to have something beautiful yet useful. Do you two like it?"

"Oh, I love it, Dalton!" Euthani exclaimed as she quickly pecked me on the cheek.

I turned to Astra to see her reaction to the gift. "This is very generous and thoughtful. Thank you, I can't remember the last time I received a gift."

"I hope that's not true, but you are very welcome. Try it on."

I offered to help her put the necklace on. Astra handed me the necklace, and I stood behind her. She raised the back of her hair with her left hand, so I could place the necklace on her. The aroma from her green hair was fucking intoxicating. As I latched the chain on her neck, I fought the urge to kiss her neck.

"So, girls, are you going to try them out?" I asked. "You press the stone in the middle, and you get a 30-second shield that will deflect light gunfire and bladed weapons.

"Wow! So, I press the gem in the middle?" Euthani asked with a giant smile on her face.

"That's it."

Euthani slowly pressed the blue crystal. There was a quick flash of blue light, and a very faint blue oval encircled her body.

A knife appeared in front of me and caused me to jump. "Dalton let's test it. Swipe at it," Astra said with a grin.

"Yeah, Dalton! Do it!" Euthani chirped.

I looked at the knife in the palm of my hand and looked at each of the women. "All right, here goes."

I raised the blade and slashed diagonally toward the floor. As soon as the blade touched the force field, my arm bounced off like it was a trampoline. The knife soared out of my hand and impaled the wall behind us.

"Fuck me!" I exclaimed with my eyes wide.

Both girls covered their mouths as they burst into laughter. "It works," Astra said sarcastically.

"All right girls eat it up. Keep laughing, and I will take return these things so quick," I laughed as I shook my head. I pulled the knife out of the wall and handed it to Astra.

Astra glared at the new hole in the wall. "Well, if anyone asks, we can just blame one of the wraiths."

"Let's go, before Dalton causes any more damage to the poor train. It has already been through enough this trip. Shame on you," Euthani playfully patted me on the cheek as she stuck out her plump bottom lip. It took everything in me not to bite down on it.

We exited the train station in Helios without any issues. The city was much more impressive than what I had seen of Osiris. There were tall buildings everywhere with heavier traffic whizzing by. It reminded me of a cyberpunk New York City. There were tons of pedestrians strolling up and down the street as we stood taking it all in.

"Okay guys let's not stand here like three dorky tourists," Astra scoffed.

"Well, we kinda are if you think about it," I replied with a wink.

"Whatever, Mr. Gundertaker."

"Oh, I like it when you call me that. Do it again,"

"Ugh, you are unbearable sometimes, do you know that?" Astra punched me in the arm.

"That I do know," I shrugged.

"As long as you know," Astra chuckled.

Euthani broke her silence with a loud exhale. "Okay, so what are we doing?"

"We're going to the haunted house full of blood sucking vampires to ask for help. Isn't that right?" I asked sarcastically.

"You are being a real pain in the ass this morning," Astra sighed.

"That's fair. My map is telling me the Shadow Scourge

HQ is about five miles in that direction. I prefer not to walk if that is ok with you two. Are their Ubers on Zorth?"

"Uber? What is Uber?" Astra grumbled.

"It is kind of like a taxi, but you don't know what a taxi is, do you?"

"Of course, we know what a taxi is dummy. There is one coming right there," Astra said as she placed two fingers in her mouth and whistled loudly while she flagged down a yellow car.

"Well shit, taxis are yellow on Zorth too? Interesting."

"You are amused by the oddest things Dalton," Astra replied with a raised brow.

I opened the door and motioned for both women to enter.

After I sat down and shut the door, I was shocked when I saw there wasn't a driver at all. There was just a computer display.

"Welcome to Helios Transportation Service. Where would you like to go?" asked a feminine robotic voice.

After Astra instructed the taxi on where to take us, it spoke once more. "This destination will cost 100 coin or 300 mojo. You may deposit your currency in the slot and port below. Once the proper amount of currency is paid, your trip will begin."

"We pay...before the taxi takes us?" I asked with a raised brow.

"Of course, how else would you do it?" Astra asked irritated.

I raised my hands to show surrender. "Hey, it is what it is. I am just learning, madam dragon girl."

"Hmm, why don't you call me that from here on out? It has a nice ring to it."

"I agree, it sounds very fancy," Euthani interjected.

"I think I'll stay with Astra. We don't want your ego to blow up any more than it already has," I replied with a cringe.

Astra rolled her eyes and deposited 100 coin in the slot.

"Thank you, we will arrive at your destination in 15 minutes. Traffic is heavier than normal, and I do apologize for any delay. Please buckle your seat belts as I will not leave until you have done so. You can't be too safe in today's world."

As soon as we clicked our safety belts, we were off. It took a bit to get off the curb due to the heavy traffic. I wondered if we would even get to the HQ in fifteen minutes.

It was a smooth ride for the most part. There were a few times where the taxi swerved in and out of traffic, but I couldn't complain about the skill of the A.I. driver. We turned on a side street and made our way to what looked like an industrial district. We turned once more into a black wrought iron gate with a demon head in the middle of it. There was a screen beside the closed gate. We would have to talk to someone on the camera in order to get in. Hopefully, the necklace would work like Choicemaker said that it would.

"You have reached your destination. Please exit the vehicle in a timely but safe manner. Thank you for patronizing the HTS this fine day. Please exit the vehicle."

"Thanks, bud, we appreciate the lift," I said as I patted the computer screen.

"What the hell are you doing?" Astra asked quietly.

"Just letting it know that I appreciate the ride. That's all."

"It is A.I., so it only needs the coin or mojo. We gave it that. It could give a shit if you liked the ride or not," Astra shook her head as she slid out the door behind Euthani.

"Well, I think it was a very nice gesture, Dalton," Euthani the fox girl replied with her usually bright smile.

"Good day, patrons," the A.I. said and then zoomed off and out of our lives. We stood and watched the yellow car for a moment before directing our attention to the demon gate and screen.

18

The demon's face on the gate was horrifying to look at. Any other time, I would stroll on past this establishment just seeing the demon face on the gate. The face had goat horns sprouting out the top of its head, and the eyes were filled with two large blood-red gems. They looked like they were enchanted. The mouth was open with a long snake-like tongue hanging downward, and there were four long fangs and a long-pointed beard on the chin.

"These red gems are enchanted. This gate has an arcane lock on it. There is no getting through that without them letting us in," Astra pointed at each of the gems individually.

Two seconds after those words left the dragon girl's mouth, the screen activated. We saw the upper body of a woman pop up on the screen. She had long red hair and red eyes, but most importantly, my eyes were drawn to the sharp fangs in her mouth. She licked her lips with her tongue before she spoke. She was jaw-droppingly beautiful, but she looked like she was ready to sink her teeth in my neck immediately.

"What is your business here?" the striking vampire asked with an exotic voice.

"We're here to see Matriarch Emberlynn. We have important business," I stated with confidence.

The woman tapped the side of her mouth with her index finger. She either had claws or long fingernails. I wasn't sure which. "Do you have an appointment?"

"No, we don't, however..." I reached into my pocket to retrieve the necklace that we were given by Choicemaker. I pulled it out and dangled it in front of the screen. "Choicemaker said that Emberlynn would be very interested in this necklace."

The vampire woman's brow furrowed. "One moment," she quickly replied, and the screen went black. After five minutes of waiting, the vampire reappeared on the screen. "Emberlynn will see you now. Walk through the gate and to the main door, and I will be there to let you inside. The door will open, and you must walk in. As you know, vampires are rather sensitive to sunlight so do not expect me to walk out to get you. If you try anything, you will be destroyed eventually. You will be toyed with until we grow tired of you and bleed you to death. Are we clear?"

I gave a quick nod and smiled awkwardly. "Crystal clear."

The screen went black again, and we heard a low clank in the door's internal mechanism. The red eyes pulsed as the gate opened. Both women hugged my arms as we slowly walked through the creepy gate. A few yards later we heard the large iron door close behind us with a deafening lock. The compound looked like an old factory but with gothic decor that you would expect from a vampire coven. Suddenly, we heard a mechanism activate and then we saw four sentry guns raise fast out of the roof. They quickly aimed for us with laser dot sights. Each of us had a red dot on our chest.

We stopped in our tracks and raised our hands in the air.

A new voice blared from a speaker system. "Who are you? Why are you here?" The voice was feminine but laced with an evil tone.

"We are here to see Emberlynn. We need her help with something," I said sternly.

"I'm Emberlynn, and why would I want to help you and your monster girls? The only thing you can do for me is offer me your neck. I can imagine the flavor as we speak, human. Don't worry we won't kill you, but we will keep you on hand for snacks."

"This was a bad idea," I muttered out of the side of my mouth.

"For the sake of Varrus, show her the necklace," Astra rolled her eyes with an exasperated exhale.

"Who's Varrus?"

"He is the God of the universe," Euthani answered.

I retrieved the black pentagram necklace from my inner trench coat pocket, and I dangled it in front of me.

"We were told this would get us in," I announced with a reserved smile.

A large steel door opened slowly a few yards away.

I looked at Astra and shrugged. "I guess he was right."

"Either that or we are going to be lunch for a coven of bloodthirsty vampires," Euthani added grimly.

As we walked through the entrance, there was no one in sight. There was red fluorescent lighting down the corridor, which was a nice touch for a house of vampires. The decor was drenched with demons, pentagrams, and skulls. I couldn't picture Choicemaker living here, but this world was full of surprises and a lot of things didn't make sense. The door slammed shut behind us, and we heard the lock click. I fully expected vampires to lunge from the shadows and sink their teeth into our jugulars.

"Hello?" I asked. My voice echoed through the corridor.

Emberlynn's voice broke the dark silence. "Welcome to the lair of the Shadow Scourge, continue forward, and you will be met by my associates. If you try anything stupid you will regret your decision."

"Fair enough," I replied

Dark figures began to move out of the woodworks; logic told me that these were vampires. There were at least a couple of dozen. They were composed of mainly women, but there were a few men that lurked in the shadows. As the women grew closer, and the light touched their faces, I saw fangs protruding out. I had no clue if we were goners or whether they were sending us a message to not fuck with them. We had to be on our best behavior or at the snap of Emberlynn's finger, we would be torn apart. We saw a throne on the other side of the room and the vampires formed a tunnel that went directly to the figure that sat on the thrown before us.

"Don't be afraid. If I wanted to kill you, it would have already happened. It may still happen, but you have piqued my curiosity. Where did you get my relic? I know who was supposed to have it, but I want to hear it from your warm lips," Emberlynn leaned over.

She had onyx black hair that was tied into a bun, and her eyes were blood red. The matriarch's skin color was pale and very close to being a bright white color. She wore a black corset which hugged breasts that spilled over the top and skintight black pants that illustrated her curves beautifully.

"Choicemaker told us it would help get you to speak with us," I said confidently. "It worked. Here we are."

The mention of Choicemaker struck a chord with the gorgeous matriarch. She held her expression as cool, calm, and collected, but I could see it in her eyes, The mention of his name was a sore spot for her.

"How is Choicemaker? It has been a long time since he abandoned me."

"He is doing okay I guess," I replied with reservation.

She sighed and slammed her fist on the arm of the throne. A chorus of gasps echoed in the room from all of the coven. I wondered if I should have told her he was doing well. Maybe telling her he was a depressed sack of shit without her would have been a better call.

"Are you part of his little heroes club, the Cosmic something?"

"Peacekeepers," Euthani interjected.

"Yes, that is it. Peace is highly overrated I think," the vampire hissed and grinned.

I wasn't sure how to respond to that, so I just stayed quiet. The matriarch glared at us as she tapped her long nails on the arm of the throne.

"What are your names?" Emberlynn asked with what sounded like a purring sound.

"I am Dalton. This is Astra, and this is Euthani."

Emberlynn smirked and moved on to her next question. "Why is it that Choicemaker didn't come with you? Is he a pitiful coward?"

"No, he just felt it might make you too angry to help us," I replied carefully.

"He is probably right. I am not sure how I would react if he stood in front of me. Now let's get to the point of your visit as I'm growing bored and thirsty," Emberlynn purred.

"We need to get to Seon 8," Astra replied.

"Seon 8? That is out of this system. What on Zorth do you need to travel there for?"

"Our friend is in need of something that can only be acquired on Seon 8. We need a starship that can take us there. It is our understanding that you have multiple," Astra replied as she stepped forward causing Vampires nearby to step toward her. The matriarch raised her hand and shook her head to instruct them to stop.

"Why would I take you there? What would possibly be my motivation?"

I stepped forward and lifted the necklace. "This would be yours again."

The vampiress let out a spooky cackle. "We could just take that from you right now. Do you not see what surrounds you?"

"Choicemaker still loves you. It hurts him to be away from you, but you wanted different things. We need your help, and we'll do whatever you ask. We need you to get us to Seon 8."

Emberlynn's face softened when she heard the word" love, but it transformed back into a scowl within a couple of seconds. "You have two options; well three actually."

"What are they?" I asked earnestly.

The matriarch's lips narrowed, and she raised a brow.

"You pay me one million coin or mojo; two...you complete a task for me; or three...you become a permanent resident here as a blood bank until we grow tired of you."

I sighed. "So, it appears that option two is the only one we will be able to do. We don't have that kind of currency, and we don't have the desire to be your slaves."

Euthani raised an eyebrow. "So, none of the above isn't a choice?"

Emberlynn leaned toward the fox girl on her throne. "Absolutely not."

"What is the task?" I asked as I crossed my arms over my chest.

Emberlynn shifted her attention to me and smiled revealing her terrifying fangs. "Slavery would be a better choice, I am afraid."

"It looks like it is our only option, so what do we need to do?" Astra asked as she stepped forward.

"In order to receive your reward, you will be required to

bring me the heart of Shadoda," a devilish grin appeared on the face of the matriarch. The coven that surrounded gasped loudly then began to cackle.

I looked around at the macabre throne room and shuddered. The cackling sounded like it originated from the depths of Hell. It seemed to go on forever and continued until I held up my hand to speak once more. Surprisingly, the coven complied with my request without any resistance.

"How do we know you will keep your end of the bargain?" I asked as I glared at the vampire. I attempted to hide my fear as I was certain that she hungered for my fear as much as she wanted my blood.

"Human, I am many things, but what I am not is a liar. Believe me, if you can pull off this feat, I will not only let you borrow a starship, but I will give Gladius to you permanently as a reward. I will also give you the pilot of the ship as she is very partial to it anyway. She will go wherever it goes, and I grow tired of her blood anyway.

I was excited and scared to my fucking core. The thoughts of being rewarded with a starship of our own was thrilling, but holy shit, this Shadoda must be an almost impossible feat.

I gulped and nodded. "We agree to those terms and will hold you to them."

Emberlynn began to cackle once more. "I like you Dalton. It isn't just because your human blood would be wonderful, but you have balls speaking to me in the way that you do. You see, I am a feared woman in this city, and I have killed more people than you can possibly imagine. It takes guts to stand in this hall, let alone be in my presence."

I gulped silently. "I apologize for any disrespect. Can you tell us more about our task?"

"Of course, I will give you the gist of it, and then you will meet your navigator, Flux. She will transport you to the coastal town of Terra on the Gladius. That should be fun for you, and it will give you some extra motivation for completing your task. Once you arrive, you will board our Hell Diver Ship and travel by the Mystic Sea to a section titled the Heartless Deep. Once you are there, you will meet Shadoda the Kraken of the Deep. She is very defensive of her home and will no doubt attack you within minutes of entering the Heartless Deep. You must kill her and return her heart to me, and it should be quite large. My coven will feast on it and absorb the power of Shadoda. Your task will be complete, and you will be the owner of the Gladius Starship as well as the pilot, Flux."

We had no interest in a slave, but we also had no clue how to navigate a starship or something called a Hell Diver. We would release this Flux once we received the Hakrium from Seon 8.

"Excuse my ignorance, but what the fuck is a Kraken?" I asked with embarrassment.

Emberlynn giggled in amusement. "A Kraken is a very large sea monster with nasty tentacles. It is the most feared creature within the Mystic Sea. Not only do we want to feast on her heart, but we have selfish business reasons as well. You see, the Shadow Scourge wants to enter into the smuggling business on a large scale, and what we will smuggle is none of your concern. Travel time to our destinations will be cut in half if we were able to navigate through the Heartless Deep, so our practices would be highly more efficient and cost effective. That is all you need to know about our business, Dalton."

I shrugged nonchalantly. "Fair enough. We would like to get started. When can we leave with the starship and Flux?"

"Impatient, aren't we? You mean you don't want to stay here with myself and my coven? We would be able to restrain ourselves...for a bit at least."

I laughed reluctantly and shook my head. "No, I think we would like to get this Kraken thing killed and get to Seon 8 as soon as possible. We appreciate your help."

"You will not be thanking me once you enter the Deep and see Shadoda for the first time."

"We'll be just fine," I replied confidently.

"I like your confidence, Dalton. It is entertaining. My associate, Nocturnus will take you to the hangar where you will meet, Flux. May the gods be with you."

One of the few men approached us from the shadows and motioned for us to follow him. He had a very formal suit on and shoulder length platinum hair. The man's eyes were blood red, and he had a devilish looking black goatee on his face. "This way."

He turned and began walking to a lit corridor behind the throne. He glided across the floor majestically with his hands behind his back. "Do not venture off. Do you understand?"

All three of us replied with a resounding yes. The

corridor went on and on for a while until we reached a steel door that automatically opened like the doors on the Enterprise in Star Trek. We entered an enormous hanger with a sleek starship that was 30 yards in length and 15 yards from the ground. It was a shiny silver color adorned with glowing lights and looked like something straight out of Star Wars. Just imagining that this fantastic starship would be ours if we bring this Kraken monster's heart back was mind-blowing. Suddenly, a door under the ship opened and a lift began to lower a female to the concrete below. She began walking as she swayed her hips in an extremely sexy way. Her skin was bright green, and she had long white hair. She wore a small sports bra looking thing over her sizable breasts. She had a flat muscular stomach that was exposed all the way to some very tight, short black shorts. Amazingly shaped thighs were met by tall tight black boots.

"Flux, I am sure you are aware of the agreement between the matriarch and these three. Correct?" Nocturnus asked.

The green goddess looked at me. "Yes, I watched the live feed of the throne room in the Gladius. Do they have any idea of what they have agreed to?"

"We have. If we want to get to Seon 8, this is the only way," I replied as I crossed my arms.

"As long as you know that we are all most likely headed to our deaths," Flux replied with a loud exhale afterward.

"That's what we hear, but we feel differently. So, we're ready to go if you are," I replied with a smile. I was smiling on the outside, but I was curled in the fetal position on the inside.

"Okay," she replied with a shrug. "Let's go."

She walked in front of us revealing an epically shaped ass, and the bottom of her cheeks hung out perfectly from the short black shorts that she wore. She stopped and turned toward us when she reached the platform. All three of us walked onto the shiny steel platform, and it began to raise slowly. I lost my balance, but I avoided falling on my ass or off the thing to the concrete floor of the hangar.

Flux giggled as she watched me squirm for a couple seconds. I looked upward and saw the glowing innards of the gladius. This was my first spaceship, and I was excited to check it out. I had only seen these things in sci-fi movies, and I can't believe that I will be at warp speed on our way to another planet. Well, that was if we killed this huge terrifying sea monster that resided in a terrifying place in the middle of the ocean called the Heartless Deep. We entered the ship at a cargo area that had a lot of lockers and crates strapped in the rear. I saw a bathroom as well, which I would be using in the very near future. Before we went up some steps to the second floor, we walked past a room that looked like a kitchen and eating area. We climbed up some steel steps and entered the bridge. It was gorgeous and highly intimidating. There were two seats at the front behind a panel of controls, and a seat on each side, and a row of three seats in the rear. It was very similar to the layout of the Enterprise. Gene Roddenberry really knew his stuff. The control panels didn't have a lot of switches or buttons. They were touch computer displays and holographic screens that looked like my interface.

"Wow, this is awesome," I murmured.

"Please do not touch anything without my approval. I

would prefer for you to sit in the three seats at the rear. Okay?" Flux asked sternly, but it was in a nice tone.

We all agreed, but we still strolled around with our hands behind our backs. There was a hallway behind the bridge with six rooms on each side. They were bedrooms, but they contained more than just a bed. There were hyper sleep capsules in each as well.

"The hyper sleep units have not been used but once as it is abnormal to travel that long of distance. Be that as it may, you do not age when you are inside. If you have any technical questions, please ask the ship. The artificial intelligence is named Beatrix. Hello Beatrix, please meet our new friends."

"I have already researched them. I have detailed files on Astra and Euthani, but I have no information on Dalton. I don't understand," a female robotic voice announced.

"Nice to meet you Beatrix. Dalton is brand new to this planet, so you wouldn't have any information on him," Euthani added.

"Nope, I am just a big ole mystery for you to crack," I smirked.

"Curious," Beatrix replied.

"How far is it to the Mystic Sea from here? This will be my first time," Astra said.

"The distance is 2,777 miles. I will be able to get you there in the next half hour. Air speeds are governed strictly by the Zorth Air Traffic Control System. I cannot travel any faster. If I could, we would be there in seconds."

"Shit," I said in a loud outburst.

"I do not detect fecal matter anywhere on the ship. Have

you had a bowel movement inside your pants, Dalton?" Beatrix asked.

Astra and Euthani busted out into laughter, and my eyes went wide as the moon.

"No, Beatrix. I might shit in my pants in the Heartless Deep, but it was just something I said that was illustrating awe. I didn't mean actual feces."

"I understand now, apologies," the AI replied. "Flux, I would advise we leave for Terra. The Hell Diver ship will have the easiest trip to the Heartless Deep at this time of day."

"Okay, please have a seat. Once we get up and running, you can walk around. It will be a fairly short trip," Flux instructed as she walked to her seat at the controls.

The three of us sat down in the seats at the rear of the bridge. We looked out the glass window ceiling to see the roof of the hangar open revealing a beautiful clear sky. The ship shook a little but smoothed out quickly. We began to rise slowly. I felt like I was in a bubble just floating upward. As we rose, we saw a beautiful view of the city of Helios. We turned counterclockwise and zoomed eastward. The speed was incredible, yet it was calm and still inside the amazing starship.

"You may roam the ship now," Beatrix announced.

19

Five minutes into the flight Flux went to a panel on the right side of the bridge. She pressed a few buttons on a touch screen and swiped toward the middle of the room. A large holographic map appeared in the middle of the bridge directly in front of us. She stood in the front and lifted her hands and opened her arms in different directions. The gesture must have been to zoom. The map centered on the Mystic Sea and showed the city of Terra.

"This is where we are headed right now," Flux zoomed in again revealing a launch pad and then swiped to a dock area where the Hell Diver was located. "We travel for three hours and then we will arrive at the Heartless Deep. It is the deepest point in the Mystic Sea, and the ocean floor is ten miles down."

"This Shadoda just stays in this area and never leaves?" I asked as I leaned forward.

"Shadoda thrives in the extreme cold of the deep water, and she loves the darkness below. Her high sensitivity to sound causes her to destroy anything that enters the Deep. She cannot handle it, so she will destroy anything that enters the area," Flux said grimly.

I leaned over and put my elbows on my knees. "How big is this thing?"

"The few that have managed to escape have said that the body of the creature is close to 30 yards, but its tentacles give her length twice that. However, we aren't sure whether Shadoda is still growing. She could be larger."

"So, why has no one killed this thing before now?" Astra asked.

"Your guess is as good as mine. Shadoda is a legendary terror of the Mystic Sea. Her tentacles can snap a wooden ship in half. If she can't snap a vessel in half, she will just pull them under the water. There is no telling how much ship wreckage there is ten miles below the surface."

"Fuck. Tell me about this Hell Diver thing we are going to use. Is it going to stand up at all to this thing?" I asked as my mouth stayed open.

"The Hell Diver is a new vessel constructed by the Shadow Scourge. The Scourge brought in many of the world's top designers and specialists to build the vessel. The process from the design to complete construction has taken three years. The vessel just became operational three months ago. Emberlynn is bound and determined to cross the Heartless Deep for her business. This vessel is roughly the same size as the Gladius. It travels on the surface of the water, and it can transform into a submarine in 1.8 seconds. The Diver is equipped with weaponry underwater miniguns and torpedoes."

"Can it withstand punishment from the Kraken?" Euthani asked with her eyes wide open.

"Well, it has not been tested against it until now, but is made from Varnothian steel which is the strongest in this star system. Emberlynn spent an exorbitant amount of coin on this thing. Not only will she be able to smuggle more efficiently, but she will charge fees to everyone if they wish to cross the Heartless Deep. She will become unfathomably rich if her plan works...if we succeed that is."

"Shit, I'm sorry you got pulled into this," I told Flux warmly.

"I am happy to do it. Either way I will escape the grasp of the Scourge. We will succeed and I will be released to you, or I will die. I would rather die than go back," Flux replied as her eyes filled with tears. Euthani knelt beside her and rubbed her arm.

The green woman turned to Euthani and smiled. "Thank you. I'm okay."

"Let's switch gears a moment, what race or species are you? Forgive me, I am new to this world. I hope me asking isn't considered rude."

Flux chuckled and wiped her nose. "No, it's not rude. There are not many of us around here. I am Mulkothian. We reside very far from here on the northern hemisphere of Zorth."

"How did you end up here?" Astra asked.

"I wanted to become a pilot, but the opportunities for that where I am from is next to zero. I entered cosmic-aviation school in Helios. It took me 5 years to acquire my cosmos aviation license. I was so excited that I looked for work right after graduation. Me being a woman and a Mulkothian worked against me in my job search. I eventually found work with the Shadow Scourge, but I was not aware of their involvement in organized crime and their complete lack of morals. I was naïve; I had no clue what a vampire was. I was just ecstatic to find work. Once I was hired, I was assigned to the Gladius which now is the most important thing to me in this world. However, I have taken vampires to do terrible things, and I have smuggled terrible things for them. I cannot speak of the evil things that I have seen...at least not right now. Eventually, Emberlynn began to call me into her quarters and bleed me. This would go on twice a week. It would have been more had I been medically able to produce enough blood. I was not only fed upon, but she forced me to do other things that I rather not speak of with her. Like I said before, if we succeed, I will be free, and if I die, I will be free of her as well. It's a win-win situation for me. That is unless we succeed and you three are horrible people as well."

"No, no. We are the good guys no doubt. You will be welcome with our group after we are done," I replied with my hands up.

Astra filled Flux in on who they were and who the Cosmic Peacekeepers were. Flux was excited to know that she would be doing good things for Zorth.

"I can't erase the evil things I have been a part of, but I

will do what I can to match them with good deeds. This is good news. Thank you," Flux replied as a lone tear spilled out of her left eye. Euthani embraced her warmly, and Astra walked over and did the same. We just met, so I wasn't sure if I would weird her out a little too much with a hug. I decided to save that for later. Luckily, Beatrix announced that we were making our descent into Terra, and I didn't have to deal with the awkwardness since she had to return to the pilot's chair.

"We will be landing at the Shadow Scourge's coastal HQ."

"Shit, I really don't want to deal with any more vampires tonight. They give me the fucking creeps," I said softly as we descended straight down into a hangar similar to the one we had just left from.

"No, you don't have to worry. There is only A.I. and a few androids here to keep things going. This place will definitely be used much more often if we pull this quest off," Flux replied with a smile.

Astra sighed and rubbed my knee. "Well, that is a relief." The sudden touch from Astra startled me and excited me. Her rubbing was traveling from my knee up to my thigh just a few inches from my dick. I felt some tingles down there as the floodgates opened for blood to fill my shaft, but she took her hand away, I was able to reel my excitement back in.

We headed to the platform and descended on the lift to the floor below. The hangar looked almost identical to the one in Helios, but it was smaller.

"Follow me, and we will make our way to the Diver. This way," Flux motioned for us to follow.

We reached a staircase that spiraled downward to another large room that resembled a hangar but on a much smaller scale. My attention was immediately drawn to what I assumed was the Hell Diver. The vessel looked like a starship. It didn't look like a seafaring vessel in the slightest. Varnothian steel was an extremely dark black steel, and there were some streaks of red coloring down the side.

"Beatrix activate the Hell Diver and run the departure sequencing. Add the navigation vectors to the Heartless Deep, please."

"So, the A.I. here is named Beatrix as well?" I asked with a brow raised.

"No, Beatrix can be transferred to other destinations for assistance. She will help us on our trip to sure death," Flux winked and laughed.

"Glad to be with you again Beatrix," Euthani spoke as she looked upward at the ceiling.

"Euthani, the pleasure is all mine. I must warn you; I do get seasick," Beatrix joked and let out a freaky robotic laugh.

"Oh snap, Beatrix has jokes," I replied with a nod.

We stood around for a few minutes while Flux and Beatrix did whatever they did to get this boat in the water.

"Dalton, you have been given 50,000 mojo by Emberlynn for you to purchase appropriate weaponry that a Gundertaker may require. Please approach the port beside Flux and insert your mojo extractor into the port," Beatrix instructed.

"Wow, that will be helpful," I replied as I walked over to

the port that Flux was pointing at. I ejected the needle from my forearm and inserted it into the port.

"Oh yes, Dalton. Right there. Don't stop," Beatrix robotically moaned.

All four of us were at a loss for words because this A.I. was joking that I was fucking her with my extractor.

"Damn, Beatrix...we are going to be good buds I think."

20

The inside of the Hell Diver was more spacious that what you would expect of a submarine...not that I had ever been in a sub before. There were three rooms that contained two bunk beds in each, and there was a small galley close by for food. The closer we got to the bridge of the vessel, the narrower it became. There were two seats in front of the controls and four seats behind. There were portholes up and down the sides of the ship that gave a good view of the surroundings. However, there were ample views on the video screen. I would assume looking through the portholes is the old fashion way of doing things. A holographic screen appeared in the center of the bridge showing the route that Beatrix had chosen for us. She considered weather, currents, and boat traffic. The route plotted by Beatrix would get us to the outskirts of the Heartless Deep in four hours. We would pause outside of the Deep to prepare and then head in to face

Shadoda. Flux finished her pre-checks and eased us down into the water under the HQ. She pushed the throttle until we shot out of the tube we were in, and we were on the ocean cutting through the waves. The ride was much rougher than the Gladius, but that was to be expected since we were on the water and not just in the air. I looked at both of my girls. Euthani had a big smile on her face like she was having a good time, but Astra had a disgusted look on her face.

"You okay, Astra?" I whispered to the dragon girl.

"I'll be okay once we get over these waves and out into the sea. If not, I'll get some meds from the mojo shop. Don't worry about me," Astra forced a smile and placed her head on my shoulder.

"We should smooth out soon," Flux said without turning toward us.

I pulled up my interface and began my search for some proper weapons and gear for our upcoming duel with a huge ass sea monster. I was becoming more comfortable with the mojo shop, and I was right at home when I accessed the firearm section. First things first, Shadoda was a big Kraken, so therefore we needed a big gun. I swiped through the shop for a few minutes until I came to the heavy weaponry section. I smiled and clicked the link, and I was bombarded by all shapes and sizes of big guns. My eyes were immediately drawn to a picture of a weapon that looked like a plasma rocket launcher. I playfully twirled my finger, then pressed on the picture. The name of the gun was the FBG 2020 Plasma Rocket Cannon. A devilish grin immediately formed on my unshaven face. The gun would fire 20 rockets per plasma battery capsule. It didn't seem like a lot, but these were rockets. Also, with my class and specialty, I should be pretty accurate at hitting this huge Kraken. I saw a video of the cannon in action on a screen to the left, and it was quick and uninformative. The rocket launched, and there was a big explosion...big whoop. The next item that caught my attention was the price tag...25,000 mojo. I cringed for a couple of seconds, but I promptly clicked the purchase button. If this Kraken was as large as Flux described, we would need a weapon of this size and power. The weapon was freaking huge as it floated in front of me.

"Holy shit, Dalton!" Astra exclaimed as she looked at the gun and then me.

I just nodded. "Yep."

Flux turned in her seat. "Beatrix, take the wheel."

"Yes, Flux," replied the A.I.

She then walked over and grasped the gun with both hands. It was heavier than she expected so I saw some struggle on her face.

"Well, help yourself there Flux," I said sarcastically.

The stock of the weapon was mechanical. When you place it against your shoulder, the gun would open the stock to the perfect size to wrap around your shoulder and armpit. There was a large digital scope and a handle under the giant barrel to hold.

All of us flinched as she began looking in the sight and moving around.

"Whoa, whoa. Careful. That thing came loaded," I said in a much harsher tone than I intended.

"Don't worry, it will only work with your biometrics until you set up access for others," Flux chuckled as she handed me the weapon.

"Sorry, captain, about snapping at you right then. I need to learn to share my toys better. My parents had to get on me about that all of my childhood."

Flux stuck her tongue out playfully and sat back down in the driver's seat.

I spent the next hour searching in the store for items to help us out. I ended up purchasing everyone a set of sticky grenades. They were glowing spheres the size of a baseball. When thrown, they will attach to any surface. Lastly, I purchased all of the crew members laser machetes, and they are as cool as they sound. You press a button on the hilt of the machete and a thick, glowing red blade materializes in front of you. Since the Kraken sounded like it was a huge squid or octopus, I figured being able to hack at the tentacles would be helpful. All three of the women agreed with my choices which surprised me. I thought that Astra would be skeptical, but she was very pleased with what I acquired. Flux had a small arsenal on the vessel already that we could use. There were several assault rifles and plasma capsules for reloading.

Flux stood from the driver's seat and smiled. "We have some time, so let's head up to the deck."

"Deck? What deck?" I asked.

"I keep the deck closed when I drive this. That way I can

dive underwater with no issues if the sudden need arises. I have opened the deck so you can check it out. There are two stationary plasma guns and one stationary harpoon gun. You can go ahead and store your weapons up there. They won't do you any good inside here. There are places to strap them for easy access. The deck will close within a couple of seconds if we need to go underwater. You don't need to be up there of course unless you want to get maimed by Varnothian steel.

We followed the gorgeous green beauty up a winding steel staircase to a heavy steel overhead door. She pressed a few buttons and an unlatching sound echoed through the depths of the Hell Diver. A burst of cool ocean air flowed through the door and throughout the vessel causing the women's hair to flutter and me to smile. I motioned for all the women to go ahead of me. Partly out of chivalry, but I also wanted to get an eyeful of their asses climbing up the stairs. I grinned and shook my head at my immaturity in the current situation we were in. We were headed straight for an almost unbeatable Kraken, and I was still infatuated with the nice asses in front of me.

The ocean had a purple tint to it that caught me by surprise. The surface of the water hand become much calmer, and the boat was cutting through the water smoothly. The port and starboard sides of the vessel sported large stationary plasma guns. They looked like those big 50 caliber machine guns on the back of jeeps in World War Two. There was one large harpoon gun at the front of the deck. I began to have flashbacks of one of my favorite films, Jaws. Would we need a bigger boat too? I had a feeling that Jaws himself would have nothing on this Shadoda monstrosity we were headed to battle. While we were up there, I took advantage of my Pure Weapons Specialist perk and trained each of the women on all of the stationary weapons, plus the ones that were just acquired by me from the mojo shop.

"So, Flux will we be able to see the Kraken coming? Or do we just wait until the ship is entrapped in slimy tentacles and getting yanked under the water?" I asked facetiously.

"The Hell Diver is equipped with the strongest sonar capabilities of any sea vessel in this hemisphere. We will see her coming which will be very helpful...at least that is my hope."

"Well, that's better than just waiting for this thing to grab us and pull us under to our deaths," Astra murmured.

"Dalton, here...catch," Flux said as she tossed something straight at me. "It's a harness if you want to attach yourself to the railing. The system will allow movement around the deck, so you don't have to worry about it restricting you very much. It's up to you if you want to use it."

I walked over to the rail that traveled around the entire deck. There was an anchor point built into the railing. The anchor point was on a track that would move around the entire deck if you chose to do so. I put on the harness just to check it out. I wasn't so sure if I would use it or not, but I would have the option available to me. I like options. The girls eagerly put their harnesses on without question.

"I am going to lock-in. I don't want to be thrown off into the water. I am embarrassed to say that I am not the strongest swimmer," Astra said apprehensively.

"Astra, not great at something? No," I joked.

The dragon girl placed her hands on her hips. "I can show you how great I am at throwing big dumbasses overboard."

I anchored to the rail quickly. "Nope, can't do it, even if you wanted to now. You are just going to have to toss Euthani over."

Euthani, who had been quiet since walking on the deck opened her eyes wide. "What? Did I miss something?"

"Yeah, Astra is going to throw you over the side. I can't talk any sense into her."

"You are such a dweeb sometimes. You think you are funnier than you really are," Astra interjected.

I placed my hand over my heart and groaned. "Astra, that hurt. I'm not very funny to you? Too far dragon girl...too far."

"I think you are totally funny, Dalton," Euthani chirped.

I simply winked at the fox girl and waited for a response from Flux. "So, do you think I am funny?"

"Why is this on your mind right now? I think you are odd...that's what I think," Flux replied with a smirk on her face followed by her tongue sticking out.

I pointed toward the southwest and squinted my eyes. "Is there a storm brewing?"

"That is just what the sky looks like over the Heartless Deep," Flux replied nonchalantly.

The closer we got to the Heartless Deep, the more demonic the sky looked. It was troubling to see blue sky surrounding what looked like a black hole in the sky. The colors were black and purple with periodic lightning flashes. The sky swirled at different speeds. A few minutes would be slow churning and then the motion would transform into violent speeds. We stopped the Hell Diver outside of the hellish quadrant of the sea.

"Yeah, this looks fucked up," I said as my blonde hair began to blow from the wind of a violent sky transformation in the Deep. "Has this place always been like this?"

"As far as I know it has, but what we need to be worrying about is Shadoda. The sky isn't going to kill you. It will just unnerve you a bit," Flux replied as she glared at the clouds.

"Unnerved? More like scared shitless," I replied with a head shake. "Well, let's get this show on the road. The Kraken isn't going to kill herself."

Euthani raised her hand. "What is the plan exactly?"

I exhaled and nodded. "This is a situation that is going to be hard to plan for. I say we start on deck, locked in with our harnesses. You and Astra will take the deck guns, and I will use assault rifles, grenades, and the rocket launcher. You need your laser machetes available for the tentacles, but there is a lot of guess work here. Anything you want to add Flux?"

"I will be able to talk to you through these earpieces. I will keep you abreast with the location of Shadoda from the sonar," Flux added as she handed us the earpieces.

"We will eventually need to go inside and drop under the water. The Kraken is bound to pull us under. The Diver has some weaponry that it can use underwater, right?" I looked at the green skinned beauty.

"Right, the Diver has torpedoes and miniguns that work underneath the surface."

Astra scoffed. "Why don't we just stay underwater then?"

"That's a fair question. The deck guns, sticky grenades, and the rocket launcher pack more of a punch. Hopefully, we can take the Kraken out from the deck. If not, we have underwater options. Now, this plan will fail awfully quick if this Varnothian steel isn't as strong as Flux says it is. If the Diver fails, then we are going to have a really bad day."

Euthani came over and gave me a hug out of the blue.

"What's all this?" I asked tenderly.

"Whatever happens, I think you are amazing. We are lucky to have you with us," Euthani replied almost in tears.

"What the heck are you talking about? I am the lucky one with you three kickass women by my side," I replied as I kissed her on the forehead.

Astra broke her silence during the embrace. "I know we had a rough start, but I have grown to like you, Dalton. It was very selfless volunteering to help me get the hakrium for Zero."

"No problem, Zero would do it for any one of us," I said as I raised my arm for her to join in on the hug. She smiled warmly and embraced the two of us tightly.

I turned my head to see Flux standing alone. I could tell that she felt awkward. "Flux, will you join us? You are part of the team now. We are huggers. You will just have to get used to it."

Flux looked uncomfortable at first, but she gave in, and we all had a large group hug on the deck of the Hell Diver. I was scared of the battle ahead, but most of that fear was whether I would be able to protect the three women who had grown to be very important to me. They were skilled like crazy, so they could hold their own, but I couldn't help worrying about them.

"Alright ladies get locked and loaded. Flux go on down there and take us into the center of hell."

21

We were seconds from crossing into the Heartless Deep. The Hell Diver bounced up and down on the waves, and that was the only sound that entered my auditory canals. I turned to look at my girls with their hands tight around the controls of the stationary guns. I could see their white knuckles from my spot at the front of the vessel. I stood behind the harpoon gun. I didn't have any plans now for using it as I wasn't sure what to do with it in the situation. I hoped an idea would present itself soon. I held a plasma assault rifle, and the plasma rocket launcher hung on my shoulder. My belt contained a row of sticky grenades, and my plasma cannon pistols were holstered. I felt I was as ready as I would ever be. My Gundertaker skills were going to be put to the test against Shadoda. There would be no zombies to help me though. However, zombie Great White Sharks might be kind of cool. If the opportunity presented itself, I would on hundred percent implement them into my strategy.

My stomach dropped as the Hell Diver broke the threshold of the Heartless Deep. The shit was fixing to hit the fan, and it was just a question of when. I was terrified, but I made sure that I didn't show it to my women. They needed me to be strong. Hell, I was strong. I was a fucking Gundertaker and KAW Heavyweight Champion! I was the fucking Cooler. My face transformed into a scowl. I spit over the railing into the water and flexed my muscles under my trench coat. The time to be a pussy was over. It was us or this fucking Shadoda Kraken bitch.

We were two hundred yards into the Heartless Deep when Flux yelled into our earpieces. "Shit, that didn't take long. We have a big ass creature headed for us. I estimate one minute before Shadoda shows herself."

"Holy shit, this Kraken bitch doesn't play games," I replied loudly. "So, do we stop or keep going?"

"Shadoda is coming from the west. I am going to turn east and speed up. If we just sit here, I think she will slam into us and capsize the vessel leaving you three just dangling underwater."

"Good plan," I replied as Flux turned us around quickly in the other directions. I had to grab the rail to stop me from falling on my ass.

"Alright, she should reveal herself in a few seconds behind us. Get ready!" Flux yelled nervously.

The girls and I turned. I sped to the rear of the vessel and aimed my gun. The women would have to be mindful not to shoot me. This was actually a moronic spot to stand, but I didn't see any way around it. I gulped as I saw something dark under the water speeding toward the rear of the boat. My blood ran cold as the top of the Kraken cut through the surface of the water. The beast had two very large glowing green eyes that stared right into my soul. Her tentacles erupted from the water and grabbed for the rear of the ship. I snapped out of my stupor and began firing the plasma rifle at the humongous sea creature. The Kraken lower her body under the water, but some of her tentacles still reached for us. Flux was able to stay ahead of the monster by a small distance. The plasma rounds that penetrated the beast didn't seem to slow it down at all. However, it did convince her to dive back under the water.

"She's under the water. I can't see her anymore!" I yelled at the girls who had yet to fire a shot. They turned their heads in multiple directions frantically searching for the hidden killer. Suddenly, a tentacle swung over the railing and grabbed Astra's stationary gun. She screamed in horror and dove toward the middle of the deck. The deck gun ripped from the deck and was thrown into the water. Two more tentacles came over the same side of the boat. One of them grabbed the railing and began to pull. The Diver began to slow down, and the engine screamed as it fought the Kraken. I heard a loud splash, and another tentacle came from the other side of the ship and grabbed the railing thirty feet behind Euthani. The fox girl screamed, but she went into immediate action. She twirled the deck gun around and began firing into the water. After a dozen rounds, she blew the tentacle from the body of the Kraken. The tentacle arm was still attached, but it dangled off the side of the Diver. The water turned red from the injury, but the Kraken slung another tentacle arm to replace the lost one. The tentacles didn't stay attached to the railing for long. Shadoda appeared to be learning from its mistakes. It swung the tentacle arm toward Euthani. She dove to the deck just in the nick of time as the arm contacted with the deck gun. The gun appeared to be bent a little, but still operational. I pulled my laser machete from my belt and began hacking at the arm. The skin was tough but the intense heat from the laser assisted the blade immensely. Red blood sprayed and squirted all over the deck as I chopped as hard as I could.

Thwack!

Thwack!

Thwack!

Thwack!

I could hear screeches muffled from beneath the ship as I chopped, and Astra chopped at another tentacle arm.

"Dalton, Shadoda is directly under the ship. I think she is trying to get a grip to pull us down. It fucking sucks, because this makes it too dangerous to us the plasma rockets," Euthani yelled in my earpiece.

More tentacles erupted from the sea and grabbed multiple sections of the boat. We were able to dismember two of the arms, but each time we got rid of one...another appeared. The deck of the ship looked like a massacre had occurred. Bloody, flesh, and fat covered the deck which made it tough to keep our footing as we ran around the boat hacking at tentacles. So far, I had sustained the only injury.

A tentacle had grazed my cheek, splitting it wide open. Luckily, it wasn't a cut above my eye causing blood to compromise my vision. If there was ever a sustained pause in the action, I would use some nanobot ointment I had purchased earlier. I ran to the back of the boat and looked over into the water. I began firing my assault rifle at whatever part of the creature was under the surface. Pink clouds appeared under the water, so I knew that I was making good contact with the beast. I shot a few more rounds into the beast causing some flesh to show itself above the water. I promptly yanked a sticky grenade from my belt and pressed the activation button on the top and tossed it hard at the exposed spot. I didn't like doing this so close to the boat, but the Varnothian steel should be able to withstand a grenade blast. The grenade dug into the flesh which held it into place.

Boom!

The grenade took a large chunk out of the Kraken, and she let go of the ship and dove deep into the water.

"Fuck you!" I screamed into the Deep.

"Speed back up," I instructed Flux through my earpiece. As we pushed forward, we say a Diver sized cloud of red in the water from the holes in the Kraken. I know we didn't kill it. Shadoda had to go regroup. She would be back any minute, and she would no doubt be pissed off.

"Is everyone okay?" I asked as I scanned the deck for my friends.

"Yeah, I'm good," Astra replied.

"Me, too," Euthani added as she breathed heavily.

Flux yelled though the ear piece again. "Brace yourself, she is coming again."

"That's what she said..." I whispered to myself.

She was approaching from the starboard side. I looked and saw the familiar black mass speeding under the water and leaving a large wake behind it.

"She's going to slam into us. Grab the rail," I exclaimed as I white knuckled the black Varnothian steel.

Shadoda plowed into the side of the boat with an amazing amount of force. I held on as tight as I could as the boat tilted toward the port side. Astra screamed as she was thrown over the railing. She splashed into the water, and then was pulled out when the boat tilted the other direction. She dangled off the side of the Hell Diver and started screaming.

"Astra!" I grabbed the cable holding her to the ship and began to pull upward as hard as I could. I then grabbed her arm and almost yanked it out of her socket as I pulled her back onto the ship.

"Thank you," Astra breathed heavily.

Four tentacle arms slithered over the opposite side of the boat and headed toward all three of us. We opened fire, shooting round after round into any part of the arms that we could. Even though they were losing chunks of flesh with each round, the arms continued to approach. Euthani's ankle was grabbed, and the Kraken began to pull her to the other side of the ship. I dove over to the arm and began axing the flesh with my laser machete. After two swipes, the arm was severed at the tip. Blood gushed from the stump like the end of a fire hose.

"Keep the tentacles off of me," I yelled as I took a grenade off my belt and began sprinting toward the starboard side of the ship. I threw the grenade, and it attached to the body of the sea monster and exploded. Blood, blubber, and meat flew in all directions as the Kraken screeched from the damage and pain. The Kraken dropped down into the water again leaving a blood cloud in its wake. Flesh floated in the water, and smaller fish began snapping at the pieces.

"Fuck, I can't get a good shot with the rocket launcher. She stays under the boat. Flux, where is she?"

"She is coming from the same direction again. This may be your chance to get a rocket off."

I immediately took the rocket launcher from my back. I looked down the sights, and I could see the dark blob under the surface. It was not the best shot, but I fired a rocket anyway. The recoil was massive, but I was able to mitigate it well. The rocket splashed into the water and exploded resulting in a horrendous screech from Shadoda. I fired again before she had time to dive. There was another explosion of gore and agony from the massive beast.

"Dalton, she has gone under again. She dove deep this time," Flux informed me.

"You think she has given up and run off?" Astra asked with a hopeful tone.

"I think regrouping is the better word," I replied as I looked over the side of the boat into the murky water. "Flux, what do you think about grabbing her with the harpoon gun?"

"She's too big. She'll just pull us around like a toy. I think

I would avoid that, but it's your call. What are you thinking about doing?"

"Well, I want to pull more of her above the surface to place some more effective shots into her." I cringed at those last few words. Really, I was thinking about sex jokes during a time like this.

"Maybe it's time to take her from below," I cringed again.

"I'm game, if you are," Flux replied.

I motioned to the other women to head toward the door inside. "Go inside, we are going to shoot some torpedoes in her ass."

Jesus, there I go again. I am on a roll with the sex puns.

We made our way inside, and the women plopped in the seats completely exhausted mentally and physically. I stood beside Flux as she told Beatrix to close the deck and prepare to go under.

"How far is she down?" I asked as I squinted at the sonar screen.

"She's a couple of miles down. Hold on," Flux replied as she began to descend below the surface and into the Heartless Deep.

"Wow, this is cool," Euthani said as she looked out of a porthole. Astra had not left her seat.

"This will definitely piss her off. Going into her domain like this will be completely new to her. See if you look right there, she has already stopped. She hears us coming," Flux said as she pointed at the screen. "I'm speeding up."

We began to descend quickly, and my stomach began to churn. I didn't usually get sick on theme park rides, so this was new to me. Playing chicken with a huge Kraken probably had something to do with it.

"She is ascending now," I pointed at the screen.

We were headed directly toward one another. Flux fired two torpedoes into the pitch-black darkness of the water. In the distance, we saw a faint light from the explosion. Shadoda stopped in her tracks on the sonar screen, so Flux had to have made contact with one of the two torpedoes.

"Good shot," I yelled and pumped a fist in the air.

"She's headed deeper. She is still alive. I'm going after her," Flux replied intently.

"How deep can this vessel go? You said the bottom of the Deep is ten miles down," Astra broke her silence from the seat behind us.

"The Varnothian steel will keep us intact easily...no problem," Flux replied confidently.

"Well that's reassuring," I interjected quietly. "Dude, Shadoda is going straight down and fast. Fuck, we would be blind without this sonar. I can't see shit."

"There are lights, but I would like her to have more difficulty seeing us. However, I am sure her underwater visibility is pretty good. We are six miles under now. I am going to descend quicker," Flux said as she pushed the throttle forward further. "See this line, that is the ocean floor. She is almost there."

Flux was a daredevil. She pushed the throttle forward even more. We were hauling ass straight down into pitch darkness.

"Eight miles," Flux announced.

A few seconds later, the green bombshell said, "Nine miles."

The Kraken was swimming away from us and hugging the floor of the Heartless Deep.

"I'm leveling off now, because we are at the bottom."

Astra gagged from behind us. "I'm going to puke."

Two more torpedoes fired from the Hell Diver at the Kraken a half mile in front of us. We didn't see any light, so we assumed the torpedoes missed their target.

"Fuck, I missed," Flux growled and slammed her fist on the dash.

"You're good, she has had enough of this shit. She is on the run," I replied as I patted Flux on the shoulder.

Not even two seconds after those words left my mouth, the Kraken made a quick turn and launched toward us at a high rate of speed. She was closing the gap fast. Flux fired off two more torpedoes. One of them made contact, but the Kraken kept coming.

"Shit, there she is. Hold on!" I screamed as I saw Shadoda in all her terrifying glory. The impact from the collision threw me backwards into the chair beside Astra. The air left my lungs, and I began to cough. When I looked out of the front of the vessel, all I saw was a throat and teeth. Shadoda looked like she was trying to swallow us hole.

"Beatrix! Damage report! Has the hull been breached?" Flux asked frantically.

"The hull has not been breached otherwise you would all be dead. Varnothian steel is as good as advertised. However, we do have a very large sea creature attached to us that does not appear interested in letting us go any time. I would also like to add that you are out of torpedoes, and the plasma mini-guns will not operate at this depth," Beatrix answered nonchalantly.

I sighed loudly and then chuckled. "So Shadoda just plans to spoon us indefinitely?"

22

Shadoda stayed locked on us for the next half hour. It appeared that the bitch was coming up with a new plan, and she was going to keep squeezing.

"She isn't letting go, is she?" Euthani asked as she investigated the massive pink maw through the glass.

"Beatrix, is Shadoda going to crack the hull if she squeezes for much longer?" I asked while I scratched the back of my head.

"Dalton, there is no way to know that for certain, but I feel that combined with the enormous pressure and her strength that the hull will crack eventually. A small crack will cause an instant bloody death," Beatrix replied.

"Alright, do you have some sort of suggestion? This is a question for you or Flux," I asked as I plopped down in a seat.

Beatrix spoke first. "An option you may want to decide upon is using the dive suit located below. It may handle the intense pressure long enough for someone to dissuade the Kraken from continuing to hold on to the vessel."

"This suit may handle the pressure. May?" I asked with a brow raised.

"The suit is equipped to handle a great deal of pressure. However, we are ten miles below the surface. It is doubtful that during testing they were able to simulate this type of environment to test the suits integrity. So, I cannot say that it will withstand the pressure. I can only tell you that it may be able to withstand the environment. The options that we have right now are not optimal, Mr. Wade."

I turned to Flux in the fleeting hope that she would have a better plan. She opened her mouth to speak but was interrupted by the loudest sound that has ever entered my ears in my life. Shadoda let out a skull splitting screech that caused me to fall to my knees and cover my ears. My teeth gnashed together with such force I was certain that I had cracked some of them. When I was able to open my eyes, I saw that all four of us were on the floor. I felt something warm stream out of my left ear, and I looked at my hand to see bright red blood.

Shadoda screamed again, this time for five hellish seconds. All of us were curled up in the fetal position on the floor. Euthani cried as blood streamed from each ear. Astra crawled over to comfort the fox girl while blood streamed from her own. The Kraken screamed twice more in the next half hour. All of us shoved small balls of tissue into our ears to deafen the horrendous screams, but it barely helped.

"Hull integrity is at ninety-three percent," announced Beatrix.

"Fuck, we have to do something. Flux, what can we power down without killing us in this thing? Maybe if we don't have any lights, no noise, or vibrations she will let go. I would really prefer not to go outside to be crushed by pressure or eaten by a fucking Kraken."

Flux nodded her head, and her expression told me she was deep in thought. "Beatrix, you heard him."

"Yes Flux, I can power down the lighting and lower the power just enough to supply oxygen. Whether this will accomplish your goal of Shadoda releasing us, I cannot comment," Beatrix replied nonchalantly.

"Do it," I said sternly.

"Yes, Dalton."

Seconds later, all the lighting dissipated, and the hum of the engine lowered to almost nothing. The control panels even dimmed, and there was almost complete darkness. There was a very minute glow emitting from the control panels, but that was it.

I put my index finger in front of my mouth even though there was no way the girls were seeing it. "Keep quiet and pray this works. Keep your ears covered in case the bitch screams at us again." I could already tell that my hearing had been damaged significantly. I hoped the nanobots in the med kit or Blowkos would be able to heal us. Not to mention the terrible headache I had that made me squint one of my eyes. I just took deep breaths and tried to relax as much as I could.

We sat there quietly for an hour in the hopes Shadoda would release us and be on her way. She hadn't budged at all. My headache had eased off some which was a welcome relief.

I heard a rustling in front of me. Someone was crawling for some reason. It had to be Flux.

"What's up? Do you see anything?" I whispered.

"Yes, I can see something moving on the sonar, or my mind could just be playing tricks on me. Just a second," Flux replied quietly. I could barely make out what she said with my fucked eardrums.

We all waited patiently to hear the verdict.

"There is something on the surface...a boat or ship perhaps," Flux whispered across the room.

I nodded in the darkness and then I felt the vessel tilt. Shadoda heard the disturbance at the surface with her sensitive ears. The Kraken growled and released the Hell Diver quickly and launched upward for the ten-mile trip to the surface.

"Power up, Beatrix," Flux yelled.

"Yes, ma'am," Beatrix replied as the lights came on, and the engine resumed. I covered my eyes from the piercing light, which caused my headache to pulse again.

"Let's get moving, follow her to the surface. Maybe we can take her out while she is distracted by whatever is going on up there," I said as I sat beside her at the driver's seat.

She pushed the throttle, and we were off. I turned to look at Euthani and Astra. Euthani had her head on Astra's shoulder, and the dragon girl rubbed her head. The fox girl was clearly traumatized by our stay on the ocean floor. I gave Astra a thumbs up, and she replied with a nod. I could see dried blood on the sides of their beautiful faces, and their eyes were red from their tears. My heart broke for them. I turned a looked out of the cockpit glass. There was some light from the front of the vessel, but it couldn't cut into the darkness with much effectiveness. Flux was navigating from her tracking system alone.

"Shadoda is almost there. I am going to speed up some more. Hold on," Flux stated as she pushed the throttle further. I was able to feel some g-forces now.

"Make sure we don't surface too close. We need room to assess the situation, but you already know that I am sure. You are a badass," I said as I rubbed the green woman's shoulder. She looked at me and smiled warmly at my compliment.

"We're close, and Shadoda is not moving. She is attacking whatever is up there," Flux said while her breathing became more rapid.

A few moments later the Hell Diver launched out of the water into the light and splashed on its belly on the surface of the Heartless Deep. Our eyes widened when we saw the Kraken wrapped around a small ship.

"Open the deck, now!" I exclaimed as I grabbed my assault rifle and rocket launcher. I could hear a mechanism unlock and began to move quickly.

"Astra follow me. Euthani stay back."

Astra nodded and got to her feet rapidly.

"There's no way I am staying down here. I'm coming," Euthani exclaimed as she shook her head.

"That's what she said," I murmured to myself as I climbed the stairs and unlatched the door. The cool sea breeze blanketed my face as I left the belly of the Diver. It felt heavenly to my skin. I sprinted to the harpoon gun too fast as I slipped and fell to the deck. I slammed my knee into the Varnothian steel and let out a grunt of pain. I picked myself back up and limped to the gun and grabbed the handles. As I aimed at the back of the Kraken, I saw two figures being crushed in the tentacle arms, and they were thrown into the sea. I aimed in the center of the mass above the water and squeezed the trigger.

Whoosh!

The harpoon launched like a missile from the gun and headed straight toward Shadoda. The shot was true, and the sharp point plunged into the dark flesh of the beast resulting in a shriek of agony and surprise. I pressed the lock button to keep the Varnothian cable in place. Then I pressed another button that was supposed to reel our catch to us, but we were the ones being pulled toward it.

"Don't fight it, just let it pull us to her."

"Got it, I will pull the throttle back. Be careful up there," Flux replied.

I turned and gave a thumbs up to the girls. "Hold on, we're going to her. Make sure you are latched with your harnesses. Get your weapons ready. It's about to get real."

I could see pieces of the other boat being strewn about the surface of the sea. There were scattered screams. Shadoda was slamming multiple arms onto different parts of the ship, smashing the hull, and ripping pieces off. I could hear her growling with each strike.

"She's pissed off," I whispered to myself.

The closer we approached my hearted pounded harder in my chest. The rocket launcher wasn't an option as it would finish the other boat off easily. I waved to the girls beside me, and we began firing round after round into the sea beast. Blood erupted like a volcano all over Shadoda's body. She was a smart creature, but she was clearly confused as to what she needed to do. I saw a couple of men fire pistols into the Kraken, but they weren't causing a lot of damage. Shadoda roared and lunged out of the water onto the crippled boat flattening the men. The boat finally gave way and snapped in two. This was my chance. The other boat was done for so now I had a shot. I swung the rocket launcher from my back and aimed quickly at the big bitch. I squeezed the trigger, and a plasma rocket tore into the beast. I immediately threw my rocket launcher to the deck.

"What are you doing? Shoot it again!" Astra yelled.

"We need the heart, remember?"

"Give me your laser machete!"

Astra's eyes widened in confusion. "What are you going to do?"

"Just give it to me!" I growled.

She tossed me the blade, and I pulled mine from my belt. I activated them, and the wicked laser blades extracted from the hilt.

I took two deep breaths and launched from the deck of the Diver and landed on Shadoda. I began hammering the blades into the eyes of the beast. Green fluid mixed with dark blood spurted from the wounds as the creature screamed.

I screamed as I stabbed over and over and over. I began cutting into the skull until I saw the Kraken's disgusting brain. I took another deep breath and dove into the hole I had made. I laid on the slimy, squishy brain, and I began stabbing and slashing until the beast stopped moving. It took close to fifty stabs across the area of the pink brain to kill her. The sea water began to fill the skull, and she started to sink with me still inside. I panicked as my head was covered by the sea water that was mixed with blood and brain fluid. I reached for the edge of the hole in the skull and pulled myself out. I was approximately fifteen feet under the water. I began to swim frantically upward. Seconds later, I shot from the water and filled my lungs with precious oxygen. I then vomited from the disgusting goo all over me. The stink was unfathomable not to mention the extreme stress I had just been under. The adrenaline in my veins dissipated, and I felt like I was going to pass out.

"Dalton! Grab my hand!" screamed Euthani as her and Astra leaned over the side of the boat. I attempted to reach for them, but they were too high.

"There is a ladder!" Astra pointed a few yards down.

I nodded and threw up once more. I slowly swam to the ladder and struggled to ascend. The girls met me near the top and grabbed me under my shoulders to help me the rest of the way. I plopped on my back on the deck. I couldn't believe what I had just done.

23

Shadoda was still attached to the harpoon and dangled under the water. All the blood from her lifeless body mixed with the Mystic Sea causing a giant circle of pink. The Hell Diver had an underwater drone equipped with arms and a laser cutter. Flux sent it down to the corpse to remove the heart. After an hour's extraction, the drone returned to the storage bay under the vessel and placed the large heart into the Diver for transport to Emberlynn. Flux sent the drone down once more in order to cut the Kraken loose from the harpoon. We watched the process through the cameras on the drone, and a quick cut caused the giant sea monster to plummet to her final resting place ten miles below.

Flux scrunched her nose and gagged. "No offense Dalton, but you reek. Please go take a shower and purchase some new clothes from the mojo store."

"There is a shower?" I raised a brow.

"Yes, it isn't very large, but it is downstairs. You didn't see it earlier?"

"Nope, I was too busy watching all three of you beautiful women strut in front of me."

Flux's cheeks reddened. "Really? Flirting after the ordeal we just went through?"

"Absolutely, I will admit that I have a bit of a crush on you. You are an amazing pilot and boat...captain, I guess. Your confidence is attractive."

"Just my confidence?" Flux smirked.

I chuckled. "Your appearance is well above attractive. Breathtaking, goddess-like...something like that."

"You are making me blush again; however, you're going to make me gag again if you don't get in that shower. We can...talk more later," Flux winked.

"Get a room you two," Euthani laughed.

Astra shook her head and scoffed sarcastically.

"Yeah, okay. I am headed to that shower now."

The warm water pounding my face felt amazing. The blood and other nastiness began to rinse from my body to the drain below. I lathered my hair and body with soap and then rinsed it off. I was good as new. It felt so good being clean again not to mention the hot water soothing my aching muscles. I closed my eyes and placed my hands on the wall of the shower. I stood still and just let the water flow on my head. I felt a draft of cool air from the shower door opening behind me. I saw two green skinned arms wrap around me and rub my chest and I felt warm lips as Flux kissed my back. I moaned as the blood began to feel my cock quickly.

"I hope you don't mind," Flux whispered in my ear. She then pressed her round perky breasts against my back.

"No, most definitely not," I replied as I turned around to admire her naked body. My eyes locked with hers and slowly descended downward to her ample chest and muscular abdomen where I saw a white-haired landing strip above her pussy.

"Am I sufficient? The other women are much more beautiful."

"They are beautiful, but my God, Flux, never doubt your perfection. You are incredible," I said as I pressed my lips to hers. We kissed lightly before I put my tongue into her warm, sweet mouth. I moved my hands up and down her back and then I cupped her perfect ass. She moaned, and our kiss became more intense as my hard cock pressed into her abdomen. She began kissing my neck, my chest, my stomach, and then she kissed the head of my dick. She twirled her tongue around the tip before taking it all in her warm mouth.

My head tilted back, and my eyes rolled to the back of my head. "Fuck," I muttered. She slid her mouth up and down slowly making me shudder. Then she began to increase her speed gradually. I put my hands into her soft, white hair as she sucked. This went on for a couple of minutes until I gently pulled her off. I lifted her to her feet and spun her around and pushed her to the wall. She gasped in surprise and anticipation. I cupped her breasts as I kissed her neck.

She squirmed and pressed her ass into my dick and moved her cheeks in a clockwise motion. I pinched her nipples causing her to let out her first audible word. "Fuck."

I slid both hands from her breasts down her stomach to her pussy. I began to fondle it lightly, then became more demanding taking her breath away.

"Dalton, I'm gonna come. Please don't stop."

I slid my index and middle finger deep into her sopping wet pussy taking her over the edge. She screamed in ecstasy. Her body shivered all over from the explosion of pleasure. The shower door opened again. We turned to see a fully clothed Euthani with a smile on her face, and her arms crossed over her chest.

"Don't mind me, I just want to watch."

"You do? I can dig it," I replied as I continued to finger the green skinned goddess.

The excitement of seeing the fox girl standing there ogling us made me even harder. I turned Flux around and put my hands under her thighs and lifted her against the wall. I lowered her on my shaft making her scream.

"Fuck me, Dalton. Fuck me hard."

"Yeah, Dalton, fuck her hard. I know you can," Euthani purred.

I bypassed the gradual thrust and began pounding in and out. The wet slapping from our drenched bodies echoed through the bathroom.

Slap.

Slap.

Slap.

Slap.

Slap.

"Dalton, I'm gonna…" Flux was cut off by another explosion of pleasure. Her pussy wrapped around my throbbing cock as she screamed at the top of her lungs. I slapped her ass hard as she came.

"Dalton, fill her for me," Euthani demanded from outside the shower. I looked over and saw the blue-eyed beauty as she smiled in the steam.

"You got it. Are you ready, Flux?" I asked as I kissed her chin.

"Oh gods, yes. Come inside me," she begged.

I began to thrust harder bringing me closer to ejaculation.

"Do it," Euthani growled.

I drove my cock in deeper which caused Flux to gasp and jerk. I squeezed her ass harder as my dick began to throb even more. I let go and spurted my seed deep inside her. My orgasm brought her to another. We both groaned loudly as my thrusts became slower and gentler. My heart pounded, and my lungs begged for air.

"That was insane," I said to Flux before I looked at a smiling Euthani.

"Thank you, see you in a few," the fox girl said as she shut the door and left the bathroom.

I exited the green skinned woman and lowered her to the floor. We kissed passionately for a few seconds, and she patted me on the cheek with her hand.

"You ready to head back and deliver this big ass heart to a scary coven of vampires?" I asked with a wink.

Flux laughed as she gave me a playful hug. "Absolutely."

The end of Monster Girl Galaxy: Book One.

Dalton Wade and his harem of monster girls will continue their journey into space in book two – COMING SOON!

Thank you for checking out book one of my new series, Monster Girl Galaxy. I had so much fun writing it and I hope you had a killer time reading it! I can't wait to deliver Book 2! Please do me a HUGE FAVOR. **Leave a review on Amazon for me**. These are so helpful to independent authors like myself and get me noticed in the store. Thanks!

--- Austin Beck

ZAMA THE LAMIA ARTWORK

Zama the Lamia

Please leave a review for Austin! He worked so hard to bring our adventures to life! Reviews are so helpful to new authors like him!

Gundertaker: Monster Girl Galaxy 1

Written by Austin Beck

BLOWKOS ARTWORK

STRANGER ZERO ARTWORK

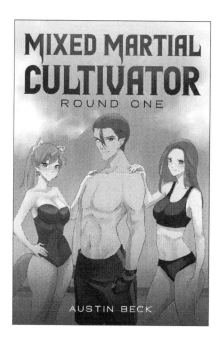

travel through a cosmic doorway that leads to the other side of the universe to a strange but beautiful world called Azura. In Azura, all things are possible, and he has the potential to gain unlimited power. This new fantasy world is desperate for his help!

Will he decide to go?

Does he really have a choice?

This Cultivation LitRPG includes intimate scenes that are described in great detail (NOT Fade to Black), graphic violence, profanity, and smokin' hot women (including monster girls) who are all in a relationship with one lucky man. So, if you don't like these wonderful things, this isn't the book for you! Otherwise, you are in for a wild ride!

Read Mixed Martial Cultivator Now!

BOOK TWO SAMPLE

The past couple of days had been utterly insane. Never in my life would I have expected to be in a deep-sea battle above water and underwater with a Kraken. My team and I took ourselves to the limit, and we succeeded in a task that Emberlynn, the vampiress matriarch of the notorious Shadow Scourge, had felt was a near-impossible challenge for a group of ragtag nobodies. I couldn't wait to see the look on her beautiful evil face when we strolled in with the big ass Shadoda heart. The starship Gladius was going to be our reward for the quest completion. Not only did that have me excited, but the gorgeous, green-skinned Flux would also be freed and one of the Cosmic Peacekeepers now. I had grown quite fond of her from the short time we had known each other. She was an intelligent, confident badass. She handled the Hell Diver like a savant and showed no fear. She didn't hesitate during the quest against Shadoda. Her looks weren't so bad either, and our little rendezvous in the shower didn't hurt her standing in my eyes either. Euthani asking to watch our fuck session only added to the hotness. So far, I really enjoyed the openness of relationships in this new world. I was falling hard for Euthani, the fox girl babe, and she seemed to be digging me as well. At the same time, she was all for me exploring other women. She was a participant in the fun threesome with Blowkos, and while not a hands-on partici-pant when I and Flux got together -- she was involved. There were no evil eyes or hissy fits from my fox girl. She cared for me and wanted me to be happy. It is almost like she thought I was so rad that other women should partake in my radness. I cared too much about Euthani to take advantage of her will-ingness to share with others. I respected the fox girl way too much to do that.

Even though she had been lenient, I was sure there was still a line that could be crossed that would piss her off. I had no desire to get anywhere near that line. Euthani was someone that I wanted by my side forever. The dragon girl, Astra, had been quiet for most of the trip back to Helios. She had been through the wringer with her emotions in the past few days. Her best friend, Stranger Zero, is hooked up to a machine that is keeping him alive while we are trying to get to another fucking solar system to get the extremely rare hakrium to save him. Then we had fought the night wraiths on the train, and we had fought a giant terrifying squid crea-ture. Astra had not been a huge fan of me when I had arrived on the block, but she had grown to like me. I am not sure whether that like will continue to a physical relationship, but I am just fine with having her as a friend. Even though Stranger Zero is a cyborg and says that he cannot pursue physical relationships, I think a part of Astra still has hopes. She is dedicated to Zero, and I don't think she has room for me. That's cool though, because Euthani, Flux, and Blowkos would be enough for me to juggle.

"We're here," Flux informed us as we began to descend straight down like a helicopter.

Astra breathed in a giant gulp of air. "Do you think Emberlynn will go back on her deal? I don't trust her."

"I don't think so," I replied as I put my boots back on.

"I have known Emberlynn for a while. She is a lot of things, but she isn't a liar. She told you the Gladius would be yours. I have every reason to believe it will be," Flux replied earnestly.

"I want to be on our way to Seon 8. I know Blowkos said Zero would be fine plugged to that machine, but I don't like putting all of my faith in something made from nuts and bolts," the dragon girl sighed.

"We are going to drop this heart off and get the hell out of here," I replied with confidence.

The heart of Shadoda was roughly the size of Andre the Giant. The robot from the Hell Diver helped with the transfer to the Gladius. Unfortunately, the robot had to stay with the vessel, so we had to figure out how to move this thing. Luckily, Flux found a cart that hovered a couple of inches off the ground, and we all grabbed a chunk and pulled it on the platform. The thing was still a mess and dripping everywhere, but I guessed vampires wouldn't mind blood on the floor. If they did, they would have to deal with it. Ember-lynn hadn't given us a special container to bring it back in. The cart was autonomous, so it followed us. We didn't have to worry about pushing it, which was a welcomed benefit. We made our way back to the throne room to be met by wide eyes from the coven. They whispered to one another as they licked their lips.

"Dalton, you've returned with something large I see. Come closer so I can have a look," Emberlynn said as she stood in front of her throne.

I nodded and directed the cart to the bottom of the steps that led to her throne. She stepped down the steps one at a time, and her smile grew with each step to the floor.

"You did it," Emberlynn said with disbelief.

"Well, we did it," I replied.

She stepped beside the heart and stuck her index finger in a puddle of blood on the steel. She put the bloody finger in her mouth and closed her eyes and moaned. "Delicious."

She turned and returned to her throne and sat. "We will feast tonight on the heart of Shadoda."

The crowd of vampires cheered and raised their fists.

"Are we done here?" I asked sternly.

"Are you in a hurry?" Emberlynn asked with a smirk.

"Yes, as a matter a fact we are. We need to get going to Seon 8," I replied surprised by her question.

"You have completed your quest, and the starship and

Flux are yours," Emberlynn leaned forward. "However, it would be rude for you to leave before we dine on Shadoda. You don't want to be rude, do you?"

"We appreciate the invitation, but we regretfully decline. We need to leave," I replied sternly but nicely.

"Ok, I will let you go," Emberlynn purred.

I did a shallow bow. "Thank you, and we hope you enjoy," I said as I motioned to the pile of cardiac muscle on the cart.

"But," Emberlynn raised her index finger.

There's always a fucking but.

"Dalton, you will eat a piece of the heart first. When I offer you a meal, you will take it. Otherwise, my feelings will be hurt. People that hurt my feelings regret it."

I exhaled and shook my head. "Alright, go cook the damn thing and give me a plate."

Emberlynn laughed. "Cook? We don't cook meat here silly. Just tear a piece off and partake. I will let the rest of your little flock out of this, but you will eat."

Astra whispered. "You don't have to do it. Let's just leave."

"I beg to differ, Astra it is?" Emberlynn smiled. "He eats, or my coven eats all of you. Simple."

I turned my head toward the women and held my hands in front of me. "It's cool. I got this. Just stay quiet."

I walked closer to the heart and began scanning it for a piece that looked less disgusting. There was no such piece. It was all a slimy, bloody mess that reeked, and it had already began decomposing. This would suck even more than I initially though. I pulled out a knife from my belt and cut off a piece that was about the size of a quarter.

"Dalton, you need to get enough to taste it. I will get you a piece," Emberlynn chuckled as she approached the table with a dagger. She walked beside me and slowly cut off a hunk the size of a 24-ounce ribeye steak. My stomach began revolting in disgust. She soaked it in a puddle of blood that had accrued on the steel. She smiled like a psychopath as she put the huge slab of bloody, decaying heart muscle in my hand. The blood dripped from my hand to the floor. The smell assaulted my nostrils, and I began to gag.

"Dalton, what are you waiting for? You may eat now, and you must eat it all in order to leave," Emberlynn purred as she licked the blood from her fingers.

She was enjoying this entirely too much. This was just a sick game she wanted to play before we left this dark shit hole. I would have to try the whole mind over matter thing. I would pretend it was just a rare filet mignon from a good steak house. I lifted the cold, squishy piece of flesh to my mouth. The fishy, metallic smell was horrendous. The smell of raw organs was bad enough, but it had begun to decompose which made it reek of decay.

I dry heaved as I brought the heart within two inches of my lips. This wouldn't be just a quick bite. This thing was huge and would take several large mouthfuls before it was gone.

Euthani broke her silence. "Why are you doing this? We did what you asked. Why are you forcing him to eat this?"

"It's okay, I got this," I smiled at the fox girl.

I took a deep breath, closed my eyes, and opened my mouth. I bit off as large a chunk as I could get in my mouth. Each chew of the soft, stringy muscles squirted blood all over my mouth. I swallowed the cold flesh and gagged again. I fought the urge to vomit. I was sure she would see it as a show of disrespect if I barfed all over the floor. After six similarly sized bites, I was done with the horrific meal. It took all my focus to avoid puking every bit of the nastiness out. As soon as I got on the ship, I would be in the bathroom with my head over the toilet puking my guts out.

"Can we go now?" Astra asked with an irritated tone.

"Yes, I think so. Dalton seems to have enjoyed his meal. Would you like some more before you go?" Emberlynn asked with a devilish grin.

I didn't reply vocally. I just shook my head slowly and turned toward the exit to the hanger. I walked slowly to avoid churning the bloody flesh that was now stuffed in my stomach. The hallway to the ship seemed so much longer this time.

"Are you okay, Dalton?" Flux asked softly as we walked.

"Not really, but thanks for asking, I guess. I just want to get on the ship. I will apologize to you all beforehand. You will hear things that may scare you from the bathroom. Just let me be, and it will all be over soon."

End of Book 2 Sample

Remember to leave a review for book one HERE!

Printed in Great Britain
by Amazon

48228478R00175